Everyone's a suspect

Tori was standing behind her desk, looking out over the town square, when he showed up, the squeak of his shoes and the pace of his gait solidifying what she knew to be true—the police car parked in front of the library was not a coincidence.

Not by a long shot.

Word had gotten out about the party moms and their feelings toward the victim. Of that she was sure. But it was the *who* behind the crime she couldn't figure out, particularly in light of the fact that each and every person at Sally's party had uttered a derogatory word under their breath where Ashley Lawson was concerned.

Including her.

Deadly
Notions

Elizabeth Lynn Casey

BERKLEY PRIME CRIME, NEW YORK

THE BERKLEY PUBLISHING GROUP
Published by the Penguin Group
Penguin Group (USA) Inc.
375 Hudson Street, New York, New York 10014, USA
Penguin Group (Canada), 90 Eglinton Avenue East, Suite 700, Toronto, Ontario M4P 2Y3, Canada
(a division of Pearson Penguin Canada Inc.)
Penguin Books Ltd., 80 Strand, London WC2R 0RL, England
Penguin Group Ireland, 25 St. Stephen's Green, Dublin 2, Ireland (a division of Penguin Books Ltd.)
Penguin Group (Australia), 250 Camberwell Road, Camberwell, Victoria 3124, Australia
(a division of Pearson Australia Group Pty. Ltd.)
Penguin Books India Pvt. Ltd., 11 Community Centre, Panchsheel Park, New Delhi—110 017, India
Penguin Group (NZ), 67 Apollo Drive, Rosedale, North Shore 0632, New Zealand
(a division of Pearson New Zealand Ltd.)
Penguin Books (South Africa) (Pty.) Ltd., 24 Sturdee Avenue, Rosebank, Johannesburg 2196,
South Africa

Penguin Books Ltd., Registered Offices: 80 Strand, London WC2R 0RL, England

This is a work of fiction. Names, characters, places, and incidents either are the product of the author's imagination or are used fictitiously, and any resemblance to actual persons, living or dead, business establishments, events, or locales is entirely coincidental. The publisher does not have any control over and does not assume any responsibility for author or third-party websites or their content.

DEADLY NOTIONS

A Berkley Prime Crime Book / published by arrangement with the author

PRINTING HISTORY
Berkley Prime Crime mass-market edition / April 2011

Copyright © 2011 by Penguin Group (USA) Inc.
Cover design by Judith Lagerman.
Cover illustration by Mary Ann Lasher.
Interior text design by Laura K. Corless.

ISBN: 978-0-425-24059-5

BERKLEY® PRIME CRIME
Berkley Prime Crime Books are published by The Berkley Publishing Group,
a division of Penguin Group (USA) Inc.,
375 Hudson Street, New York, New York 10014.
BERKLEY® PRIME CRIME and the PRIME CRIME logo are trademarks of Penguin Group (USA) Inc.

PRINTED IN THE UNITED STATES OF AMERICA

10   9   8   7   6   5   4   3   2

For my friends, Lynn Cahoon and Joe Richardson.

*There's no one I'd rather stash a body with than
the two of you.*

Acknowledgments

As always, writing is largely a solitary endeavor. It means long conversations with myself and even longer periods of time hunched over the computer—alone.

That said, the most wonderful bursts of sunshine creep through the process in the form of my family. Without them, I wouldn't be half the writer I am.

And then there are my readers, the people who make writing this series all the more fun. Thank you. Your emails and letters mean the world to me. Keep 'em coming!

Chapter 1

Tori Sinclair held up the next picture in the pile and looked around at the fourteen kindergarteners sitting cross-legged on the braided rug. "Who drew this face?"

A hand shot into the air. "Me!"

"Okay"—she dropped her gaze to the nametag slung around the child's neck—"Bobby. Can you tell us what this face is feeling?"

"He's mad as a bear with a sore backside." The redhead rose onto his knees, swiping the back of his hand across his nose as he did.

"Mad as a bear with a sore backside?" she repeated.

Bobby nodded. "Uh-huh. Means he's real mad. 'Cept when my daddy talks 'bout the bear, he doesn't say *backside*, he says *butt*."

"Ah, I see." She pointed at the picture, mentally filing away yet another southern expression to add to her ever-growing list—a list that had started the day she moved to Sweet Briar, South Carolina, and that still showed absolutely no sign of completion more than a year later. "Can you tell us how you chose to show his anger?"

The little boy jumped to his feet and came to stand beside her, his moment in the spotlight no doubt responsible for the face-splitting smile that boasted two missing front teeth. "I made his mouth go down right here like this." He poked at the face on his drawing then lifted his finger up to the curlicues shooting out from the sides of the perfectly round head. "And see this part? That's the smoke comin' out of his ears."

"Wow! He *is* madder than a bear, ain't he?" Sally Davis sat up straight in her spot near the center of the circle, her large brown eyes round as saucers. "My mee-maw says Jake Junior"—the child paused and looked around at her classmates—"that's my big brother in case you didn't know that, gets smoke out his ears when he's mad, too. 'Cept I ain't seen it yet."

"Keep lookin', Sally. If it's there, you'll see it." Bobby turned back to Tori and flashed yet another smile. "I did good, didn't I, Miss Sinclair?"

"You did a very nice job, Bobby, thank you." Shifting his picture to the bottom of the pile, she looked back at the rest of the class, her voice a poor disguise for the laugh that was becoming harder and harder to stifle. "And who drew this one?"

Jackson Calhoun skipped back into the room from his bathroom trip, his dark brown hair curling at the ends in an exact replica of his father. "Ooooh, that's my picture, Miss Sinclair!"

She waved him over. "Would you like to tell us what *your* face is feeling, Jackson?"

"Sure I—" He stopped midway across the room and stared at his drawing, the corners of his mouth slipping downward.

"Could I change one—no, *two* things first? Please? Pretty, pretty please? I'll do it mighty quick. I promise."

Waving off his teacher's hesitation, Tori nodded and handed the little boy a pencil. Two seconds later the picture was back in her hand, this time sporting a few lines on each side of the eyes and a long rectangle draped across the center of the mouth. "Those are interesting changes, Jackson. Would you like to tell us about it?"

Jackson nodded. "My face is worried."

"Worried?"

Again, the child nodded. "My mamma says that's what happens when grown-ups give small things big shadows."

"That's the same as being worried," Bobby interjected.

Tori nibbled her lip. "Have you ever considered being an interpreter, Bobby?"

"What's that?" Sally asked.

"That's someone who translates words from one language to another," explained Tori. "For example, if I spoke Spanish yet your class spoke only English, I would need an interpreter to explain what I'm saying so you could understand."

"Nah, I wanna be a race-car driver." Bobby grabbed his make-believe steering wheel and moved it back and forth, car noises emerging from between his lips. "And I'm gonna be so good I won't never be worried like Jackson's face."

Jackson's face.

She motioned toward Jackson's picture with her head. "Okay . . . tell us."

"Well, his eyebrows come down here and he's got lines right here"—Jackson imitated the illustration with his own face—"and this right here? Why, that's his finger pushed up against his mouth. Like he's trying to figure something out to make it all better . . . but he can't."

"That's very good, Jackson."

"Mrs. Morgan helped me."

"Hey! That's not fair," whined a blonde from the back of the group. "You said we had to draw these faces on our own."

"Mrs. Morgan helped you?" she echoed as her gaze left Jackson and traveled around the children's room of Sweet Briar Public Library. Not seeing her assistant, she looked back at the little boy. "When?"

"Just now . . . when I went to the potty." Placing his hands on his hips, Jackson turned to face the little girl who'd questioned his integrity, his voice taking on an injured quality. "She didn't tell me what to draw. She didn't even talk to me."

"Then how did she help you?"

He looked back at Tori, his eyes wide. "You said to close our eyes and try to think how someone looks when they're happy or sad or worried . . ."

"Or *mad*, don't forget mad," Bobby reminded.

"Yep, mad, too. And well, I closed my eyes and I did what you said and that's why the eyebrows are upside down like that." Jackson pointed at the squiggly caterpillar-like marks on the top half of his drawing. "But when I went to the bathroom, Mrs. Morgan helped me think of the lines and the finger."

The little girl in the back stamped her foot, dislodging a golden blonde tendril from her perfectly coiffed little head in the process. "No fair! I'm going to tell my mother!"

Jackson's hands found his hips once again. "She didn't *tell* me, Penelope. She *showed* me . . . like this." Scrunching up his face, he stuck the index finger of his right hand in front of his mouth.

"Did you *ask* her to demonstrate?" Tori asked as she looked from Jackson to his teacher and back again, her mind warring with itself over the urge to laugh at the child's demonstration.

"No. She didn't even see me. She was just standing there behind the desk like this." Again he made his worried face and again she tried not to laugh, only this time she wasn't any more successful than his teacher.

Forcing her attention onto the task at hand, she painstakingly went through the rest of the pile giving each kindergartener a chance to point out the expressions they opted to use to illustrate their chosen emotion. When they were done, she handed the pictures out to their rightful owners. "Bobby, how did you know what a mad face looked like?"

"I just do." Bobby shrugged. "Everybody gets mad."

She looked at Jackson. "And you knew how to draw worry because of Mrs. Morgan's face?"

The little boy nodded.

Shaking off the questions that followed in her thoughts, Tori stood and gestured toward the various shelves in the center of the children's room, her time with Mrs. Tierney's class drawing to a close. "As you get older, some of the stories you read won't have pictures. But that's okay. Because if you use your imagination and your own personal experiences—as you just did with your drawings—you can still picture the characters and the places in your mind based on what's being said in the story. And you want to know something?"

Fourteen heads nodded as fourteen sets of eyes fairly glued themselves to her face, waiting.

"Sometimes books are even more fun *without* pictures. Because then you can imagine a character the way *you* want to imagine them."

"Wow!"

"That's cool!"

"I still like pictures best."

You win some, you lose some . . .

Mrs. Tierney clapped her hands softly, bringing instant calm to the room. "Class? What do we say to Miss Sinclair for spending time with us this morning?"

"Thank you, Miss Sinclair," chorused fourteen voices as Sweet Briar Elementary School's morning kindergarten class lined up at the door, the promise of snack time under the hundred-year-old moss trees more than enough to keep them quiet.

One by one the students filed out of the room like baby ducks waddling after their mamma. And, true to form, the last of the bunch strayed from the pack. "Miss Sinclair?"

She looked down, a smile tugging her lips upward at the sight of her friend's son. "Yes, Jackson?"

"Will you make sure she's okay?"

"Who?"

"Mrs. Morgan."

Smoothing back a strand of soft brown hair from the little boy's forehead, she nodded. "Of course I will. But I'm sure she's okay. She was probably just trying to answer someone's question. We get a lot of those at the library."

Jackson shook his head, displacing the same strand of hair once again. "She was all by herself. There wasn't anybody else in the li-berry 'cept Sally's mom."

Melissa.

She squatted down to the child's eye level and gave him a quick hug. "I'll check on her, okay? But I don't want you to worry. I'm sure Mrs. Morgan is fine."

For a moment he looked as if he was about to protest but, in the end, he was lured back to the line by the promise of a snack with his friends. "Mommy said she packed me a chocolate cupcake."

Her stomach growled at the thought of Debbie's chocolate cupcakes . . . and her black-and-white cookies . . . and her pies . . . and her—

Shaking off the mental inventory of her friend's bakery, she tapped the tip of Jackson's nose. "Then you better hurry along before I take a taste and end up eating the whole thing."

"Okay." He took three steps toward the door and then stopped once again. "But you'll really check, right?"

"I'll really check. Now run along before Mrs. Tierney gets worried."

And with that Jackson was gone, his little white and blue sneakers smacking softly against the tiled floor that led from the children's room to the main library, Tori's own heels making a pitter-patter sound just a few steps behind. When he turned left toward the door, she continued on, her gaze riveted on her assistant's face.

Her *worried* face.

Tori hurried across the room and over to the information desk, her eyes making a quick sweep of her surroundings. "Nina? Is everything okay?"

The woman shook her head, her finger pointing in the direction of a solitary figure hunched over a stack of books. "I tried to help but it was no use. She kept saying she had to come up with something special. Something better than last year's."

Tori bobbed her head to the left, the long dirty blonde ponytail registering in some dusty corner of her brain alongside Jackson's sweet voice . . .

"She didn't even seem to notice that Sally's class just walked out the door," Nina continued, her eyebrows furrowed. "And she's not the kind of mamma that doesn't notice her own babies."

"I'll take care of this, Nina. Why don't you go ahead and take your lunch break."

Nina pulled her attention from Melissa's weary form and fixed it on Tori. "Are you sure, Miss Sinclair? Because I can wait if you need a moment to relax after the class visit."

She touched her assistant's shoulder with a reassuring hand. "I'm sure. The kids were great, they really were."

"Okay. But if you need anything I'll be right outside." Reaching down, the woman pulled a brown paper sack from the bottom shelf of the information desk and held it into the air. "I'm hoping a little fresh air will help chase away this sluggish feeling I've been having lately. Though the thought of food doesn't sound terribly appealing at the moment, either."

"Are you feeling sick?"

Nina shrugged. "A little under the weather, maybe, but nothing to worry about." Flashing the shy smile that was as much a part of her as the thick hair that hung to her shoulders, Nina made her way across the room and out the door, her lunch sack clutched tightly in her petite hands.

Turning back to the object of both Jackson's and Nina's worry, she made a beeline over to Melissa's table. "Melissa? Is everything okay?"

Slowly, the thirty-something mother of seven lifted her head from the eight-book-high stack and shook her head. "I'm done."

"Done?" Tori echoed as she plopped into a chair on the opposite side of the table, her eyes skimming the various titles in front of her friend.

Melissa gestured toward the books. "Sally's birthday is next week and I can't find a birthday that will impress without having to take out a double mortgage on the house."

She stared at her friend. "I don't understand. You threw

a great birthday for Lulu a few months ago. Why can't you just do one like that again?"

Raking her hands across her makeup-free face, Melissa shook her head. "Because Lulu doesn't have to invite Penelope Lawson. Sally does."

"Penelope Lawson?"

Melissa nodded. "Penelope's last party was a circus. Literally."

"They hired a clown?"

"And a lion tamer . . . and a master of ceremonies . . . and someone to run the cotton candy stand . . . et cetera, et cetera. Of course there was also the mother elephant with her baby, the pair of snow-white horses, and a lion for the tamer to tame. Oh, and let's not forget the firework display that evening. The kids all liked the ones that looked like smiley faces the best."

Tori's laugh died on her lips as Melissa stared back.

"You're *serious*?"

"Completely." Melissa sat back in her seat, her hands running down the spines of the books she'd considered and apparently discarded. "And the year before that? Her mother had a truckload of beach sand shipped in, along with an internationally known sand artist who shared some of his tips with the bucket and shovel crowd."

"A sand artist?"

Again, Melissa nodded. "And the year before that? Well, that was the year the kids went through stations complete with a professional storyteller, the country's top balloon artist, and none other than Barney the dinosaur. Flown in from Texas, no less."

"Um . . . how?" It was all she could think to ask.

Pushing the rejected books to the side, Melissa shrugged. "I have no idea. But nothing is ever too good for Penelope."

Tori racked her brain for a name to go with the face. "Is she the one with the heart-shaped face and blonde curls?"

"That's the one. She always threatens to tell her mom if someone so much as looks at her crooked."

"Okay, I know who she is. She accused Jackson of cheating today in story time. And, just as you said, she claimed she'd tell her mom."

Melissa rolled her eyes. "That's not a surprise. She's not the kind of little girl most kids want to befriend. Not by choice, anyway."

"So why do you have to invite this little girl?"

"Because Sally would be blackballed if we didn't."

Tori felt her mouth gape open. "Blackballed?"

"Blackballed," Melissa repeated. "Not that she won't be anyway if I have a party consisting of homemade birthday cake and pin the tail on the donkey."

"But that's what a kid's party is supposed to be. That's what you did for Lulu and her classmates loved it."

"I repeat . . . Lulu doesn't have to invite Penelope Lawson. Sally does. Which means I need to come up with something. Something creative and different that won't result in Jake and me splitting the blanket over the expense."

"Splitting the blanket?"

"Getting divorced."

"Like that would happen." She reached across the table and gave her friend's hand a squeeze. "Jake adores you. You know that."

"But to throw Sally the kind of party I need to throw is going to cost money. Money we don't have."

"What does Margaret Louise say?" she asked, surprised that Melissa's mother-in-law hadn't stepped in already. "She usually has great ideas."

"Oh, she has a great one all right. Only strangling

Penelope's mother and stuffing her in a closet isn't the most viable option." Melissa brought her hand to the base of her neck and widened her eyes in theatrical fashion. " 'My daughter's dress touched *what*? Take it away . . . I can't have *that* touching *her* skin. It might be bad for her complexion and overall scores.' "

Tori couldn't help it, she laughed, the sound bursting from her lips before her surroundings registered her faux pas. Leaning across the table, she lowered her voice to a more acceptable level despite the momentary lapse in patrons. "What are you talking about?"

"Beyond the fact that precious Penelope is a pageant kid, her mother, Ashley Lawson, is Regina Murphy's head designer and she's apparently very good at what she does."

"Regina Murphy? I'm not sure I know who that is."

"Tall leggy blonde, wears tailored pantsuits to go jogging"—Melissa met her gaze for any sign of understanding—"lives on the eastern side of town . . ."

"I'm not sure I've ever met her."

Melissa waved away her confusion. "Anyway, Regina owns Pageant Creations—a company that makes and sells little girls' dresses specifically designed for pageants."

"Oh, okay. That's what Beth does, too. Only I think her company's name is Spotlight something or other."

"Who's Beth?" Melissa mumbled as she flipped open yet another party book.

"Milo's college sweetheart. She's coming into town later this week for some sort of business meeting and wants to get together with him."

Melissa glanced up at the slight shake in Tori's voice. "Are you worried?"

"Beth was years ago. If he felt that strongly for her, he wouldn't have married Celia, right?" It was the same mantra she'd been telling herself all week. A mantra she hadn't questioned until he'd pulled out a few old photographs after dinner one night.

One look had told her everything she didn't want to know. Beth Samuelson was drop-dead gorgeous. And, based on the stories he'd shared while flipping through the photographs, she'd been Milo Wentworth's first true love. The one who'd broken his heart and drove him into the arms of his late wife.

"Makes sense. Besides, Milo is crazy about you. Everyone knows that." Melissa flipped through another page or two before closing the book with a resounding thud. "You know something? Margaret Louise's idea looks better all the time. It would certainly make pin the tail on the donkey an acceptable party game once again."

Shaking her thoughts free of Beth Samuelson, Tori willed herself to focus on the change in conversation. "Margaret Louise's idea?"

"The one about strangling Ashley Lawson and stuffing her body in a closet."

The corners of her mouth tugged upward. "Did Margaret Louise really say that?"

Melissa made a face. "You know my mother-in-law."

And she did. Thankfully. In fact, since moving to Sweet Briar, the sixty-something woman had become one of Tori's dearest friends both inside and outside of the Sweet Briar Ladies Society Sewing Circle. The sometimes loud, sometimes opinionated woman had shown her nothing but loyalty and kindness through some of her darkest days, including a bout as a murder suspect. It was the kind of friendship she worked hard to reciprocate.

"I've got it!"

Melissa's eyes rounded in surprise. "What?"

"What do you think of having the party in the children's room? The kids could use the dress-up trunk and put on little shows based on the stories we read to them."

"I don't know. Could we really use the room?"

Tori nodded. "With a donation to the library, and my assurances the room will be cleaned afterward, I'm sure the board will grant permission. And if we have it after hours on Sunday, it won't conflict with our patrons at all."

Feeling the excitement start to build, she continued, giving words to the ideas cycling through her head. "We could have Debbie make a cake highlighting Sally's favorite story, and we could bring in a few tables and chairs and set that part up outside under the moss trees."

Melissa sat up. "It would certainly be different . . ."

"And relatively cheap," Tori added.

"Kids love to play dress up."

"And, if we got our hands on a video recorder, we could even tape their performances to be watched during cake time and then send a copy home with each child as a memento from Sally's party."

"That's it! That's perfect." Jumping up from her chair, Melissa ran around the table and threw her arms around Tori. "Oh, Victoria, thank you! You just saved two lives."

"Two?"

"Mine . . . and Ashley's."

"Sally would love you no matter what kind of party she did or didn't have. You need to remember that, okay?" Tori grabbed the pile of party books and stood, the last part of Melissa's statement bringing a smile to her lips. "And as for this Ashley woman . . . perhaps we should keep any and all rope away from Margaret Louise that day. Just in case she can't hold back the urge any longer."

"That's a good idea. Though, keeping it out of sight from the rest of the moms who come to the party might be a good idea, too."

"Why is that?" she asked.

"Because Margaret Louise is one of many who has had enough of Ashley Lawson. *One* of *many.*"

Chapter 2

Shifting the plate of homemade gingerbread cookies to her left hand, Tori knocked on Dixie Dunn's front door, her hand making a crisp rapping sound against the trim.

"Oh, thank goodness I'm not the only one who's late." Beatrice Tharrington stepped onto the weather-beaten front porch beside Tori, a foil-covered plate in her hand. "Luke was being a little devil this evening. Didn't want me to leave."

"Isn't Monday evening supposed to be special time with his parents?"

Beatrice nodded. "It is. But he's gotten a might bit attached to me."

"And this surprises you?" She looked from Beatrice to the screen door and back again, the sound of footsteps in the distance her only indication the knock had been heard above the gossip that was as much a part of the group as needles and thread.

"It does, indeed. I'm just the nanny."

"Just the nanny?" she echoed as she sized up the only other member of the group who didn't sport a southern accent. "You make Mary Poppins look inattentive."

A flush rose across the British nanny's young face. "Victoria, you shouldn't say such things."

"Why? It's the truth." She glanced back toward the door, the footsteps growing still louder. "I can't believe this is the first time I've made a meeting at Dixie's house."

"I wish I could say the same."

Startled, she met Beatrice's shame-filled eyes, her mouth unable to form words before a retraction was offered.

"Oh, Victoria, can we please pretend I didn't say that? It was . . . unkind. And most unfair of me to say."

She reached out, gently squeezed her friend's hand. "It's already forgotten."

"Well look who's here. I thought for sure you weren't coming since we were supposed to start ten minutes ago."

Beatrice's face flushed still deeper. "Dixie, my apologies for being late. Luke got rather upset when it was time for me to leave and I felt it only fair to help settle him down for his mum."

Dixie nodded, her crop of white hair barely moving as she turned her scowl in Tori's direction and waited.

"I had a few last minute things to tie up at the library this evening before I could break away." Tori stepped back as Dixie pushed the screen door open and motioned them inside. "Then it was just a matter of running home and grabbing the cookies and my supplies and—"

"It's simply a matter of getting better organized, Victoria. Why, when I was head librarian, I had the door locked every day at five o'clock on the dot."

Biting back the urge to toss around words like *flexibility* and *public service*, she simply smiled instead, her propensity toward good manners winning out. Besides, some battles simply weren't worth fighting. Especially when the other side was elderly and still carried a grudge where her forced retirement was concerned.

Dixie's nose scrunched. "Do I smell gingerbread?"

"You do. I made some this morning before work." Tori held the plate in the host's direction.

"You made *gingerbread men*? In *spring*?"

"I made gingerbread flowers."

"Oh." Dixie sniffed and reached for Beatrice's covered plate instead. "And what did you bring?"

Beatrice gulped. Loudly. "I helped in Luke's classroom this afternoon and lost track of time. Before I knew it, it was too late to whip anything up on my own. So I stopped by Leeson's Market and ordered up a few blueberry scones."

A soft yet noticeable cluck emerged from Dixie's mouth followed by a sigh to end all sighs. "Things are certainly different these days, aren't they? Good manners and grace have simply gone right out the window."

"Yes, apparently, they have." Tori looked down as a sheet of white paper was thrust into her free hand. "What's this?"

"That, Victoria, is an example of organization."

"Organization?"

"It's our agenda for the evening."

She looked from the paper to Dixie and back again, the reality of what she was hearing and seeing taking root in some dusty corner of her brain. "An agenda? For sewing circle?"

Dixie turned on her penny loafers and headed down the hallway from which she'd just come, the flick of her hand an indication they should follow. "That's right. It will keep us on task."

Setting the gingerbread cookies on the kitchen table along with the various offerings from her fellow circle members, Tori hurried to follow, her brain processing the words on the page in her hand.

7:00 p.m. Arrival

7:10 p.m. Sewing commences

7:30 p.m. Moderated discussion

7:40 p.m. Return to sewing

8:00 p.m. Dessert

8:15 p.m. Final round of sewing

8:30 p.m. Departure

"It's like this all the time when we meet here," Beatrice whispered as they fell in step with each other, their hostess leading the way amid grumbles about the perils of tardiness. "It's why I said what I said earlier."

"And no one says anything?"

Beatrice's too-thin shoulders rose and fell. "Margaret Louise and Georgina speak at will anyway. So, too, does everyone else. But it's met with eye rolling and exasperated sighs from Dixie."

"No wonder she's irritated with us," Tori said mid-chuckle. "We've arrived when sewing is supposed to be commencing."

Dixie looked over her shoulder, her chin grazing the bold floral print of her housecoat. "Shhh . . ."

"Good heavens, Dixie, who are you hushin' out there?" Margaret Louise's voice bellowed into the hallway, earning a sigh from Dixie in the process.

"It's just us," Tori said as she rounded the corner and drew to a stop in the doorway of what appeared to be Dixie's version of the Sweet Briar Public Library, right down to the rickety table and chairs Tori had thrown out shortly after taking over the position of head librarian. "Is that the same—"

"Come sit with me, dear, I've saved you a spot." Leona Elkin lowered her latest travel magazine to her lap and patted the rusty folding chair on her left, her voice dropping to a level only Tori could hear. "It *is* one and the same. Only she'll deny plucking it from the trash in favor of something much more martyr-like. And if you inquire, she'll find a way to go at you for throwing it away in the first place. Need I remind you of the way Dixie likes to accuse you of stealing her job out from under her?"

"Roger that."

"Roger that?" Leona looked over her glasses at Tori. "I'm fairly sure that's not one of the acceptable southern responses I've tried so hard to teach you this past year."

"Lots of people use that expression, Leona."

"Where? In"—the sixty-something woman curled the corner of her lip upward ever so slightly—"*Chicago*?"

"No. Everywhere. Including the south."

"And who in the south might say that?" Leona demanded in a whisper.

"My uncle."

"You mean the uncle who lives in Florida, dear?"

"Yes, exact—" And then she stopped, Leona's protest playing through her thoughts before the woman even uttered a word.

"For the thousandth time, dear, Florida is not the south." Raising her voice for everyone to hear, Leona took command of the conversation, steering it into calmer waters. "Margaret Louise has been telling me all about the party you and Melissa are planning for Sally this weekend."

"Would you believe my twin is thinkin' about helpin'?" Margaret Louise bellowed.

Tori swung her gaze back and forth between the mismatched pair. "You do realize it's a child's party, don't you, Leona? That means *children* will be there."

"I can wear earplugs if necessary," Leona countered as laughter erupted around the room.

Dixie tapped her watch. "It's not seven thirty yet."

"Oh, stuff a sock in it, would you?" Rose Winters, the group's oldest member, stamped her foot against the linoleum floor. "This is sewing circle, not story time."

Dixie's face turned crimson. "But if we talk we won't get our work done."

"And the sky won't fall down around our ears, Dixie." Rose leaned forward in her chair and released a cough that nearly shook the room, her failing health not missed by anyone in the room. Least of all, Rose. "I've only a dozen years left if I'm lucky and I don't plan on living them by the hands of a clock."

The former librarian opened her mouth to speak only to let it snap shut, any protest she could offer stifled by the large eyes staring at her from atop a pair of bifocals. "Now that's better." Turning to Tori and Beatrice, Rose continued, the sharp edge to her voice all but gone. "It's nice to see you this evening."

Tori flashed a smile at the woman. "And you, too, Rose."

Georgina Hayes's wiry figure perked up from behind one of the group's portable sewing machines, a sympathetic smile on her face. "Victoria, how are you faring with this Samuelson woman in town?"

"Samuelson woman?" Leona set her magazine down once again. "Who's that?"

Willing her voice to remain even, she shrugged. "Beth Samuelson is Milo's old college girlfriend."

"What's she doin' in Sweet Briar?" Margaret Louise asked.

Tori looked down at the tote bag in her lap. "She's here on business."

"Is that what they call it now, dear?" Leona drawled, her gaze locked on Tori's.

"Leona!" Georgina reprimanded. "There's no need to get Victoria all worried about something silly. Milo adores her. You know that. I only brought it up because she came into the town hall today to ask for directions and happened to mention knowing Milo."

"Is she pretty?"

"Leona!" Rose stamped her foot. Hard. "What difference does that make?"

"It's okay, Rose." Tori inhaled every ounce of courage she could muster in order to answer the question as accurately as possible. "Actually, Leona, she's beautiful."

"That don't mean nothin'." Margaret Louise shot a daggered look in her twin sister's direction before turning a softer one on Tori. "Besides, you can't tell much 'bout a chicken potpie 'til you cut through the crust."

"That's true," Debbie Calhoun echoed.

"In Leona's case we've already cut through the potpie right down to the ill tastin' insides." Rose's voice elevated above the chatter in the room, earning a gasp from Leona and laughter from everyone else.

"Oh, quit your gaspin', Twin. You had that one comin'." Margaret Louise stretched her pudgy hands over her head and worked to stifle a yawn. "Good men may be as scarce as deviled eggs after a church picnic, but Milo is a good man. Just like my son, Jake."

Tori closed her eyes, willed her mind to embrace the words she knew to be true. Just because Jeff had cheated on her during their engagement party didn't mean Milo would break her heart as well. He wasn't that kind of man.

"So tell us about this party you and Melissa are working on for Sally." Rose settled back against her cushioned chair. "It sounds very clever."

Grateful for the change in conversation, Tori removed the wooden box from her tote bag and set it on the table to her side, her hand returning to the bag for the pale yellow skirt she needed to hem. "I don't want to duplicate what Melissa might have already told everyone . . ." Her words trailed off as she looked around the room, her gaze skimming across her fellow sewing circle members—Georgina, the town's mayor, Debbie, Leona, Margaret Louise, Beatrice, Dixie, and Rose. "Wait, where's Melissa? Isn't she coming tonight?"

Margaret Louise shook her head, her plump hand gripping a needle as it zipped in and out of a piece of eyelet draped across her lap. "When I stopped by to check on the young-uns, she was sittin' at the table agonizin' over the loot bags for Sally's party. I tried to tell her the DVD would be enough but she's convinced it won't be. Not with Penelope Lawson there."

"Did you say *Penelope*?" Dixie groused.

Stilling her needle beneath the eyelet, Margaret Louise transitioned to a nod.

"Sadly, Melissa is right," Debbie interjected. "A DVD won't be enough. Not for that little girl and her mother, anyway."

"Last year? After the circus? Luke came home with a porcelain picture frame complete with a professional photograph of himself and the party girl atop the elephant." Beatrice laid the pieces of a cowboy vest across her lap and set about the task of finding the perfect color thread, her soft British accent bringing a hush to the room. "And the year before that? He came home with a beach towel and his own blow-up pool."

"And don't forget the sandals, the beach ball, and the photo album complete with pictures from the party that were taken and developed before the children even left." Debbie shot her hands above her head and stretched, her dirty blonde hair reaching halfway down her back. "That's why I did Jackson's birthday out of town this year. To escape the pressure."

"Pressure?" Georgina peeked out from behind the machine once again. "Debbie, you are grace under pressure. Just look at the way you handle being a mom to Jackson and Suzanna, and a wife to Colby . . . all while running the bakery seven days a week."

"A piece of cake compared to keeping up with Penelope's mother. That's pressure I can't take."

"Is she really that bad?" Tori asked. "I mean, truly?"

Debbie, Beatrice, and Margaret Louise nodded simultaneously.

"Just this morning at the bakery Caroline Rowen and Samantha Smith were talking about Sally's party. They were saying how badly they felt for Melissa. How they're glad they don't have to jump through the annual party hoop for another few months." Debbie rubbed at her left shoulder with her right hand and moved her head from side to side. "Wow, I must have spent too much time hunched over Melissa's cake design this afternoon—my neck and shoulders are killing me."

"What were they sayin' about Sally's party?" Margaret Louise looked up, her fingers poised around her needle.

Shrugging, Debbie picked up her own needle and thread and began working on the pale blue skirt she was making for her daughter. "They didn't get to say much. Regina Murphy came up behind them in line and everyone shut up. Fast. Though, based on the way her brows furrowed, I imagine she heard enough. I only hope for their sake she doesn't relay things back to Ashley."

"If she does, their children are done."

"Done?" Rose repeated, stealing the sentiment from the tip of Tori's tongue.

"Done." Beatrice shot a glance in Debbie's direction, leading Tori's eyes to follow.

"Beatrice is right. If you say or do anything to put Ashley's daughter in a bad light, your child is blackballed from everywhere—scouts, the playground, school, everywhere. Happened to a little girl named Abigail about a year ago. Her mother made a comment about Penelope being pampered and that was it. Poor little Abigail was shunned from that day forward. Her family moved out of Sweet Briar just a few months ago."

"Sounds to me as if Penelope isn't any nicer than this hotshot mother of hers." Dixie set her latest sewing project on her lap.

"She's not," Debbie stated matter of factly. "And trust

me, I don't like expressing a feeling like that about *any* child. Even one that belongs to *that* woman."

Rose coughed to clear her throat. "Then I still say Melissa should have left her off the guest list."

"She can't. It would be like signing the death certificate on Sally's social life if she did."

Tori heard the gasp as it escaped her mouth. "But Debbie . . . they're *children*. Having *birthday parties*."

"Not if they're the same age as Penelope Lawson."

Chapter 3

If Tori didn't know any better, she'd have thought someone called an emergency meeting of the Sweet Briar Ladies Society Sewing Circle.

At her library, no less.

But she *did* know better. The troops had simply assembled in a show of support for one of their own—support Melissa would have appreciated had she been aware of its presence.

Which she wasn't.

Instead, their fellow circle member was running between the children's room and the picnic tables outside, attending to every birthday party detail imaginable. Balloons were suspended in trees, streamers hung from branches canopying the party table, red tablecloths had been cut and attached at the seams to create a red carpet effect from the parking lot to the children's room, makeshift spotlights were pointed at the tiny stage where children would act out their favorite stories, and Colby Calhoun's video player was poised on its tripod in anticipation of the stellar performances Sally Davis's party guests would undoubtedly give.

"Land sakes, that child is fixin' to have a nervous breakdown," Margaret Louise declared as she huffed and puffed her way through the back door of the library only to have Melissa turn midway down the hallway and head outside once again. "She's here, she's there, she's all over the place. Heck, I think she's even harder to keep up with than those seven grandbabies she and Jake have given me."

"She's stressed, that's for sure, but I think she's going to realize fairly soon that this is going to be one amazing little birthday party." Tori peered into the children's room, her excitement over the library addition she'd created rearing its head all over again. It didn't matter that it had been in place for over a year, the newness still hadn't worn off. Not for her, anyway.

She turned to Leona. "You sure you want to be here when the guests start arriving?"

"You might get chocolate or jelly smeared on that fancy schmancy suit of yours." Rose pulled the flaps of her thin cotton sweater tighter against her body. "Chocolate can be tough to get out of silk."

Leona drew back. "I'll stay away from the cake."

"Have you ever seen a five-year-old after they've eaten cake?" Dixie inquired as she looked around the children's room, her gaze skimming the shelves that had been pushed to the side for the party.

"Why?" Leona roamed a questioning eye between Rose and Dixie. "What's wrong with them?"

Rose snickered. "Perhaps we should simply let you wait and find out."

"Isn't that just like you, you old goat. Stir the pot and then run. Classic Rose Winters if I've ever heard it." Leona sniffed, her off-white heels making a clicking sound on the tile floor as she spun around and headed toward the door, Rose's gasp of indignation bringing an undeniable sparkle to her eye.

"Did you hear what that old biddy just called me?"

Tori shrugged innocently. "I'm not sure, Rose, I think I zoned out for a minute or two."

"The heck you did." Rose stamped her foot on the ground. "Why, I have a good mind to—"

Melissa breezed back inside, her cheeks red. "Has Debbie gotten here with the cake yet? The kids are going to be arriving in"—the woman's face paled as she stole a glance at her wrist—"five minutes!" Grabbing hold of Tori's left arm, Melissa began pumping it up and down. "They can't come yet. I'm not ready."

Tori slowed the movement of her arm by capturing Melissa's hand with her right. "Melissa, relax. Everything is more than ready. The stage looks great. The costumes are hanging on the little portable rack Jake assembled. And the decorations you've made couldn't be more perfect." She bobbed her head to the left to capture Melissa's worried eyes. "It's going to be okay. Great, even."

"But the cake . . ."

Margaret Louise strode across the room, her boisterous voice taking on a soothing quality. "You don't want the cake here too soon. Otherwise it won't be a surprise when it's time for the kids to sit down."

"But what if the design I gave Debbie didn't work?"

"It'll work," Tori assured. "Debbie is amazing with her cakes, Melissa. You know that."

Inhaling sharply, Melissa nodded. "I do. And you're right . . . both of you. I need to relax. It's just that I want everything to be perfect."

"It is," Tori, Margaret Louise, Rose, and Dixie said in unison.

Flopping into a nearby child-size chair, Melissa dropped her head into her hands. "I don't want to disappoint Sally. Molly is a wonderful baby but she's certainly claimed a lot of Sally's mommy time."

"Sally is fine. She loves that baby. And she loves you." Margaret Louise waved her hands in the direction of the stage and the parted curtain of balloons Melissa had created. "And when that young-un sees this setup, she's goin' to be beside herself. Absolutely beside herself. You just wait and see."

Melissa nodded again as she, too, ran a visual inventory across the room. "I suppose you're right. I just hope . . . Oh, never mind." Shaking her head, the woman rose to her feet, the first sign of a smile beginning to nudge her lips upward. "You're right. This evening is about Sally. And as long as she's happy, nothing—and *no one*—else matters."

"Mommy, Mommy, I'm here!"

They all turned as Sally pushed open the back door and ran inside. Dressed in a baby pink pinafore-style dress with a white frilly blouse, the birthday girl stopped just inside the door of the children's room and clapped her hands together. "Wow! Wow! Wow! I'm gonna have the bestest birthday ever!"

Tori grabbed hold of Melissa's arm as the woman dropped back down to her chair, relief moistening her eyes. "See?" she whispered. "It's going to be great."

"Thank you." Melissa reached outward and wrapped her arms around her daughter. "So you like it?"

"I do! I do!" Sally hopped from one patent leather shoe to the other, her curly pigtails bouncing above her shoulders. "When does everyone come? When does everyone come?"

"How about right now?" Margaret Louise asked as she winked at her granddaughter and pointed toward the door.

Sure enough, in walked a smattering of five-year-olds led by Jackson Calhoun. "They're here! They're here!" Sally shouted, her smile threatening to split her face in two. "Mommy, they're here!"

The children milled around, oohing and ahhing over the balloons and the carpet, their anticipation for the party contagious. "Looks like it passes muster to me." Rose nudged her chin toward the handful of children. "Seems a shame Melissa had to worry so much for nothing."

"You haven't met the reason yet. When you do, you'll understand," Margaret Louise explained.

"Hello? Hello? Is anyone here to greet the party guests?"

Heads turned toward the door once again as a woman, dressed in a pair of white silk pants and matching silk top, stepped into the library. On her heels was a little girl with the same strawberry blonde hair and high cheekbones as the woman. She, too, had ocean blue eyes and an upward turn to her nose, yet was dressed in clothes more befitting her age if not the event.

Dixie squared her shoulders. "Why is *that* one here?" she asked through clenched teeth.

"That's Penelope," Margaret Louise whispered. "The spawn of the woman who is single-handedly responsible for Melissa not sleeping this past month."

"Not that nasty little thing," Dixie snapped. "The bigger one."

"That's Penelope's mother, Ashley Lawson."

"I didn't realize ya'll were talking about *that* Ashley the other night." Dixie narrowed her eyes as she swept her gaze from Margaret Louise back to the topic at hand.

"And I certainly had no idea she went with that hateful little thing."

"Good heavens, what is that child dressed in?" hissed Rose as she leaned her head forward to afford a better view. "If I didn't know any better I'd think that child was wearing cash—she *is*! She's wearing cashmere!"

Melissa jumped off her chair and shoved Sally forward in the child's direction, nervous panic taking over where relief had been. "Ashley . . . Penelope . . . we're so happy you made it."

"We are?" Dixie hissed through teeth that were suddenly clenched.

Ashley Lawson looked past Dixie as if she wasn't even there, her gaze traveling, instead, down Melissa's choice of jeans and a cotton blouse before skipping to Sally's birthday dress. "Happy birthday, Sally, don't you look . . . *quaint*."

Tori grabbed hold of Margaret Louise as the woman lunged forward. "Not now," she whispered.

"I saw the little picnic table outside. Your paper products look so . . . *cute*, Melissa. So—so *homey*."

Rose's lips pursed.

Dixie's mouth gaped.

Margaret Louise's hands fisted at her sides.

"Did your Mommy and Daddy have your cake shipped in from Belgium, too?" Penelope asked as she swayed from side to side, her fingers holding out her royal blue dress as if it were made from spun gold. "They really do have the best chocolate, don't they, Mother?"

Ashley smiled behind her flawlessly manicured hand. "They most certainly do, Penelope. But Sally's cake won't be shipped in from Belgium, precious. They can't afford the kinds of things that Daddy—well, it's just simply too costly."

"Where is that cake?" Rose hissed beneath her breath.

Tori forced her attention from the pampered pair in front of her and focused it on her elderly friend. "Why? I'm sure it'll be here soon—"

"I hope Debbie's made a duplicate."

"A duplicate?"

The woman's gray head bobbed. "The first one really ought to be shoved—"

Tori shot a hand across Rose's mouth, successfully cutting her off mid-sentence. "Not now, Rose," she hissed. "Today's about Sally, remember?"

"It's a good thing it is or *I'd* be fixin' to—"

Melissa cleared her throat, cutting Margaret Louise's tirade short. "Sally's cake is from right here in Sweet Briar and she's gonna be tickled when she sees it, isn't that right, Mee-Maw?"

Margaret Louise nodded then grabbed hold of her granddaughter's hand. "That's right. She is." Turning on the soles of her Keds, the plump woman addressed the party guests. "Who's ready to have fun?"

"I am!"

"Me, too!"

"I like fun, Mizz Davis." Jackson Calhoun turned to the birthday girl. "Sally, I'm sure glad you invited me. This is gonna be the best birthday party ever."

Ashley Lawson gasped. "Why Jackson Calhoun, don't you remember coming to Penelope's party last spring? With the elephant rides and the clowns?"

"I do. But this looks even funner. And besides, Sally is always nice to me. Sometimes Penelope can be kinda—"

Tori stepped forward, closing a hand over Jackson's shoulder as Ashley's face grew pale. "Shall we look through the books Sally's mom has chosen and decide which ones we want to act out?"

Eleven little bodies jumped up and down, their feet clad in everything from sneakers to patent leather party shoes. Or, in Penelope's case, miniature versions of something that looked an awful lot like Prada. Falling in line, one behind the other, the children followed Sally's grandmother into the children's room like eleven obedient little ducklings.

Pulling her shoulder bag higher on her arm, Ashley thwarted Melissa's move to follow suit. "I'd prefer that Penelope not be placed beside Jackson Calhoun. That little boy is trouble."

"Trouble?" Melissa asked as she exchanged looks with Tori. "Jackson Calhoun? You can't be serious."

"Yes, trouble. And yes, Jackson Calhoun. Didn't you hear him just now? The way he tried to disparage my daughter? I simply won't stand for that." The woman turned on her own Pradas. "I'll be right back. I must get Penelope's costumes from the car."

"Oh, you don't need to do that." Tori stepped forward and extended her hand in Ashley Lawson's direction. "We have costumes to go with all of the stories Melissa selected for the party. All your daughter has to do is choose the story she wants to act out and then find the costume that goes with that part."

The woman's chin rose into the air. "And *you* are?"

Despite everything she'd witnessed since the Lawsons' arrival, she still found herself taken aback by the woman's rudeness. It was unnecessary and more than a little uncalled for. Yet, as she herself had reminded Rose, it was Sally's birthday. And for Sally she would find the restraint she needed to address her classmate's mother. "My name is Victoria Sinclair and I'm the head librarian here."

"Oh. That's why I don't know you. I prefer bookstores over libraries. The books are new and there isn't that"— Ashley raised her nose into the air and sniffed—"musty smell that libraries always seem to have."

"Then suit yourself," Rose interjected, her voice dripping with ice. "We'll show your daughter to a chair so she can wait for you to return with suitable costumes."

"Thank you." And with that, the bane of the kindergarten birthday circuit was gone, the only remnant of her presence the hint of her five-hundred-dollar-a-bottle perfume.

And her daughter.

"Just who does that woman think she is?" sputtered Rose.

"She's Ashley Lawson." Melissa inhaled deeply, squaring her shoulders as she did.

"No, she's rude. With a capital *R*." Rose pulled the flaps of her sweater still tighter against her frail body and shuffled her way into the room, the sound of happy laughter doing its best to dispel the tension that still hung like a cloud over the hallway. "C'mon, Dixie, let's make ourselves useful."

"Do you think Miss High and Mighty would have a fit if she knew her precious daughter was inhaling bona fide library air just the other day?" Dixie mumbled as she fell in step behind Rose.

Tori turned to join them only to stop as the back door shot open and Beatrice entered with her charge, the nanny's eyes moist with tears. "Beatrice? What's the matter? Is everything okay?"

"I thought so. Until I saw that woman in the parking

lot." Beatrice handed a brightly wrapped package to Luke
and gave him a gentle shove toward the children's room.
"Run along now, Luke, I'll be outside helping Jackson's
mum if you need me."

When the little boy was out of earshot, Tori tried again,
the tension hovering around Beatrice's body too hard to
ignore. "What happened?"

"Nothing."

"Beatrice, you look like you're on the verge of crying."

"I really shouldn't complain. It's not like I was the only
one."

"The only one what?"

"To have a run-in with Penelope's mum."

"What are you talking about?"

Beatrice pointed through the window in the center of
the door, her finger trained on two women and two little
girls. The children were peering at the cake over Debbie's
shoulder while the women paced around the outdoor party
table. "You know Caroline Rowen and Samantha Smith,
right? The little redhead, Zoe, belongs to Caroline, and the
brunette belongs to Samantha. We all arrived at virtually
the same moment . . . just as Ashley Lawson was heading
out to her car to fetch a few outfits."

Tori stared out the window, her gaze seeking and finding Penelope's mother, who was removing a large garment
bag from her trunk. "Did something happen?"

"She commented on Zoe's hair, said she could provide the name of a good hairstylist when Caroline finally
decided to do something about that wretched color. That's
what she said . . . that *wretched* color."

Without taking her eyes off Ashley, Tori posed the
question that was begging to be asked in light of Beatrice's
shaky demeanor. "And what did she say to you?"

The nanny rummaged around in her purse and pulled out a tissue. Quickly she dabbed at each eye, her voice barely more than a trembling whisper as she leaned against the door. "I opted not to have Luke get dressed up since I figured he'd be wearing a costume for much of the party. I considered asking his mum what she thought but she left early this morning for a breakfast meeting."

"Okay . . ." Tori turned and looked into the party room, locating Luke in quick fashion. "He looks fine, Beatrice."

"I thought so, too. But Ashley doesn't agree."

She stared at the woman. "Ashley doesn't agree?"

Beatrice shook her head, her mouth tugged downward with worry. "No. She said I should be ashamed dressing him like . . ." The nanny's words trailed off as she shifted from foot to foot.

"Dressing him like what?" Tori prompted.

Looking slowly from side to side, Beatrice's voice grew softer, her cheeks sporting a slight shade of crimson. "Like . . . . . . like one of the Davis kids."

"What's that supposed to mean?"

"Like a"—Beatrice released an audible sigh—"a commoner."

"You mean like a normal kid?" she spat.

"I don't know, Victoria. I just know that Ashley Lawson and Luke's mum socialize from time to time. I can't afford to lose this job."

She reached out, rested a reassuring hand on Beatrice's shoulder. "If Luke's parents were to fire you, that little boy would never forgive them."

"I hope you're right." Beatrice jumped forward as the door opened against her back. "Oh . . . Mrs. Lawson, can I help you with those?"

Mustering up every ounce of goodwill she could find, Tori closed the gap between them, her hands seeking to lighten the woman's load. "Yes, please, let us help you with that."

Ashley waved off Tori's assistance, opting instead to toss the heavy garment bag into Beatrice's waiting hands. "Penelope, of course, will need privacy for any and all costume changes." Beckoning the nanny to follow, Ashley strode into the children's room, firing off orders over her shoulder. "And we'll need to adjust the lighting before Penelope takes the stage."

"Yes, Mrs. Lawson."

Tori jogged forward until she was in step with Beatrice. "What are you doing? You don't have to take orders from her."

"She's friends with Luke's parents and I'm their employee."

"Beatrice!"

"It's okay. Really." Beatrice touched Tori's arm then continued on, following Penelope's mother to the clothing rack.

For a moment Tori considered marching over to the rack as well, her desire to put Ashley Lawson in her place more than a little potent. But, in the end, she resisted, the sight of Sally Davis prancing around in a white eyelet Bo Peep costume enough to convince her it was neither the time nor the place for such a confrontation.

"You remembered to put away the rope, right?"

Tori nodded, the sound of Melissa's voice in her ear bringing a much needed smile to her lips. "I assumed you were overreacting, painting this woman as some sort of monster."

Melissa released a tired snicker. "And now?"

She glanced across the room in time to see Penelope's mother shoo the other party guests from her more elegant and elaborate costumes, the momentary hurt on their tiny faces tugging at her heart. "I'm surprised strangulation is the only method Margaret Louise considered."

Chapter 4

Tori couldn't help it, she'd fallen far harder for Milo Wentworth than she'd ever intended, especially in light of her post-Jeff vow to steer clear of anything resembling serious. It was a vow she'd made with good reason and a vow she'd intended to keep . . .

Until Sweet Briar Elementary School's third grade teacher swept her off her feet with his kind ways and even kinder heart.

Suddenly, it hadn't mattered that her former fiancé had cheated on her in the coat closet of the very hall they'd rented to celebrate their engagement with friends and family. Sure, the sting from such a humiliation was still there—probably always would be. But somehow, some way, Milo had made her believe in love and honor again.

"I stopped by the bakery and bought you a brownie today." Milo disappeared into his kitchen only to return with Debbie's trademark white bakery bag with the powder blue cupcake emblem emblazoned on the front.

"I was torn between the brownie and the caramel cake for a while but, in the end, the brownie won out."

She smiled up at him from her spot on his sofa, her gaze riveted on the man who'd stolen her heart before she had a clue what was happening. Handsome in the same quiet, understated way he moved through life, Milo sported a crop of burnished brown hair that complimented his amber-flecked brown eyes. "Tell me again how I found you?"

"You didn't. I found you." Placing the bag on the coffee table, he bent his leg at the knee and dropped onto the sofa beside her. "And it just gets better all the time."

And it was true. It did. What had started out as a shy attraction between two people had blossomed into the kind of relationship that was almost too good to be true—a rare example of give and take that had propelled them firmly into keeper status. For his part, he was an amazing listener, remembering the things that mattered to her and making her feel special—always. For her part, she was supportive of his teaching career and his need to spend time together.

"The kids loved the tire swing you tied in that tree behind the library. It was one of the many highlights of the party." She snuggled back against his chest, savoring the feel of his arms around her body. "I know Melissa really appreciated you dropping by before the party to do that. Especially since you had plans . . ."

"My pleasure."

Closing her eyes against the wave of self-doubt that threatened to stymie her mood, she dove headfirst into the conversation she knew she should be big enough to initiate. "So? How was it?"

He nuzzled the top of her head with his chin. "How was what?"

"Your dinner with Beth." There. She said it. She released a burst of air from her lungs. "Was it good to see her again?"

"It was. It's been a lot of years. Which meant a lot of catching up."

Nibbling her lower lip inward, she closed her eyes again, willed herself to embrace the calm his arms provided. "Did she know about Celia?"

His chin bobbed against her head. "She did."

"Did she *know* Celia?"

His chin slid side to side. "No. I met Celia when I was student teaching. We were married inside a year and she died six months later. This is the first time I've actually seen Beth since before all of that."

"Oh." She tugged his arms more tightly around her. "Um . . . is she married now?"

"To her career, I suspect, based on how much she talked about it. But not to a person." Whispering a kiss atop her hair, he continued, his deep voice rumbling against her back. "She seems pretty happy with being single. And she looks spectacular."

Great.

"Owning her own business certainly seems to agree with her. Especially now, when things are looking so good."

"Especially now? How so?" she made herself ask.

He shrugged. "I don't know specifics. Beth has always been the type that's really superstitious. She never liked to say how she did on a test until she got the grade back. If she forgot her keys or her purse when we were going out on a date, we had to go back into her dorm room and sit for a few minutes before we could leave."

"Oh."

"From what she *did* share though, she had an appointment earlier today that virtually inked some deal she's been working on for months. She wasn't ready to divulge details yet but said she'd show me as soon as the labels were done."

"Labels?"

"I don't know. I tried to ask but she prattled on about taking the pageant world by storm."

"What's her company called again?"

"Spotlight Fashions. At least for now. That's apparently one of the changes she's making in conjunction with whatever this new acquisition is."

She pondered his words. "Sounds neat. Did you . . . did you tell her about us?" The second the words were out she regretted them, the overall question—coupled with the slight tremble to her voice—making her seem more than a little pathetic. "You know what? Scratch that. It doesn't matter."

"Hey. Slow down a minute." Ever so gently he scooted her forward then turned her to face him. "Of course I told her about you. We were there to catch up on each other's lives and you, Tori Sinclair, are a huge part of my life."

Reaching up, she traced the side of his face with her hand. "Thank you. I needed that more than you can know."

"We all need to hear the truth." He jerked his head toward the coffee table as dimples carved holes in his cheeks. "And we all need chocolate, yes?"

She laughed. "Wow, I've really trained you well, haven't I?"

"Never better." Grabbing the bag, he pulled it onto his lap. "So tell me more about this party. The swing really went over well?"

"It was a huge hit." She took the piece of brownie he

held out to her and popped it in her mouth. "Though, as the party wore on, I couldn't help but think the rope was a mistake."

He looked a question at her as she rushed to explain. "I was afraid it might make things a little too tempting."

"Things?" he asked around a bite of brownie.

"Strangulation, for starters."

He choked on his dessert. "Come again?"

"It's top on Margaret Louise's method of choice at the moment."

"Method of choice for what?"

She stuck her hand into the bag and broke off another piece, the promise of chocolate far stronger than her willpower. "Don't you mean for *whom*?"

"Okay, sure . . ." Milo paused with his second helping mere inches from his mouth. "Wait. Does this have to do with Ashley Lawson?"

"You remembered."

"How could I not? After hearing how stressed Melissa's been getting ready for this party, it's hard not to remember. Though, in all fairness, I have to believe she took it a bit far. I know this woman has a reputation for being a little overbearing, but to be as over-the-top as Melissa said? It's hard to imagine."

"Have you spoken to her?"

"Not directly. But Penelope is only in kindergarten."

She swiveled her body to afford a better look at Milo. "See, I thought the same thing in the beginning. You know, that Melissa and the rest of them had to be exaggerating a little where this woman was concerned."

"And now?"

"And now I know they weren't. In fact, they may have *under*stated things."

"You can't be serious."

"I can. And I am." Grabbing the bag from his hands, she peered inside, the remnants of the brownie nothing more than mere crumbs. Her lower lip jutted over her top lip. "I think I liked it better when you were wary of chocolate."

He made a face. "So Margaret Louise wants to strangle this woman, eh?"

She looked into the bag again, her finger chasing crumbs across the bottom of the sack. "She does. But so does Melissa, and Beatrice, and Rose, and Dixie, and Caroline Rowen, and Samantha Smith."

His laugh echoed around the living room of his modest two-bedroom cottage. "And you? Where do you fall in all of this?"

"It would be unkind to the rope." She held up her hands and gave her head a little shake. "I'm kidding, really . . . but I have to tell you, Milo, this woman is mean personified."

"That bad, huh?"

"And then some." She set the bag on the coffee table and snuggled into the crook of Milo's arm, the warmth of his body making her eyes heavy. "Her boss, Regina Murphy, showed up toward the end of the party. Just to help collect the dress-up costumes Ashley insisted on bringing to the party. Did Ashley appreciate it? No. Yet the woman still seemed to be her biggest champion, casting an evil eye on the other moms who so obviously had had enough of Ashley Lawson."

"Maybe there's something good there after all."

"Maybe . . ." she allowed, albeit grudgingly.

"Word on the street is she's a fabulous designer."

"Well, designing dresses for pageants is all well and good—even better if she's truly that good at it—but being a decent human being should mean a little more, don't you think?"

"Agreed. But people place different importance on different things. Makes it easier to sort the apples from the lemons that way." He nudged her chin upward until their eyes met. "It's finding the little diamonds underneath all of those apples and lemons that isn't always easy."

She smiled up at him, his honesty and his openness catching her by surprise for what had to be the millionth time. "Oh trust me, I'm well aware of that."

Chapter 5

Tori, of all people, knew life could change in an instant. She'd lived it when she'd found Jeff in the closet with a mutual friend. She'd lived it when she'd become the top suspect in a murder she didn't commit. And she'd lived it when she made the conscious decision to give love another try.

She just hadn't counted on living it when Milo's first love walked into the room, proving once again that pictures don't always capture a person's true beauty. The hair that had looked blonde in the college photographs he'd shown her was golden in real life, the exact shade reminiscent of the fair-haired beauty in Rumpelstilskin. The eyes that had looked as if they were just regular blue were actually blue as blue could be, their ocean-colored hue popping against her flawless porcelain skin. And the figure that had been that of a young college coed was suddenly all woman.

"Oh my," Tori mumbled under her breath as she

noticed every male head in the room look up at the same instant, their jaws dropping in time with hers.

"Do you know her?" Debbie asked as she wiped her flour-dusted hands across the front of her apron.

"No. Not personally. But that's . . . um . . . Milo's old girlfriend."

The bakery owner looked from Tori to the woman and back again. "Oh. Okay. That's who that is. She's kinda pretty I guess."

"Kinda?" she echoed. "Kinda?"

"Her name is Beth, right?"

"Yes. Beth Samuelson."

"Victoria is a much prettier name," Debbie said as she nodded to Emma, her college-aged employee, to take the register. "Much prettier."

"Because let's be honest, men notice names." Tori heard the hint of sarcasm in her voice and was instantly ashamed. "Hey, don't mind me, I didn't get home until late last night and I was so wound up from sugar it was hard to sleep."

Debbie studied her closely, her eyes nearly burning a hole into her soul. "*You're* prettier, too."

She laughed. "Perhaps *you've* had too much sugar."

Her friend shook her head. "No, seriously, I think you're prettier. I really do. You're the whole package, as my Colby likes to say."

Pulling her gaze from Milo's former love, Tori fixed it on Debbie instead. "My package isn't wrapped like that . . ."

"There's something to be said for beauty that just *is*, rather than beauty that is because it's been fussed into place." Debbie filled the to-go cup with hot chocolate and topped it with whipped cream before handing it across the counter to Tori. "You, my friend, just *are*. She"—Debbie cast a sidelong glance at the woman now talking to Emma—"on the other hand *is* because she *tries*."

Tori glanced back in Beth's direction. "I don't know . . ."

"Have you met her yet?"

She shook her head. "No. Milo invited me to go to dinner with them last night but I'd already promised Melissa I'd help with Sally's party."

"Then I think you should introduce yourself now. It's like my grandmother used to say, Victoria, 'sometimes what we imagine is far worse than reality.' And besides, when I saw her in here yesterday morning she seemed fine to me."

Was Debbie right? Was she making this woman out to be something she wasn't? Besides, she knew Milo. Trusted Milo. And knowing she'd gone out of her way to be kind to someone he knew would make him happy.

"Okay, I'll do it." She stepped forward, her hot chocolate cup in her left hand. "Beth? Beth Samuelson?"

The woman turned, her eyes wide. "Yes?"

Tori held out her right hand. "I'm Tori. Tori Sinclair. Milo Wentworth's girlfriend?"

"Tori Sinclair? Hmmm, I don't remember hearing your name but I certainly know who Milo is." Beth reached out, shook Tori's hand firmly as a megawatt smile stretched across her face revealing snow-white teeth. "He's quite a man, isn't he?"

Tori swallowed along with her nod, her brain suddenly incapable of forming a coherent thought around the memory of Milo's voice in her head . . .

"Of course I told her about you. We were there to catch up on each other's lives and you, Tori Sinclair, are a huge part of my life."

"I've prided myself on good decisions in life—decisions that are really starting to pay off in ways I never imagined. But breaking things off with Milo all those years ago? That's the one decision I've regretted." Beth released her grip on Tori's hand and brought it to the strap of her Coach bag. "But that's what's so wonderful about life, isn't it? We have the power to change mistakes if we want to badly enough."

She felt her jaw drop.

"Not that you should feel threatened, of course." Beth pulled her gaze from Tori's face and fixed it on the menu that hung on the wall behind Emma's head. "I wouldn't think of actively stealing another person's man. Things like that need to be two-sided, you know?"

"I—uh—" She stopped, all intelligent responses absent from her brain.

"Hello . . . I'm Debbie Calhoun. Welcome to my bakery."

Grateful for her friend's interruption, Tori took a moment to catch her breath, her mind still too jumbled to truly analyze everything that had been said.

Beth looked around, her blue eyes sparkling in the morning light that streamed through the large plateglass windows along the eastern wall of the bakery. "I was in here just yesterday and fell in love with the place. I love the motif on the menu and the bags, too. It's very nice."

"Thank you."

Tori closed her eyes, willed herself to remain the calm and sensible person she knew she was. Yet somehow, despite her best efforts, she found herself wanting Debbie to dislike this woman.

Realizing her thoughts were ludicrous and more than a little childish, she forced herself back into the conversation.

"I lived in Chicago for years before moving to Sweet Briar and Debbie's bakery beats anything I found there."

A hint of pink spread across Debbie's cheeks. "Thanks, Victoria."

"It's easy to speak the truth." Unless, of course, the truth involved how much she wished the floor would open up and swallow Beth Samuelson whole . . .

As if she hadn't spoken a word, Beth stepped closer to the counter, closing the gap between her and Debbie. "Perhaps we could get together one afternoon for coffee. You know, two entrepreneurs getting together to swap business ideas."

Debbie smiled. "That would be great. Tori, would you like to join us?"

"Oh? Do you own your own business as well?" Beth asked as she turned to acknowledge Tori.

"No. I'm the head librarian at Sweet Briar Public Library."

A slight smirk chased the model-like smile from the woman's face. "A librarian and a teacher? Oh, how very Milo."

"Well, as you know, Milo *is* a smart man," Debbie interjected as she slung a protective arm across Tori's shoulder. "And he certainly knows a good thing when he's got it."

Beth's gaze roamed its way down Tori's body, taking in everything from the light brown skirt that skimmed her knees to the off-white sweater set that hugged her petite frame. Tori shifted from foot to foot under the scrutiny, all the while wishing she'd opted for the boots instead of the flats and the cascading hair instead of the high ponytail.

"I think I'll just take a mocha latte to go. I've got a lot of work to do this morning." Setting her purse on the counter, Beth extracted a sparkly change purse. "How much do I owe you?"

Two minutes later, drink in hand, the woman turned back to Tori. "Tori, it was nice to meet you. I'm sure we'll be bumping into each other again." She walked a few feet, only to stop and glance over her shoulder. "Give my love to Milo."

Her love . . .

"Wow. I didn't see that in her yesterday. But, ignore her. She's trying to get under your skin."

Without taking her eyes off the woman's receding back, Tori addressed her friend. "She's succeeding, Debbie."

"Don't let her. That's what she wants. That's what her type always wants. They live to shake up other people's lives."

"Maybe . . ." Her words trailed off as she watched two different men jump from their seats just to hold the door open for Beth Samuelson. Good and decent men she'd met since moving to Sweet Briar. "But guys never seem to see it, do they?"

"Colby does."

She nodded, suddenly aware of an uncharacteristic slump in her mood. "Hey . . . I better get going. Nina will be wondering what happened to me." She took a few steps toward the door only to have her progress thwarted by the sound of Debbie's voice.

"Victoria?"

She turned.

"Milo loves you. Remember that."

And so she tried, Debbie's words replaying their way through her mind as she walked to work, the early morning temperatures hinting at the gorgeous spring day looming on the horizon. Traditionally one of her least favorite months, March was gaining favor now that she lived in the south.

Her feet slowed as she approached the library, the hundred-year-old moss trees that lined the grounds suddenly calming her troubled heart. Here, she could be herself—the same Tori Sinclair she was whether a man was part of her life or not.

Rounding the building's western corner, she stopped short, her gaze riveted on the tire lying in the middle of the grass. Glancing up at the tree, she searched in vain for the rope that had hung there just the night before, giving flight to Sally Davis's friends as the tire it held spun round and round.

"What on earth?" she mumbled to herself before opting to rephrase the question for someone who might be able to offer an actual answer. She pulled open the back door and stepped inside the hallway. "Nina? Are you here?"

"Right here, Miss Sinclair." Nina popped her head out of the tiny office they shared behind the main room. "So how'd the party go last night?"

"Great. The kids had a really good time." Tori stopped outside the entrance to the children's room, the tension in her shoulders beginning to dissipate. "They loved dressing up, loved having their little performances taped, loved playing outside." She turned and met her assistant's eyes. "Hey, Nina? Do you have any idea what happened to the tire swing Milo hung for the party?"

Nina shrugged. "I saw the tire, too. I just figured you cut it down."

"No. I didn't. And the rope is missing, too."

"Maybe one of the board members decided to take it

down before we opened this morning? Maybe it's a liability issue or something."

"Maybe but I—"

The sound of the office phone cut short any further conversation.

"Should I get that?" Nina asked.

"No, I'll take care of it. Would you just do a quick look through the main room and make sure everything is ready? Doors open in five minutes."

"Of course, Miss Sinclair."

Tori strode into the office and over to her desk, the phone's ring echoing throughout the tiny room. Grabbing the receiver from its base, she held it to her ear. "Good morning. This is the Sweet Briar Public Library. How may I help you?"

"Victoria?"

She strained to pick out the whispered voice on the other end of the line. "Melissa? Is that you?"

"Yes."

Sensing the stress in her friend's voice, she gripped the phone still closer, a sudden and inexplicable chill making her shiver. "What's wrong? Has something happened to one of the kids? Or to Margaret Louise?"

"No."

"Then what's wrong?"

"It's Ashley. Ashley Lawson."

A sense of relief flooded her body and she dropped into her desk chair, the morning sun streaming through the window and warming her body from the outside in. "Phew. You had me worried for a minute."

"She's dead."

Tori sat up tall. "What did you just say?"

"She's dead," Melissa repeated. "Ashley Lawson is dead."

"What—when? How?"

"They just found her in her car."

"In her car?" she echoed in disbelief. "But how? What happened? Was she sick or something?"

"No. She was strangled to death."

Chapter 6

Tori was standing behind her desk, looking out over the town square, when he showed up, the squeak of his shoes and the pace of his gait solidifying what she knew to be true—the police car parked in front of the library was not a coincidence.

Not by a long shot.

Word had gotten out about the party moms and their feelings toward the victim. Of that she was sure. But it was the *who* behind the crime she couldn't figure out, particularly in light of the fact that each and every person at Sally's party had uttered a derogatory word under their breath where Ashley Lawson was concerned.

Including her.

"Here we go again," Tori mumbled as she blew a strand of light brown hair from her forehead and turned to face Sweet Briar Police Chief Robert Dallas. Sure enough, he was standing just behind a wide-eyed Nina, his hat secured beneath his upper arm.

"Miss Sinclair? Police Chief Dallas w-would like a word with you."

"Thank you, Nina." She strode across the twelve-by-twelve-foot office and extended her hand in the chief's direction, his firm handshake and stalwart face doing little to ease the tension seeping into her neck and shoulders. "Chief Dallas, it's nice to see you. How can I help you this morning?"

Glancing quickly in Nina's direction, he motioned toward the library's main room with his chin. "I need a moment of your time, Victoria. Alone. It's important."

She nodded then addressed her assistant with as much cheerfulness as she could muster. "Nina, can you hold down the fort for a while? This shouldn't take too long—" She looked to the chief for confirmation, the words dying on her lips as he shook his head.

"I've got it under control. You take your time, Miss Sinclair." Nina turned on her heels and scurried down the hall, her back disappearing around the corner in record time. Squaring her shoulders, Tori gestured into her office. "Chief, won't you come in and sit down? I wish I had some of that chocolate mousse pie you like so much but I wasn't expecting a visit. Maybe next time?"

"Maybe next time." He reached into his pocket and pulled out a notepad and pen, his fingers flipping it open as he walked. "Are you aware that Ashley Lawson was found dead in her car early this morning?"

She rounded the corner of the desk and sat down, her hand waving toward the folding chair on the other side. "Please, sit. Make yourself comfortable."

"Thank you." When he was situated he met her gaze, repeating his question once again. "Are you aware that Ashley Lawson was found dead in her car early this morning, Victoria?"

She considered her words. "As of about an hour ago . . . yes."

"And how did you come to learn of her death?"

"A friend called and told me."

His eyes narrowed. "May I ask who this friend was?"

"Melissa Davis."

"I see." He scribbled something in his notepad. "May I ask why she would call and tell you? Were you friends with Mrs. Lawson?"

She pulled a pen from the wooden holder between them and tapped it on the top of her desk. "I met Ashley Lawson for the first time yesterday evening. At a birthday party Melissa threw for her daughter right here in the library."

"Go on."

Flipping the pen onto its other end, she slid her fingers slowly down the shaft only to repeat the process all over again when she reached the bottom. "That's it."

"Did anything unusual happen during the party?"

"No. It was your basic child's birthday party. They played games, they dressed up as their favorite storybook characters, they ate cake, they swung on a tire swing—"

"And where did this tire swing come from?" the chief asked,

"Milo Wentworth set it up about an hour before the party started. He had an old tire out in his garage and offered it to Melissa to use for the party. The kids loved it."

"And the rope?"

She shrugged. "I think he had some of that, too."

He nodded then jotted a few more notes in his pad while she continued. "I'd show it to you except someone took it down after the party. The tire is still there but the rope isn't."

"That's okay, I've seen the rope. Or, rather, what I suspect is the rope."

"Oh, okay, good. I was wondering what . . ." The words trailed from her mouth as he looked up from his notepad and simply stared at her.

She closed her eyes as a wave of nausea racked her body. When she opened them, he was still staring at her. "Tell me you're not saying what I think you're saying."

"What do you *think* I'm saying, Victoria?"

"The rope? Was it used to . . . to kill Ashley Lawson?"

He sat back in his chair, his lips set in a grim line. "Yes, I believe it was."

Pulling her hands upward, she dropped her face into them. "Oh, how awful."

"Yes, it is. For her and her family."

It was like a switch turned on in her brain, reminding her of one simple fact—no matter how unpleasant or rude Ashley Lawson may have been, she was someone's mother. Penelope's mother.

Blinking against the sudden moisture in her eyes, she popped her head up. "Do you have any idea who did this to her?"

"That's why I'm here. To ask you that very same question," he said, pinning her eyes with his own. "Because, from what I've heard, there were more than a few women present at yesterday's birthday party who expressed an interest in doing exactly what was done."

She looked a question at him, her mouth suddenly too dry to speak.

"She *was* strangled, Victoria, remember? Which leads me back to my question. Do you know of anyone who may have wanted to kill Ashley Lawson?"

"Of course not," she gasped. "Who would want to murder a little girl's mother?"

"I can think of several people who might fit that description thanks to a witness who stood right outside this library yesterday evening and heard the threats."

"The threats?" She leaned back in her chair, her mind rewinding back to the previous evening. The part of the party that had been outside had involved the cake and presents as well as time on the tire swing. And unlike the costume changes and subsequent little shows that had taken place inside the children's room, that part of the party had needed little more than visual supervision, allowing the moms plenty of opportunity to talk.

And talk they had.

About Ashley . . .

And how they'd like to strangle her . . .

She gripped the edge of the desk as reality hit with a smack to the head. If a witness had conveyed what was said, that same witness had surely pointed fingers at specific people.

Like Margaret Louise . . .

And Melissa . . .

And Beatrice . . .

And Rose . . .

And Leona . . .

And Debbie . . .

And Dixie . . .

And Caroline Rowen . . .

And Samantha Smith . . .

And me.

She gulped. "Chief Dallas, people say things out of frustration all the time. Especially when they've been pushed the way Ashley Lawson pushed them both last night and during countless other events for their children."

"Go on . . ."

"People say stuff like that all the time. It doesn't mean they're going to run out and do it."

"Say stuff like what, Victoria?" the chief prodded.

"Like, she makes me so mad I could strangle her. Or like, sometimes I could just kill her." She raked a trembling hand through her hair as she tried to convince him she was right. "It's normal, Chief. Everyone says that kind of stuff at one time or another. It doesn't mean someone is actually going to *do* it."

Chief Dallas shifted in his seat, his unreadable gaze fixed squarely on her face. "But see that's where you're wrong, Victoria. Someone *did* do it. To Ashley Lawson. In the very same manner that was volleyed around by as many as ten people yesterday evening."

"Ten?" she repeated as her mind began to count the culprits.

He nodded and flipped to an earlier page in his notepad. "Margaret Louise Davis, her daughter-in-law Melissa Davis, Leona Elkin, Beatrice Tharrington, Dixie Dunn, Rose Winters, Debbie Calhoun, Caroline Rowen, Samantha Smith . . ."

She mentally followed along with his list, her thoughts sifting through the various names in order to come up with anyone who hadn't uttered a derogatory word about the high maintenance mom who'd stood poised and ready to ruin Sally's party any number of times. That is until her boss had shown up and cast an evil eye over their fun.

Ashley's boss. Regina Murphy. The woman who had pointed Chief Dallas in their direction.

"Oh, and *you*, Victoria."

At the sound of her name she snapped her head up. "I'm sorry, did you say something?"

His eyes narrowed to near slits. "Did you express a desire to strangle Ashley Lawson, Victoria?"

Pushing back in her chair, she stood, anger clipping her words. "Was I one of the ones who verbalized a desire to strangle Mrs. Lawson? No. I wasn't. I did, however, speculate it was a good thing the rope from the tire swing had been secured by a former Boy Scout."

"And why would you say something like that?"

"Because Ashley Lawson brought new meaning to the word *rude*. And in doing so she rubbed everyone at the party the wrong way, including me. Only instead of saying the words your witness overheard on the tongues of many, I simply took the joke in a different direction." She walked to the door of her office and waited, her actions making her intent crystal clear. "And that's what those comments were, jokes. Jokes made in an attempt to diffuse the unnecessary tension spread across a special event by the victim. Nothing more."

Chief Dallas rose to his feet, stuffing his notepad into his back pocket as he did. With several long strides he met and passed her in the doorway before stopping to swing his hat onto his head with an air of authority. "Murder is no joking matter, Victoria. You of all people should know that." He stepped into the hall only to turn one last time. "I'll be in touch."

Chapter 7

For the first time in more than a dozen or so visits, Margaret Louise's home didn't exude its normal happy aura. Sure, the alphabet magnets and finger-painted pictures that covered nearly every square inch of the proud grandmother's refrigerator were in place just like always. Nothing would ever change that.

But as certain as those things were, so, too, was the downtrodden mood that threatened to suffocate the life out of that evening's sewing circle.

"Do you know how many times I said I wanted to kill Thomas after what he did?" Georgina mused from her spot beside an overturned teddy bear on the navy blue sofa in the far corner of the room. "Why, when I heard what he'd done, I could have strangled him with my bare hands."

Tori studied the town's mayor from the sunlit corner she'd claimed as her own, the last of the day's lingering rays growing weaker. For over a year now, the woman had forged ahead with dignity and determination despite the humiliation of having been married to a murderer. "But you wouldn't have done that. You're too good."

"There were days in the aftermath of his arrest that I doubted that, Victoria. Especially after the hell he put you through."

She held her hands up. "The truth finally came out, Georgina, and that's all that really matters. Now it's done and over and I'm doing just fine."

"I know. But that doesn't mean I didn't think about strangling him, or tripping him just as he approached the edge of a cliff, or running him over with my car, or locking him in a cellar and watching him starve to death. These are the things I thought about back then. Still do on some days."

"And that's only natural if you ask me," Rose grumbled from behind the portable machine she'd commandeered the second she arrived. "I think anyone in this room would be hard-pressed to say they've never had thoughts like that about someone who's wronged them."

Heads nodded around the room.

"But that doesn't mean we act on them." Dixie's chin rose into the air. "Victoria wouldn't be here if we did."

"We?" Leona drawled.

Dixie's face reddened. "Okay . . . me. But she took my job from me—a job I devoted my life to from the time I was her age."

"Good heavens, Dixie, would you get down off that cross, 'cause someone else surely needs that wood." Rose pulled the sweater she was hemming from the machine and stamped her foot on the ground. "Victoria didn't take your job. She was given it. By the board. And they did that because it was time for you to retire."

Dixie opened her mouth to speak only to slam it shut as Rose continued. "I don't like being old any more than you or"—she lowered her chin and peered over the top of her glasses as she scanned the room—"Leona, over there, does. But it's life. Get over it."

"You're the one who's older than dirt, Rose." Leona sat up straight in her chair, her latest travel magazine slipping from her flawlessly manicured hands. "I'm a good quarter century younger than you."

"A quarter century?" Rose shook her head.

Margaret Louise let out her first laugh of the evening. "Twin, don't you know that twistin' the truth is like puttin' perfume on a pig?"

"Oh shut up, Margaret Louise," Leona groused as she pulled her magazine off her lap and opened it in front of her face.

Feeling the corners of her mouth twitching upward, Tori took a moment to savor the momentary burst of playful energy that was synonymous with their group—a burst that disappeared the moment Melissa opened her mouth.

"I know I said some unkind things about that woman after Sally had opened her gifts but she'd pushed me to the brink. She really did." Melissa jumped to her feet and peeked outside the window, the path of her gaze no doubt traveling in the direction of her own home. "But I couldn't hurt a flea. Just ask my Jake."

"Oh, Melissa, there's not anyone in the world who could think you would hurt another human being," Beatrice said, her soft British accent making them all pause. "Police Chief Dallas will figure that out soon."

"There ain't no difference between a hornet and a yellow jacket when they're both buzzin' in your pants," Margaret

Louise said from her spot just inside the doorway. "Every single one of us in this room 'cept Georgina is guilty of saying somethin' off-color about that nasty woman. And there's not a one of us who could hurt a flea, either, yet the chief's still circlin' like a vulture waitin' for his supper, ain't he?"

Heads nodded again.

"Which is why fingers are going to start pointing before long, you just wait and see."

"They already have," Tori said as she glanced in Dixie's direction. "How do you think Chief Dallas knew about the comments?"

"How *did* he know?" Debbie mumbled around the needle she held between her teeth.

"I imagine it was Regina Murphy. She showed up at that point during the party when everyone had hit their limit with Ashley Lawson, remember?"

Beatrice's face paled. "Oh no, you're right. She heard me say—" The nanny sat up straight, shock and fear skittering across her face. "Oh no!"

Debbie pulled the needle from her mouth. "Don't you worry none, Beatrice. Everyone said something at one time or another. And Victoria is right, Regina heard just about every last comment. But just as she was getting ready to give us a piece of her mind, Samantha got a hold of her and started gabbing away."

"That's probably why she was practically frantic to talk to Ashley by the end," Margaret Louise mused. "Woo-eee that Samantha Smith can talk."

Dixie cleared her throat, halting all further conversation. "That's not the finger pointing I was talking about."

All eyes turned in Dixie's direction. "What are you

babblin' about, Dixie?" Georgina asked as her hand paused above the blouse she'd been working on for the past month. "Who's pointing fingers?"

"We all will be if it serves us well."

"What are you talking about?" Beatrice whispered.

Crossing her arms in front of her stout frame, Dixie took her moment in the spotlight. "If Chief Dallas were to show up at your doorstep, Beatrice, and badger you about what you said regarding Ashley Lawson what would you say?"

"I—I . . ."

Dixie turned to Leona. "And if he showed up at your doorstep and badgered *you*, what would you say?"

Leona lowered her magazine. "I'd tell him I was only repeating what I heard Rose say."

Rose gasped along with everyone else.

"Leona!"

"It's okay, Victoria." Rose leaned forward in her chair and narrowed her eyes to near slits as she stared at Margaret Louise's twin sister. "And when he showed up at my door telling me what you said Leona, I'd tell him it's always the dirty dog that howls the loudest."

"You wouldn't," Leona spat.

"Try me," Rose countered.

"I rest my case," Dixie said as she settled back against the cushions of the rattan chair she'd claimed for the evening. "It's just like I said, fingers will start their pointing sooner than any of us realize. You mark my words."

Tori swallowed over the lump that sprang to her throat. Was Dixie right? Would everyone start throwing each other under the bus that was Ashley Lawson's murder simply to save their own skin?

"There is another way." Debbie's voice, quiet yet firm, rang out from her place beside Margaret Louise.

"What's that?" Beatrice asked.

"We band together."

Dixie looked up. "As a united front?"

"No. As friends." Debbie pulled a spool of thread from her sewing box and held it to the lamplight on her left. "We all know we didn't do it. So why on earth would we give the impression otherwise?"

"Someone had to have done it," Georgina interjected. "And you must admit that the way in which it was done is more than a little curious in light of everything I've heard about Sally's party."

"You're right, someone did it. But let's not forget the fact that two of the women at that party are not in this room right now." Debbie unraveled a piece of the baby pink thread and threaded it through the eye of her needle. "And they were every bit as fed up with Ashley Lawson as the rest of us."

Beatrice bristled. "Caroline Rowen and Samantha Smith are no more capable of murdering someone than any of us are."

"That might be true if Ashley hadn't insulted Caroline's daughter."

"But if you follow that logic, then you're just as much of a suspect," Melissa pointed out.

Debbie set her needle and thread down. "How do you figure that, Melissa?"

"Ashley may have commented on little Zoe's red hair, but she also called your son a troublemaker. Even refused to let her daughter sit anywhere near him during the party."

Debbie's face turned crimson. "Can you imagine any-one saying that about my precious Jackson? That woman was out of her mind."

"I seem to remember you were, too, after you heard what

she had to say about him." Dixie scooted to the edge of the rattan chair and struggled to her feet. "*And* your cake."

Margaret Louise turned and looked at Debbie. "She said something about the cake? I didn't hear that."

"Neither did I," Tori said.

Gritting her teeth, Debbie flashed a look of annoyance in Dixie's direction. "It wasn't a big deal."

"Oh no?" Dixie's stout frame moved across the sun porch. "Then why did you point to the rope the kids were swinging from and speculate how much it would take to wrap around that woman's neck?"

Margaret Louise clapped her hands sharply. "Dixie, that's enough."

"Seems to me you'd like me pointing that out on account of the fact it deflects attention from the things *you* said."

"It's already been established I wanted to strangle her," Margaret Louse reminded Dixie in a voice that was uncharacteristically sharp for a woman who seemed to smile twenty-four/seven.

"But has it been established that you talked about the best way to untie the kind of knot Milo used to secure the rope to the tree in the first place?"

More gasps erupted around the room.

"Dixie, why are you doing this?" Tori pleaded, her heart sinking at the fear in her friends' eyes. "You made a comment or two yourself that night."

The elderly woman stopped just short of the hallway that led to the bathroom. "You're right, I did. And I suspect those words will come back to bite me just as all of yours will do for you. But knowledge is power, Victoria. And knowing what can be used against us will help us to prepare."

Leona tossed her magazine onto the coffee table and swiveled to face Dixie. "Prepare?"

Dixie nodded then offered an explanation that made perfect sense. "To prepare a defense."

"A defense against what?"

"The kind of scrutiny that comes with a murder investigation. The kind of scrutiny each one of us is going to be under until Ashley Lawson's killer is finally caught."

Chapter 8

She wasn't sure how long she'd been sitting there in the dark. Maybe a half hour, maybe more. It was hard to know exactly without getting up off the couch to check her cell phone—an effort that seemed too great.

In fact, if Tori was honest with herself, she knew the effort to do much of anything at that moment seemed too great. Especially when the events of the past twelve hours were weighing on her shoulders like a pile of bricks.

The moment she'd heard of Ashley Lawson's death, she'd known the offhand comments made during Sally Davis's birthday party would come back to bite them. But it wasn't until that evening's circle meeting that she'd truly begun to realize just how ferocious that bite might be.

There was no doubt about it, Dixie had gotten the circle riled up, her stick poking offending more than a few members. But when Tori had allowed herself to step back and be objective, she knew Dixie was right. People tended to look out for themselves. Self-preservation, after all, was part of human nature.

Knowing that, though, didn't make the fallout from Dixie's comments any easier to take. Never in the past year had Tori ever seen Debbie get as defensive about anything as she did regarding her feelings for Ashley Lawson. And never, in that same amount of time, had she ever known Margaret Louise to be anything but happy and fun-loving—a far cry from the demeanor the woman had exhibited on the heels of Dixie's cross-examination.

Even the normally shy Beatrice had shown something resembling a spine when Dixie had mimicked the victim's opinion on what constituted correct party attire, the nanny's flaming red cheeks and trembling hands merely a hint to the animosity she still harbored.

Pulling her knees to her chest, Tori wrapped her arms around them and stared at the swath of light streaming in through the blinds from the street lamp two doors down. She knew she should probably consider getting ready for bed, or, at the very least, laying out her clothes for the next day, but she couldn't. Her mind was simply too keyed up—and her heart too heavy—to move.

A soft knock at the door made her look up, her eyes squinting toward the transom window that framed the right side of the door. Suddenly, a hand rose up against the glass and waved, the identity of the person on the other side of the door all but certain.

She dropped her feet to the ground and stood, a smile tugging her mouth upward as she closed the gap between them in record time. When she reached the door she yanked it open. "Milo! Hi!"

"Hi." Smiling sweetly, he held a white paper sack into the air. "I brought you back some dessert. The waiter called it Death By Chocolate and the second he did, I immediately thought of you."

She tried to smile. She really did. But on the heels of what had transpired that day, the name of the dessert didn't sound quite so appealing.

"Hey, what's wrong?" He lowered the sack to his side and glanced down at his wristwatch. "I didn't wake you, did I?"

"No."

A frown furrowed his brows. "Are you feeling poorly?"

"No."

"Then what's wrong?"

"It's been a rough day with Ashley Lawson's murder and all."

Milo's mouth hung open. "What?"

She stared at him, his reaction not what she had expected. "You didn't hear?"

"No. What happened?"

Stepping back, she waved him inside. "She was found in her car this morning."

He strode into the darkened living room and then stopped, retracing his steps over to the light switch on the wall. With a flick of his finger, her living room was bathed in light. "And they think she was murdered because . . ."

"Of the rope that was tied around her neck."

"Wow."

That was one word for it.

She followed him over to the sofa and sat down. "Even more of a wow is the fact that I'm pretty sure it was the same rope you used to secure the tire swing for Sally's birthday party."

He dropped onto the cushion beside her, his mouth gaping open once again. "What?"

"I suspect that's one of the reasons Chief Dallas was in my office just after ten o'clock this morning." She heard the wooden quality to her voice yet could do little to stop it. The day had taken its toll on just about every ounce of her being.

"Huh?" Milo swiveled to face her, his hand reaching for hers. "Wait. Tell me he's not looking at you for this."

She shrugged. "If he is, I'm one of many."

"I don't get it."

She closed her eyes as his fingers entwined with hers. "Do you remember what I told you last night after the party? How I was afraid the rope might be too tempting for Margaret Louise after expressing her desire to strangle Ashley Lawson?"

His face paled. "Oh my God, I forgot about that. You don't think—no, there's no way. Margaret Louise would never do something like that."

"Do you remember how I told you she wasn't the only one who wanted to strangle her?"

He nodded. "Oh. Wow."

"Unfortunately those feelings were muttered aloud—shared behind hands and hinted at via whispered innuendos by the likes of Margaret Louise, Debbie, Beatrice, Rose, Dixie, Leona, Melissa, Caroline Rowen, Samantha Smith, and in a roundabout way, me. And they were overheard, and then shared with the police shortly after Ashley's body was found."

"Shared?" He released her hand, raking his own through his burnished brown hair. "Shared by whom?"

"Ashley's boss, Regina Murphy." She grabbed the throw pillow to her left and hugged it to her chest, the memory of Regina's face crystal clear in her mind. "I remember when she walked up. The kids were taking turns on the swings and Ashley was holding back the line so Penelope could take a ride without having to wait like the other kids."

Milo rolled his eyes.

"When Penelope's turn was over, Jackson was waiting. Penelope asked to ride again and Ashley agreed. When Jackson started to cry, she told him to grow up. That's when Debbie muttered her desire to strangle Ashley. A desire that was seconded several times over by everyone standing there."

"And Regina heard that?"

She nodded. "And now it's all one big mess." Resting her chin on top of the pillow she closed her eyes. "You should have seen our circle meeting tonight. By the time it was over, everyone was pointing at everyone else just to get the heat off of themselves."

His arms came around her and pulled her close. "I'm sorry, Tori. I really am. But don't you worry, Chief Dallas will figure out who really did this and the heat will dissipate. It has to."

She willed herself to keep the doubt silent. Expressing it didn't do any good. Instead, she opted for something a little closer to wishful thinking. "You're right, Milo. It'll be okay." For a moment she simply breathed in his nearness, allowed it to bolster her spirits as much as possible. "Wait! How was your dinner with Beth?"

"It was okay," he said. Ever so gently he stroked the side of her face with his hand in a gesture she'd grown to love. "It would have been better if you'd been there with us."

"She might have been surprised if I was."

His hand stopped. "Why would you say that? She knows about you."

"To hear her talk she doesn't." The second the words were out she wished she could recall them, the general sentiment sounding almost bitter.

"When did you see her?"

She told him about meeting his college sweetheart at Debbie's Bakery just that morning, describing, in detail, the things that had been said. Including the part where Beth seemed clueless as to Tori's place in Milo's life.

When she was done, he simply scratched his head. "I don't know, Tori. Maybe she was more distracted than I realized last night when we met. I mean, she was all keyed up about everything from some deal she'd just ironed out to the new company name she needs to design into a logo and how all of that is going to take her to the top. Maybe she was so focused on *that* she didn't really listen to the things *I* had to say."

"Maybe." She grabbed his hand in hers and rubbed it against her cheek until he took over on his own once again. "Or maybe she just wants you all to herself."

He laughed. "Not likely."

She sat up straight, unsure of the tone in which his words were spoken. Had she heard disappointment? Or wishful thinking? Or was her imagination in hyper I've-been-hurt-by-love-before mode? "Wh-what's not likely?" she stammered.

"That I'd ever let that happen."

"No lingering feelings? No haunting what-ifs?"

"None." His hand dropped to her shoulders and squeezed. "How could there be when I've got someone a gazillion times better?" His back pocket vibrated against the sofa, making them both jump. "Hey now, who on earth would be calling at this hour?"

"You could answer it and find out," she teased.

"Good idea." She nestled into the crook of his arm as he flipped open his cell phone and held it to his ear. "Milo here."

A woman's voice fairly purred from the phone, filling the miniscule gap between them. "It's Beth. I wanted to call and tell you what a lovely time I had with you again tonight, Milo."

He turned his head and whispered a kiss across Tori's forehead. "Uh, me, too, Beth. It was great. We'll have to do it again sometime soon . . . when Tori can join us."

"Tori?"

"My girlfriend. I told you about her last night and you met her at Debbie's Bakery this morning. In fact, I'm here with her now."

"Oh." Silence followed only to be cut short by a giggle. "My timing never was very good, was it, Milo? Remember when I called you on your wedding night?"

Tori tilted her head upward to meet his gaze. His nod confirmed the woman's words. "You're fine, Beth."

A long sigh emanated from the phone. "I've been working on my company's new logo ever since I got back to my room. And you know what? I think I've finally found the perfect font for the P and the C. Which is great because all that's left then is the overall color scheme."

He leaned his head against the sofa, his breath warm against Tori's head. "I'm sure you'll get it."

"I need to get it *perfect*. So the clientele associates the company's name every time they see these—" The giggle returned. "Oh, look at me. I get so excited talking to you, Milo, that I almost let the cat out of the bag. And I can't. Not yet, anyway. Everything needs to be just perfect before I do."

A thought struck Tori and she met his gaze again. "Her company does something with pageants, right?" she whispered.

He nodded.

"Does she know about what happened to Ashley Lawson?"

He shrugged. "I don't know."

"Know? Know what?" Beth interjected through the phone.

"Tori was wondering if you knew a woman named Ashley Lawson?"

When there was no response, he pulled the phone from his ear and checked the screen. Realizing they were still connected he held it loosely to his ear once again. "Beth? You there?"

"I'm still here."

"Did you hear my question?"

"Uh, no, I'm afraid I didn't. There was a—a sound out in the parking lot just now. I guess I was distracted."

"Tori was wondering if you knew a woman named Ashley Lawson?"

"Vaguely. I mean, we're in the same business but that's all. Why?"

"She's dead."

A gasp sounded between them. "Dead?" Beth echoed.

"She was found in her car this morning."

"I—I don't know what to say . . ." The woman's voice trailed off only to return in a slightly softer pitch. "What happened?"

"It appears that she was murdered."

A second gasp was followed by more silence.

"Beth, are you okay?"

"I'm fine, Milo. It's just . . . I don't know, sad, you know? I mean she had a—I think she had a little girl, didn't she?"

"Yes. Penelope."

"That's a shame." Beth's voice returned to its earlier purr, the sound tickling Tori's ear despite its distance from the phone. "Oh, Milo, it's so nice to be able to talk to you again. I've missed that so much since we broke up."

"We broke up fourteen years ago, Beth."

"We were together for a full year . . . . "

"A year that ended fourteen years ago," he said gently.

"And I've missed it ever since."

Tori tried not to roll her eyes as she snuggled closer against Milo's chest.

"Then I hope you find someone as special as I have."

Silence was followed by a third—yet different—giggle. "Then perhaps it's time I get to know this special lady of yours."

Milo glanced down at Tori, gestured toward the phone with his chin.

Realizing what he was asking, she sat up tall, her mind sifting through her various appointments and obligations for the rest of the week. "I have a little time tomorrow morning. I'm not due into the library until noon."

He winked at her as he spoke into the phone. "Any chance you're free tomorrow morning, say around"—he glanced at her for confirmation—"ten?"

"I can do ten. Where?"

"How about Debbie's?" she whispered up at him.

"How about Debbie's? The same place you met this morning."

"Debbie's? You mean that darling little bakery in town? Oh yes. That sounds lovely." Beth paused. "Can she hear me right now?"

"Who? Tori?"

"Yes."

He held his lips to her forehead for just a moment before replying. "Yes, she can."

"Wonderful. I'll see you at ten, Tori, okay?"

He held the phone outward to allow her to respond and then cocked it toward his ear once again. "So you two are all set now?"

"We're all set. Unless, of course, you'll be joining us, Milo?"

"I'm afraid I can't. I'll be in the middle of third grade math at ten o'clock."

Another giggle sounded in their ears. "Oh, that's right. It's probably for the best. I imagine it would be rather awkward for Tori to watch us together anyway."

Milo met her silent question with the rise of his finger. "Watch us together? I'm not sure I understand, Beth."

"Oh, Milo, c'mon. You know what I'm talking about."

"I do?"

"Fourteen years is no match for chemistry, my love."

Chapter 9

She wrapped her hands around the ceramic powder blue mug and glanced at the clock over the door.

10:15 a.m.

Beth Samuelson was late.

The simple fact that she was fifteen minutes late didn't really bother Tori. It happened. To everyone. But after the things the woman had hinted at on the telephone the night before, all it served to do was give her more time to think.

And worry.

It wasn't that she didn't trust Milo, because she did—or as much as she could given the fact she'd trusted once before only to be humiliated in a way she wouldn't wish on anyone.

No, it had far more to do with the unknown and its impact on her psyche.

Sure enough, the more she tried to forget about Milo's college sweetheart, the more the woman plagued her mind. The more she tried to take comfort in the things Milo loved about her, the more she noticed all the things Beth had that she didn't. And it was driving her batty.

The sound of her cell phone broke through her wool-gathering. Flipping it open, she held it to her ear. "Hello?"

"Good morning, beautiful."

She grinned. "Isn't this a nice surprise." She glanced at the clock again, her mind immediately leaping to his day. "I thought you were in math right now."

"I am. Alice took them outside for a few minutes just to give them a change of pace."

"What are they working on today?" She lifted the mug to her mouth and took a quick sip.

"Multiplication."

"No wonder they need a break."

"Oh, they're not getting a break. They're actually doing multiplication right now."

"Outside?"

"Alice is a whiz. The kids love her."

Tori couldn't help but smile. She, of all people, knew the wonders of a good assistant.

"So? Is she there?" His voice rumbled in her ear.

"No. Not yet."

"I guess that's no real surprise. Beth has been known to take the notion of fashionably late to a whole new level unless . . ." His voice trailed off.

"Unless what?"

"Forget it. It doesn't really matter."

She sat up straight, her curiosity aroused. "C'mon now, you don't get to do that. Finish your sentence."

A sigh filled her ear only to be thwarted by a reply she wished she hadn't pursued. "Unless she was meeting me. Then she was never late."

"Oh." She took another sip, this time closing her eyes as the warm liquid slid down her throat.

"Tori?"

"Uh-huh."

"Please don't pay any attention to what she said last night on the phone. There was no chemistry between Beth and I over dinner either night. None. Zip. She's an old friend. Nothing more. Nothing less."

An old friend.

An old friend he happened to have loved deeply at one time.

An old friend who had opted to end a relationship that meant the world to him.

"I know." And she did. She just needed her head to stop messing with her heart.

"Good."

The bell over the entrance to Debbie's Bakery jingled and she looked up, her heart sinking at the sight of Beth Samuelson.

To call Milo's college flame pretty would be an understatement of epic proportions. Beautiful didn't truly cut it, either. Stunning, gorgeous, breathtaking—these, on the other hand, were far more accurate and equally ego crushing.

"Milo, I have to go. Beth just walked in." Without waiting for a response, she flipped the phone shut and stood, her heart keenly aware of the simple black pencil skirt and white satiny blouse she'd chosen for the day—clothes that seemed almost dowdy compared to the form-fitting charcoal gray designer pantsuit that made every male in the room turn in Beth's direction. Only in Beth's case it wasn't merely the outfit that caught their attention. It was the whole package—the sexy curves, the flirty smile, the long golden hair, the ocean blue eyes . . .

Swallowing over the lump of dread in her throat, she forced a smile to her lips. "Beth, hi. I'm so glad you made it."

The woman nodded, her heels clicking across the floor in Tori's direction. "I got hung up at the inn."

Tori gestured toward the table she'd claimed. "Busy working on that logo?"

Beth deposited a large brown portfolio against the table leg then climbed onto the white lattice-back stool, her hair swishing against her back. "Logo?"

"The one for your company's new name?" She sat up tall in an effort to catch Emma's eye. When she did, she motioned the girl over. "Would you like something to eat, Beth?"

"I'm not much of a breakfast girl. But I'll have a latte." Beth turned to Emma and flashed her megawatt smile. "I'll take a latte. Small."

When Debbie's employee had retreated behind the counter, Tori leaned forward. "It must be so exciting to run your own company, deciding everything from product to marketing and all aspects in-between."

"It is."

"I know a little bit about that with the library." Tori pulled her mug closer to her body and inhaled slowly. "It's fun and challenging all at the same time."

For a moment Beth said nothing, her gaze pinning Tori as if she'd grown two heads. "You work at the *library*, don't you?"

"I do. I'm the head librarian."

"And you actually liken that to owning a business?"

Tori laughed at the surprise in the woman's voice. "In some ways, sure. Just like you, I'm concerned with getting patrons in the door. And to do that, I have to do marketing of my own. Although it's not usually done with commercials and full-page ads in magazines like you probably do."

Emma reappeared beside their table, a baby blue ceramic mug in her hand. "Here you go, ma'am."

"Thank you." Beth leaned back in her chair as Emma set the drink in front of her. "I never heard of marketing a library."

"The more people we have using the library, the more funding we receive." Tori clasped her hands together and rested her chin on top. "The more funding we receive, the more programs we can offer."

"Interesting . . ." Beth clicked her nails against the mug. "Does Milo enjoy hearing these sorts of things?"

She smiled, dropping her hands to the table as she did. "He does. He's wonderfully supportive and he's great to brainstorm ideas with, too."

A quick laugh burst through Beth's lips. "He's great to do a lot of things with."

Tori forced the smile to remain on her face even as her heart threatened to tug it downward at the innuendo in Beth's words. "So tell me about your company."

The woman studied her for a moment, her gaze moving from Tori's hair to her face to her clothes. When the visual inspection was over, Beth pursed her lips ever so slightly. "Do you know *anything* at all about fashion?"

"I know quite a bit, actually. I've been sewing since I was a little girl and I try to keep up on the latest fashions."

The woman dropped her gaze to Tori's attire once again. "Oh?"

Nibbling back the urge to say something unkind, Tori merely nodded.

In a flash, an unmistakable glow of excitement shot across Beth's face. "Would you like to see my new designs? The ones that are going to put Spotlight Fashions on the map in the pageant world—and beyond?"

"Spotlight Fashions? I thought you were changing the name."

Beth stared at her. "Changing the name? Where would you have gotten that?"

"Milo. He said something about you working on a new logo?"

"Oh. That. Well"—she grabbed hold of the leather portfolio and hoisted it onto the table—"I've had a change of heart." With a yank of her hand, Beth unzipped the case and spun it around to give Tori a better view of the plastic-sleeved pages inside. "Wait until you see my latest designs."

Pushing her mug to the side, Tori leaned forward, her attention captivated by the first dress in Beth's lineup. "Oh my gosh, Beth, this is—this is gorgeous."

Beth nodded, her hand sweeping across the first design. "Do you see the way the corset bodice is long and narrow, accenting the top of the waist?"

"I do." Her gaze skimmed across the design, stopping to inspect various aspects more closely. "And I really love the sweetheart neckline and the gathered skirt."

"Just wait. They get better." Beth turned the page to reveal a dress fit for a princess. "Do you see this one? The scallop-edged neckline really draws the eye, don't you think?"

"The ruched bodice is a nice touch as is the full princess skirt." She leaned closer. "Will the skirt be detailed with beads?"

"Scattered, yes." Beth turned to the third design. "Now this one is my favorite . . ." Her words trailed off as she stared at the drawing. "Don't you just love the embroidered bodice and the charmeuse waist?"

"It's beautiful." Tori pointed at the bottom half of the dress. "Are those appliqués cascading down the skirt?"

Again, Beth nodded. "They are. And they look stunning against the full skirt, don't you think?"

"Absolutely." Page by page they studied each of the six designs, stopping to discuss the various touches that made each one memorable. "Beth, they're gorgeous. Absolutely gorgeous." She shook her head softly, the woman's talent nothing short of mind-boggling. "Milo didn't tell me you did your own designs. They're amazing."

"A woman's got to keep a few secrets to herself just to keep them guessing, don't you think?" Beth ran her hand down the last of the six designs and sighed. "Besides, until recently, I used a different designer."

"Why didn't you design your own stuff from the beginning?"

Beth paused. "Well, because I—I was concentrating on getting the company up and running. It would have been too much trying to design everything myself."

"Oh." She watched as the woman closed the portfolio and zipped it closed. "Okay. So when will you roll these out?"

"Soon. I'd hoped to have twelve but, well, six will do."

"I can't imagine six more. These"—Tori gestured toward the leather case—"are really spectacular. You have an amazing talent, you really do."

"I know." Beth giggled. "Now I just need to make sure everything is in place."

"What do you mean?"

"When these designs hit, Spotlight Fashions will be *the* choice for pageant dresses."

Tori studied the woman closely, the glow of excitement making her all the more alluring. "Is the pageant business really that big?"

"When you have virtually *all* of it, it certainly is."

"Wow. I don't know how you do it."

A cloud passed across Beth's eyes. "Do what?"

"This." She pointed to the portfolio. "Designing these kinds of dresses while running the company, and traveling, and having a personal life. It seems like a lot."

"I don't have a personal life."

"Too busy?" Tori turned the mug in her hands, the ceramic material no longer warm.

"No. I just haven't seen the point in wasting time with anyone who isn't perfect."

"Perfect?"

"For me."

She reached across the table, patted Beth's hand atop the portfolio. "You'll find him."

"Oh, I found him. I found him a long time ago." Beth wrapped her long slender fingers around the handle of the leather case and stepped down off her stool, the click of her heels and the sexy purr of her voice making more than a few heads turn in their direction. "Fifteen years ago, to be exact."

Chapter 10

She pulled the ordering sheet closer to the computer and splayed her fingers across the keyboard. The best-selling author had always been wildly popular but his latest effort had blown away everyone's expectations. The result? A lengthy wait list that was simply unacceptable for her patrons.

"How many more copies are you going to order?" Nina clutched a pile of books to her chest and peered over Tori's shoulders.

"Two. That'll get us up to six copies." She typed in the necessary information and then pressed Send, the order form disappearing from her screen. "That should help cut down on the frustrated phone calls asking whether a copy has been returned yet."

Nina laughed in her ear. "I think Mr. Monting has called every day for the past week."

"When did the copies go out?"

"They all went out about the same time. Maybe nine days ago?"

"We should be seeing them back soon." Tori punched in the title and read the names of the four people who had checked it out on the very first day. "Wait, maybe not. Tina Stewy took it on vacation. And, knowing her track record, she'll be calling on the day it's due asking for an extension. The second copy went to Carter Johnson, the third to his wife."

"They both checked out a copy?"

Tori nodded. "They're both huge fans and want to be able to talk about it the second they finish."

Nina set the pile of books down to the left of the computer, her hands beginning the sorting process before they were even officially on the counter. "And the fourth?"

"The fourth . . . the fourth," Tori repeated under her breath as she scrolled down the page. "The fourth went to Leona."

"Leona?" Nina stopped sorting and turned toward Tori with rounded eyes. "I didn't know Ms. Elkin read anything besides travel magazines."

"She doesn't usually. But when it comes to a Joseph Cappy book, she reads. And looks."

"Looks?"

"At his author photo. Again and again and again."

"She likes Joseph Cappy?" Nina asked.

"How could she not? Have you seen that mischievous crinkle beside his eyes? Those dimples in his cheeks?" They looked up as Leona, clad in a mint green skirt and jacket, strode across the room and plunked the coveted book on the counter beside Nina's pile. "And let's not forget those shoulders. They're so broad, so powerful."

Tori laughed. "Were your ears burning? Is that why you chose this very moment to walk in?"

"My ears are just fine." Leona flipped the book over and

pointed at the author photo on the back cover flap. "I think the photo he used last year was even better. I preferred the full body shot. It made it easier to picture the two of us together."

"The two of you together?" Tori cast an amused glance in Nina's direction.

"Of course, dear. We'd be perfect together. His strong, towering frame would compliment my smaller, more feminine shape."

"I, uh, don't know what to say." She considered the head-and-shoulder shot the author had opted to use with his latest book. "And this picture doesn't allow you to, um, picture the two of you together?"

"It's a bit more difficult, dear. The arms are essential."

The arms?

"Do you picture this often?"

Leona waved her manicured fingers in the air. "All the time. I bought a copy of last year's book the second I saw the picture."

"The second you saw the picture? Don't you mean the second you realized it was such a good book?"

Tilting her head down, Leona pinned her with a stare across the top of her glasses. "No, dear, I mean precisely what I said. It's why that book is still backside out on my bookshelf a year later."

"Backside out?" she repeated, the hint of amusement in her question nearly impossible to miss. "That's a book placement you don't hear often, huh, Nina?"

Nina's face grew darker as she nibbled back her infamous shy smile. "I better get back to work. Are you going to take your dinner before I leave for the day?"

Tori glanced at her watch, noted the late afternoon hour.

"I probably should." Turning to her friend, she motioned toward the hallway. "Would you like to come sit with me in my office, Leona? I have enough for both of us."

"I'll come sit, dear. But I'm not hungry."

Shrugging, Tori grabbed her purse from beneath the information desk and led the way toward her office, the pitter-patter of Leona's shoes following closely behind. When they reached the room she shared with Nina, she gestured her friend inside. "Mr. Monting will be very pleased with you, Leona."

"Calob Monting?"

Tori nodded.

"I'd be surprised if he wasn't."

"Oh?"

A knowing smile spread across the sixty-something's face. "We had quite the evening a few years back."

Tori held up her hands, palms out, and dropped into her desk chair. "More details than I want to know, Leona."

Leona's brows furrowed as she, too, sat. "Then what are you talking about, dear?"

"The book? The one you just returned?" She set her purse at her feet then reached into the bottom drawer for her brown paper dinner sack, her hands finding the opening in record fashion. "Mr. Monting is top on the wait list."

"Oh." Leona made a face then swept her gaze around the room. "You really should paint this place. Give it a more romantic feel."

"A romantic feel?" Tori slipped her hand into the sack and pulled out a tuna salad sandwich, an apple, a chocolate chip cookie, and a napkin. "It's just an office, Leona. It really doesn't need a romantic feel."

For a moment Leona said nothing, her gaze following Tori's every move as she spread the napkin across her desk and situated her food on top. "Does Milo ever come to visit you here at work?"

She raised the sandwich to her mouth and took a bite. "He does."

"Are you ever alone in here?" Leona looked from the sandwich to Tori and back again, a hint of disgust tugging her lips downward. "Really, dear, you should consider what you eat. Bread is just not good for your figure."

"My—" She stopped mid-chew and glanced down at her satiny blouse and pencil skirt. "My figure is fine. Slight, but fine."

Leona opened her mouth to say something but closed it once again.

"And as for your question about Milo, sure, he comes to my office at times when Nina is either busy on the floor or off work. Why?"

"Romantic colors on the wall would set the mood better."

Tori set the sandwich down on the napkin and stared at her friend. "We're talking about my office, Leona. Inside the Sweet Briar Public Library."

"I'm aware of that, dear." Leona swiveled a hairbreadth in her chair then crossed her ankles delicately to her side. "How are things going with Milo?"

Bringing the apple to her lips, she shrugged. "They're good. Why?"

Leona leaned forward and dropped her voice to a near whisper. "Because you've got to be on your toes with that woman in town."

"Woman?" The crunch of her apple echoed around the room. "What woman are you talking about?"

Leona rolled her eyes skyward. "The old college flame. The one who looks as if she stepped out of the pages of a fashion magazine."

She dropped her apple-holding hand to the top of the desk. "You saw her?"

"No, dear, but Debbie has."

"Debbie said that? About the fashion magazine?"

Leona nodded. "We need to make sure she doesn't win, dear."

"Win?" She glanced down at the food on her napkin just in time to feel her appetite go riding off into the sunset. "Win what?"

"Milo."

Pushing the napkin off to the side, she leaned back in her chair, the thoughts she'd managed to shrug off in favor of work resurfacing with a vengeance. "I'm not out to *win* Milo."

Leona peered over her glasses. "Oh?"

"Milo and I are happy together. Beth Samuelson was years ago. Fourteen years ago to be exact."

"Time has a way of slipping away, dear. Especially when someone's on a mission."

"I'm not sure what you mean."

"She's after Milo."

She closed her eyes against the words she didn't want to believe, words Beth, herself, had certainly alluded to that morning at Debbie's Bakery. "No, she's not."

"Oh no?" Leona crossed her arms. "Then why did Debbie say you looked so miserable after your little meeting with her this morning?"

Damn.

"I didn't. I just—" And then she stopped, all further denial futile. "He says he's not interested."

Leona waved her hand above her head. "Which is neither here nor there, dear. A woman can break down virtually all walls of resistance if they want to. It's a matter of
using the proper tools."

Tucking an errant strand of hair behind her ear, Tori
slumped back in her chair. "And she's got those. In spades."

Leona pulled her purse onto the desk and unzipped it,
her hand locating and displaying a plethora of makeup products. "Anyone can highlight their tools, dear. That's easy."

"It is?"

The woman gestured around the room. "It's the aura,
the *mood* a man feels when he's with you that really seals
his fate."

"You think it was mood that made every man in the
bakery turn and stare at this woman?"

"No. Men are very predictable. They like the shiny
object. It's why I get so many looks everywhere I go."

Tori nibbled back the urge to laugh. If there was one
thing Leona wasn't lacking, it was an ego. Granted, it was
justified—she looked amazing for her age—but still, it was
there. And then some.

"But it's what you *exude*, dear, that keeps them
focused—for the long haul . . . or as long as you decide."

"Okay . . ." Tori spun her chair just enough to afford
a view of the library grounds and the town square just
beyond its perimeter. "Then I should be okay, right? Milo
and I have a lot in common."

"Common, schmommon. I'm talking about the attraction, the excitement, the *passion*."

She spun back to view her friend. "Milo and I do fine.
Just fine."

"That's exactly what I'm talking about, dear. There

shouldn't be any *just* about passion. Not the kind that will make him stick around, anyway."

Was Leona right? Did she need to spice things up a little? Had they gotten too comfortable with each other?

Comfortable is good.

She shook her head. "Can we not talk about this right now? Please?"

"I'm just trying to help, dear."

"I know. And I appreciate it, Leona, I really do. It's just—"

The ring of the branch phone cut her off mid-sentence. She picked it up and held it to her ear, glancing at the clock on the wall in the process.

"Good evening. Sweet Briar Public Library, how may I help you?"

"Yes, this is Regina Murphy."

Tori gripped the phone tighter. "Oh, yes, Miss Murphy, how may I help you?"

"I had a call on my answering machine from a Nina Morgan. Is she in?"

She looked a question at Leona, noted the way her brows rose in response despite the woman's inability to hear any part of the phone conversation. "She is, she's on the floor right now."

"Oh." The tone that had sounded rushed now adopted a hint of tension as well. "Are you the one who was at that birthday party the other night?"

"Yes. Is there anything I can do to help?"

"You can figure out which one of your friends murdered Ashley. Unless, of course, that someone was you."

She felt her hand moisten around the receiver. "Miss Murphy, I'm sorry to hear about Ashley, I truly am."

"Oh, give it up. You're not sorry at all. None of you are." A pause gave way to a secondary rush of words. "Look, I'm calling for one reason and one reason only. My bracelet."

"Your bracelet?" She peered at Leona, the woman nearly falling out of her chair in her effort to hear as much of Tori's conversation as humanly possible.

"Apparently this Nina person found a bracelet of mine on the library grounds. Her message said she saw the inscription on the inside and suspected it was me."

Tori pushed her chair back and stood, her gaze skimming the top of Nina's desk. Sure enough, a silver bracelet sat dead center with a sticky note bearing Regina Murphy's name attached. "Oh yes, I see it right here."

"Can I put you on hold for a moment, my dinner just arrived." Without waiting for a response, the woman disappeared from the line, the sound of her footsteps in the background the only indication it was still an active line.

Covering the mouthpiece with her hand, Tori provided a name to go with the caller. "It's Regina. Regina Murphy."

"I got that, dear." Leona's eyebrows rose still further. "Shall we ask her which one of us she truly suspects of murder? Or do you think she imagines it was more of a *group* effort?"

"Shhh. Not now." She pulled her hand from the phone and listened to the voices in the background. "She's getting pizza," she whispered.

Rolling her eyes to the ceiling, Leona lifted her shoulders momentarily. "So tell me about this meeting with Milo's girlfriend."

"Milo's ex-girlfriend, Leona." She reached for the phone cord and wrapped it around her finger. "I guess Milo thought it would be good for us to meet."

"And?"

It was Tori's turn to shrug. "It was awkward at first, but then it got better. She showed me the six designs she's just completed for Spotlight Fashions. And Leona? They're amazing. The beaded detail on the skirts, the charmeuse waists, the ruched bodices—they're incredible. I had no idea Beth Samuelson was such an amazing designer."

"It matters naught as long as you keep the passion alive, dear, remember that—"

Breathing in her ear brought her focus back to the phone. "Regina?"

"One minute, I'm not ready yet."

She moved her mouth to the side and made a face at Leona.

"Where's this relationship-wrecker staying while she's in Sweet Briar?"

Tori tapped her fingers on the desk, her attention caught between the breathing in her ear and the challenging set to Leona's brows. "The Sweet Briar Inn, where else? But, really, Leona, what difference does it make?"

"She's too close."

Regina returned to the line. "I'm here now. My dinner arrived a full five minutes sooner than it was supposed to, otherwise we'd have been done with this charade of a conversation before it arrived."

Charade?

"That's fine." She glanced back toward the bracelet on her assistant's desk. "I was just saying that I see your bracelet right now. It's on Nina's desk."

"Wonderful. I'll send someone by to get it within the hour."

"It'll be here." The click of the phone in her ear signaled

the end to their call and she returned the receiver to its base. "There's certainly no love loss there."

Leona shrugged. "We threatened her employee and now that employee is dead. Can you blame her?"

"We didn't do it, Leona." She sat back down in her chair and released a louder than intended sigh.

"*Someone* did, dear."

"Can we talk about something else? Please? My head is starting to pound."

"We're running out of topics, dear."

"I know." She grabbed the cookie off her napkin and broke a piece off the end. Popping it into her mouth, she chewed and swallowed in rapid succession. "What do I do, Leona?"

Leona ran her index finger along the edge of the desk then held it upward. At its relatively clean appearance she nodded in appreciation. "Do about what, dear?"

She swallowed back the lump that threatened to render her speechless. "Milo."

"I thought you said you didn't want to talk about that."

"I didn't."

The woman sniffed. "I see. Well, you can make your next date something special, something extra creative."

"Creative," she whispered.

"I realize we're limited on culture in this town but perhaps you could call on the circle for a little help."

"What kind of help?"

"Margaret Louise could whip up one of her culinary delights. You could borrow Rose's china. You could—"

"Extra creative," she repeated as images began to flood her mind.

"That's right, dear."

Creative . . .

"But—" She stopped, squared her shoulders and then forged ahead, the question needing to be asked even if Leona wasn't the one to answer. "What happens if he falls for her again?"

"He won't." Leona's chin rose upward. "Because we won't let him."

Chapter 11

She knew she was merely caving, letting Leona-induced fear rule her actions, but she didn't really see any other way. Beth Samuelson had her sights set on Milo. Of that, Tori was virtually certain. And while her mind was just as certain about Milo's feelings for *her*, her heart was squirming just a little.

Okay, maybe a lot.

Perhaps some of it was the sucker punch Jeff had dealt her during their engagement party, his presence in the reception hall's coat closet with a mutual friend just about as humiliating as it came. Perhaps it was a sign of even bigger confidence issues than she'd realized. Or perhaps it truly was the effects of Leona Elkin.

But, regardless of what it was, she was prepared to fight for what she wanted. And what she wanted was Milo Wentworth.

Pulling the oven door open, she backed up to peek inside. The tantalizing aroma of the beef brisket wafted through the opening. "Mmmm, perfect."

"Do I get to know what it is you're making?"

She smiled to herself as she lifted out the tray and set it on top of the stove. "When I call you to the table," she responded.

The dinner had been a last-minute idea, the handcrafted invitation she taped to the steering wheel of his car close on its heels.

"Do you have any idea how cool it was to find that note like that?"

Carefully, she unwrapped the foil package that housed the brisket, the trapped heat warming her cheeks. "I'm glad you liked it."

"I loved it."

Point One—me.

"In fact, I was so engrossed in your note I didn't notice the photograph Beth had slipped into the passenger seat sometime during the school day."

She stopped, mid-fork-poke. "Photograph?"

"Yeah. Just some picture from a school formal we went to together my junior year." His voice hitched a bit indicating he'd risen from the sofa and was walking around the living room. "Gosh, we looked so gaga over each other."

"*Gaga*, huh?" she mumbled beneath her breath. "Isn't that wonderful." Taking a step back once again, she reached into the oven a second time, this time to retrieve a tray of piping hot dinner rolls.

Point One—Beth.

"It was, at one time. But, whatever, enough about that now. Anything new on the Ashley Lawson front?"

She set the tray of rolls on a hot plate then lifted the lid from the homemade mashed potatoes, transferring all to the china serving dishes she'd retrieved from the cabinet above the refrigerator. "No, not really, except I got a call from Regina Murphy yesterday."

"What about?"

Slicing a few pieces of butter from the stick in front of her, she plopped them onto the potatoes and mixed them together, adding a sprig of parsley to the top. "She dropped a bracelet out on the grounds during Sally's party the other night. She wanted to claim it."

"Oh, okay. That makes sense."

She shifted the brisket to a cutting board and began slicing. "Of course she took the opportunity to let me know my friends and I are killers."

"All of you?"

"Essentially." Piece by piece she moved the brisket to a delicately flowered serving platter. "Okay, Milo, you can come to the table now."

"Music to my ears." His footsteps sounded on the wood floor as he moved from the living room to the eat-in kitchen. The second he rounded the corner she felt the butterfly brigade take flight in her stomach just like always. "Whoa, candles?"

She looked at the table and nodded, her gaze riveted on the flames that danced atop their wicks. "I just felt like doing something special for you tonight."

He crossed the kitchen and pulled her into his arms, his breath warm against her forehead. "You do special things for me all the time."

"I hope so, I really do." She stepped from his embrace and pointed at the table. "Take a seat. Everything is ready."

Peeking over her shoulder, he inhaled deeply. "Mmmm, that smells delicious. My mom would love this."

She smiled at the mention of Milo's mom. It had only been a little over five months since she'd met Rita, yet in that time they'd grown close, brought together over their shared love for Milo and solidified thanks to their similar easygoing, people-pleaser personalities. Learning of their shared interest in sewing had simply been the icing on the cake.

"When will Rita be here again?"

"A few weeks. She wants to come for Heritage Days this year."

Steeling herself for an answer she didn't want to hear, she placed the brisket platter on the table and returned to the counter for the potatoes, rolls, and carrots. "Do you think Beth will still be here then?"

He grabbed hold of the serving platter and forked a few pieces of brisket onto his plate. "I don't know. I suppose it's possible. She mentioned the other day that she can work remotely from just about anywhere."

She placed the butter on the table then grabbed the wine bottle she'd placed in the center. At his nod, she poured the wine into the crystal goblet she'd set beside his plate. "Does your mom know Beth?"

"She does." He handed the platter to Tori and then reached for the potatoes. "They met a few times during that year we dated. Beth met my father, too."

"Oh." For a moment she warred with the desire to ask the one question that still remained on her tongue, curiosity winning out in the end. "Um, was your mom sad when you broke up?"

He shrugged, his broad shoulders rising and falling in short order. "I guess. She never really said much either way. But I can tell you this, she never gushed over her the way she does you."

Tori grinned.

Point Two—me . . .

"I'm glad."

Pausing his fork just shy of his mouth, he studied her closely. "You're not worried about Beth, are you?"

She blew a rebellious strand of soft brown hair from her face only to watch it fall, undaunted, against her forehead once again. "I'm trying not to be, Milo. I really am. It's just that Leona . . . Well, let's just say she has a way of playing on insecurities I wasn't aware I really had."

He set his fork on his plate and reached for her hand, his touch calming her nerves instantly. "You've got nothing—absolutely nothing—to worry about, Tori. Putting my long-gone romantic feelings for Beth in the same camp as my feelings for you is like trying to say hamburger and filet mignon are one and the same."

Blinking against the sudden moisture in her eyes, she squeezed his hand in response. "I'm sorry, Milo. I really am. I'm not sure why I let Leona get in my head like that."

His fingers left her hand in favor of her face. "This stuff with Ashley Lawson has thrown you for a loop, that's all. When a person is stressed about one thing, silly things tend to balloon up as well. It's human nature."

She cocked her head to the left and studied him, his amber-flecked brown eyes a perfect compliment to the dimples she saw growing in his cheeks. "What? What's so funny?" she asked.

"It's kind of nice knowing you care so much."

Turning her head, she caught his fingers with her own and planted a kiss on their tips. "Don't let it go to your head—"

The ring of his cell phone cut her short and she released his hand. Rummaging in his pocket he pulled out the silver device and checked the screen.

"It's Beth."

Point Two—Beth.

"This will only take a second, I promise." He tugged the phone open and held it to his ear. "Hey, Beth, what's up?'

The familiar voice poured from the phone, this time so

shrill and so loud it was impossible for Tori to miss. "It's Beth. I need you to come quick. Please."

He sat up tall, his hand tightening around the phone as he met Tori's gaze across the table. "Beth, what's wrong? Are you okay?"

"Someone just tried to kill me."

Tori, too, sat up, the woman's words striking a sense of fear in her.

"What did you just say?" Milo repeated.

"I—I said I think someone just tried to kill me."

"What happened?" he snapped.

Sniffling was followed by the woman's throaty, yet broken voice. "I—I w-was walking through the parking lot of the inn just now and I heard footsteps behind me."

"Okay . . ."

"I turned around once and didn't see anyone so I figured I was wrong. Then I heard it again, and just as I was starting to turn around a car pulled into the lot and whoever it was dove behind a parked car."

"Did you see who it was?"

"No. But they had a knife."

His eyes widened along with hers. "A knife? Are you sure?"

"It dropped to the g-ground when they d-ducked behind the car. As soon as I saw it, I—I r-ran." And then the sobbing started, loud racking sobs that left them feeling more than a little helpless.

Tori looked at Milo. "Ask her if she called the police," she whispered.

The crying stopped. "Is someone there with you?" Beth asked between whimpers.

"I'm with Tori." He tipped the phone at an angle to make it easier for her to hear. "Did you call the police when this happened?"

Beth sniffed once, then twice. "I th-thought about it. B-but I don't want any publicity r-right now. Nothing that might d-detract from the unveiling of the designs."

Tori closed her eyes, recalled the breathtaking dresses the woman had shown her just the previous morning.

"Do you think that's wise?" Milo asked. "If you're right, and someone meant you harm this evening, the police really should know."

"And I'll tell them. If it happens again," Beth promised. "But not now, Milo. Please."

Tori watched as his leg began to bounce ever so slightly, a sure sign Milo was feeling stressed. His words simply served as secondary confirmation. "I don't know, Beth . . . You've got me worried now."

The sniffing stopped. "You're worried about me?"

Milo nodded.

"Milo, are you there?"

"Oh. Sorry. Yes. I'm worried about you. How could I not be?"

Beth hiccupped into the phone. "It was scary. So very, very scary. And to tell you the truth, I'm still scared, Milo." The woman's voice paused a moment before resurfacing with a noticeable shake. "Do . . . do you think you could come by and take a look? Just to make sure no one is lurking outside my door?"

He raked a hand through his hair then met Tori's eyes with the question she knew he was hesitant to verbalize. Instead, she beat him to the punch. "Why don't you go have a look? It'll make the both of you feel better."

Covering the phone briefly, he searched her face closely. "Are you sure? You went to so much trouble for this dinner."

She nodded, her hand finding his free one and holding it close. "I'm sure. It's the right thing to do, Milo."

He pulled his hand from the front of the phone and whispered a kiss across her forehead. "I love you, Tori." To Beth he said, "What room are you in?"

"What room am I in?"

"That's what I asked."

For a moment there was nothing. And then, "Oh, c'mon now, Milo . . . you *remember*."

She stared at Milo, her heart unwilling to consider the implication of the woman's words. Or the way they resurrected the sound of Leona's voice in her head.

"No," he stammered, his face suddenly crimson. "I met you at the restaurant both nights."

"Oh. Okay, Milo." A flirty laugh escaped from the phone in much the same manner as an open hand to Tori's face. "I'm in 3B."

"Okay. I'll be right there."

The sudden yet audible smile in the woman's voice sent a shiver down Tori's spine, the words that followed kicking off a wave of nausea that was virtually impossible to ignore. "And Milo? I'll be waiting for you."

Chapter 12

Tori shielded her eyes from the sun and studied the faces of the women who'd become her closest friends over the past year—women who had helped her move forward in a life that was as close to perfect as anyone could ever hope to have.

In fact, each and every member of the Sweet Briar Ladies Society Sewing Circle had taught her something.

Rose had taught her what it meant to soldier on despite an aging process that had its own agenda at times.

Debbie had taught her the reality that dreams—no matter how big or how many—could happen if you simply put your mind to it. Owning her own bakery while excelling at her marriage and motherhood was proof of that.

Beatrice had reinforced the importance of not judging a book by its cover. The nanny, although painfully shy, had a heart of gold and some great ideas if one only gave her a chance.

Melissa had shown her that mothering went far beyond kissing boo-boos and getting dinner on the table by six every night, her constant encouragement of each of her seven children a joy to witness.

Georgina had taught her about resilience in the wake of humiliation, her positive spirit despite her former husband's murder charge nothing short of commendable.

Margaret Louise had taught her about loyalty in a way no one ever had, the woman's steadfast and unconditional friendship a rarity in a world where everyone seemed to look out for themselves and their best interests.

Leona had taught her the ways of the south—or, rather, the ways of the south according to Leona Elkin. The woman's on again, off again ornery demeanor simply served as tangible proof that good things came in the most interesting of packages.

Even Dixie had taught her a few things, most noticeably the fact that everyone needed to feel important no matter how young or old they might be.

"Earth to Victoria, earth to Victoria, come in Victoria."

The sound of her name jolted her back to the here and now—a here and now that had her sitting at one of the bakery's outdoor tables alongside the rest of the sewing circle.

"Oh, I'm sorry," she said by way of a smile at Margaret Louise, the woman's plump form decked out in one of her trademark polyester warm-up suits, this one in lavender. "Did you say something?"

"I asked if Chief Dallas has paid you another visit."

"Um, no. Not yet." Shaking her thoughts into focus, she looked around at her friends. "Has he come to see anyone else?"

All but two hands shot up—hers and Georgina's.

Her mouth gaped open. "And?"

"He asked about the party and about the things that were said regarding Ashley. You know, the same sorts of things he asked you," Debbie said, her voice barely more than a whisper. "He talked to Caroline Rowen and Samantha Smith, too."

"Did you tell him we were just irritated at Ashley's attitude?"

"We all did, dear. Though I'm not sure what good it's done." Leona looked down at the blueberry scone on her plate then pushed it aside. "I don't know why I order these things."

"Maybe because they look delicious?" Debbie shook her head, a sparkle in her eye belying the exaggerated hurt in her voice. "Maybe because I made them from scratch while you and the rest of Sweet Briar were catching a few extra hours of beauty rest?"

"Some of us don't need sleep to achieve that distinction. We simply are."

Rose snorted from her spot across the table. "Leona, why don't you wish in one hand, spit in the other, and see which ones gets full faster."

Tori laughed out loud. "Excuse me? What did you just say, Rose?"

"It's akin to saying Aunt Leona is spouting something that's no more than wishful thinking on her part." Melissa dipped a soft-tipped spoon into a jar of bananas and then brought it to Molly's lips, the youngest of her brood razzing out as much as she consumed.

Leona made a face as the pale yellow fruit ran back down the baby's chin. "She's never going to attract a man that way."

"I'll worry about that in, I don't know, maybe twenty years or so." Using the edge of the spoon, Melissa collected the missed bananas from Molly's little chin and re-deposited it back in the baby's mouth.

"As for that expression Rose just uttered, dear" —Leona

trained her focus on Tori—"don't you be adding that to our list of southernisms, understand? That one is just plain ignorant not to mention backwoods."

"I think *accurate* describes it better, Twin," Margaret Louise bellowed from her spot on Molly's other side. "Don't forget what Grandmammy used to say. 'The easiest way to eat crow is while it's still warm, 'cause the colder it gets, the harder it is to swallow.'"

"That's why I preferred Grandfather." Leona shifted in her seat and directed her attention toward Debbie. "Now don't get me wrong, Debbie, I think a late morning gathering has potential, but really, if we're simply going to sit here and listen to the likes of my sister and Rose Winters all morning, I really must be heading out. I have inventory to price at the shop."

Tori lifted her hot chocolate to-go cup to her lips and took a quick sip. "Did you get a new shipment of antiques?"

Leona nodded. "I did. It's not big but there are some really exquisite pieces."

Dixie pushed back her chair and stretched her swollen legs outward. "Why *did* you ask us here, Debbie? Other than to assemble all the suspects in one place should Chief Dallas be hoping for a short workday?"

The bakery owner's pale blue eyes skittered from one face to the next, her wider than normal smile simply adding to their near constant sparkle. "I have a request I'm hoping you'll all consider. Something to keep us busy while the vulture circles."

All eyes turned in Debbie's direction.

"A sewing request?" Beatrice asked, her soft British accent a nice contrast to the southern drawl that was as much a part of life in Sweet Briar as sweet tea and gossip.

Debbie nodded.

"A group project?"

"Yes, Margaret Louise, a group project. *If* everyone's willing." Debbie reached beneath her chair and extracted a small brown felt bag that resembled a child's lunch sack. Laying it in the middle of the table she stuck her hand inside only to pull out a hand-painted cardboard container.

"What's that?" Dixie asked as she leaned forward for a closer look.

Rose, too, leaned forward. "Did you make that?"

"I did." With a quick turn of her hand, Debbie opened the container and began to pull out something resembling potato chips.

Margaret Louise took one in her hand and turned it over. "Felt? You made a potato chip with felt?"

Dixie snatched it from Margaret Louise's hand and held it in front of her thick glasses. "You've even stitched it in such a way to give the chip a curved effect."

Reaching inside the felt sack once again, Debbie pulled out two pieces of bread and a clump of lettuce.

Melissa stopped feeding Molly long enough to grab hold of the lettuce and turn it over in her hands. "You made play food?"

"It's cheaper than the store-bought stuff and it allows the kids to have the items they want rather than what is dictated by some company." Debbie turned the sack upside down to reveal a slice of ham, two tomatoes, and a brownie. "Suzanna and Jackson love to play with this stuff."

"It's darling," Tori said. "Absolutely darling."

"Thanks, Victoria." Debbie swept her hand across the contents of the felt lunch sack. "This is just some of the food I've made with felt for the kids. They have pizza, pancakes, cake, hamburgers with all the trimmings, peanut butter sandwiches . . . you name it. And all it takes to make it is a little creativity, various colors of craft felt, a simple pattern you can draw up on your own, and either a needle and thread or a machine depending on what you're doing."

"So what do you need from us?" Dixie asked between bites of her cinnamon crumb cake. "Do you want us to help you stock Suzanna and Jackson's toy closet even more?"

Margaret Louise rushed to soften Dixie's question. "Because we will if you need us to."

Debbie shook her head. "I've already made enough for the kids. But the other day, Colton Granger came into Jake's garage. He had a flat tire that needed patching."

"I heard, through the grapevine, that Colton is out of work," Rose said.

Beatrice nodded. "I saw his wife, Eloise, at the playground day before last and she said the same thing. People aren't fixing up their homes these days and Colton's boss doesn't have the funds to employee him any longer."

"Such a shame," Dixie mused. "It's hard to see folks out of work like that—whether there's simply no work for them or they're forced out to make room for younger, cheaper employees."

Leona met Tori's gaze before rolling her eyes skyward. "You watch, she'll stick to it until the last pea is out of the pot."

A gasp rang up around the table.

"Why, Aunt Leona, if I didn't know any better I'd think you just used one of Margaret Louise's expressions," Melissa chided.

The woman's face drained of all color. "I—I did no such thing . . ." The words trailed from Leona's mouth as Tori laughed out loud.

"It's okay, Leona, every dog ought to have a few fleas now and again, isn't that right, Dixie?" Rose winked at Tori before turning her focus on the retired librarian. "Dixie?"

The elderly woman with the crop of snow-white hair looked up, the expression behind her glasses hard to decipher. "Colton and Eloise have young-uns, don't they?"

"Yes, they do," Debbie affirmed. "Two little girls—Abby and Sophie. And both have birthdays coming up at the end of the month."

Rose sat up tall, a smile softening her wrinkled features. "And we're going to make them play food?"

Debbie's eyes shone. "That's what I was hoping."

"Count me in," Tori said as she reached for the slice of bread, turning it over and over in her hands. "I'll also donate some of the felt. I'm fairly sure I have a bunch in the same color as the top and crust of this bread."

"Count us all in." Dixie pulled her legs back toward her chair. "Let's plan on working on this at our next meeting at"—she looked around at the group—"who's having the next one again?"

Tori raised her hand. "I am."

"Shall we invite Chief Dallas, ladies?" Margaret Louise brushed a kiss across her granddaughter's messy face. "That way he can save the town a little gasoline."

Georgina cleared her throat. "He's only doin' his job. A woman *was* murdered after all."

Margaret Louise pointed at Dixie. "Did you murder Ashley Lawson?"

Dixie shook her head. "Though I'd be lying if I didn't say I was tempted."

Her finger shifted to Rose. "Did you murder Ashley Lawson?"

Rose shook her head.

Her finger shifted to Debbie. "Did you murder Ashley Lawson?"

Georgina held up her hands before Debbie could answer. "What does this prove, Margaret Louise?"

"It stops time from bein' wasted, that's what." Margaret Louise reached in front of the baby and capped up the empty jar of bananas as Melissa moved onto Apple Delight. "We've all lived in this town for years—'cept Victoria and she's no more capable of murderin' someone than the rest of us are. Chief Dallas is barkin' up the wrong tree is all."

"Ashley Lawson was murdered. There is an investigation going on in order to catch her killer. Everyone at this table was overheard making threats against her just hours before she was killed." The town's top elected official folded her napkin and tossed it beside her crumb-ridden plate. "I'm sure you can see how that makes me caught where the wool is short."

"That's all well and good, Georgina," Rose stated as she, too, tossed her napkin onto the table. "But remember this: You can put your boots in the oven, but that don't make 'em biscuits."

Tori looked a question at Leona only to have it answered by Margaret Louise.

"Rose is right, Georgina. The chief can ask us if we murdered that nasty woman until the cows come home. But askin' and investigatin' won't change the answer none. He's barkin' up the wrong tree, plain and simple."

Chapter 13

"I feel bad for Georgina," Tori said as she walked side by side with Leona on the way toward their final destinations. "I mean, think what that must be like, being elected to oversee every aspect of a town's well-being. Only in order to do that, you must ruffle the feathers of your friends."

"The ruffling wouldn't last nearly as long if everyone would just play along."

She considered her friend's words as they crossed Center Street and headed south along the sidewalk that bordered the town square on the east. "You don't mind being questioned in Ashley's murder?"

Leona shrugged, her surprisingly toned arms rising and falling beneath the pale pink Donna Karan suit she wore. "Why should I? I didn't do anything wrong."

"You said some not-so-very-nice things about a woman who wound up dead less than twelve hours later."

"She deserved them. She brought rude to a new level that night." Leona's heels clicked against the concrete.

"My grandmammy used to say some people are so full of themselves, you'd like to buy them for what they're worth and sell them for what they think they're worth. A perfect description of that woman, don't you think?"

"It is. I guess. Though she's not the only one who seems—"

"*Seemed*," Leona corrected.

"*Seemed* to be affected with that disorder." She cast a sidelong look at her friend. "Is that better?"

"Yes." Leona slowed as they neared a spot on the sidewalk that was buckled thanks to an exposed tree root. "Georgina would do well to have that removed before someone trips and sues."

She stepped to the left to allow Leona to clear the spot then fell into step beside her once again. "Though I'm not sure Beth is like that with everyone."

"Beth?"

"Milo's college sweetheart." The second the words were out of her mouth she couldn't help but cringe at the tone in which she'd spoken them—the hint of hurt and fear as tangible as the gentle spring breeze that lifted their hair from their heads. "You know what? Scratch that. Can we pretend I didn't bring her up just now?"

"We could, but we won't." Leona wrapped her fingers around Tori's forearm and tugged her onto the Green, pointing her manicured finger toward a bench beside the town's famed gazebo. "Let's sit."

"Don't you have to inventory the antique shipment you just got?"

"It can wait, dear. Problems with men can't. They need to be addressed and eliminated without delay." When they reached the bench, Leona sat down primly, tugging Tori down beside her. "So tell me. What happened?"

That's all it took for the floodgates to open.

"I decided to take your advice last night . . ."

Leona beamed. "Yes, dear?"

"I left a dinner invitation on the steering wheel of Milo's car while he was still at work. Then I rushed home and made a beef brisket with all the trimmings."

"Attacking through the stomach certainly does have potential . . ."

She winced. "I wasn't trying to attack. Not really, anyway. It was more about trying to show him he's special to me."

"Semantics, dear."

"So he came over and I lit some candles. Then I set the table with my best china. And made one of my best recipes."

"And how did it go?"

She shrugged. "Fine. For all of about ten minutes. Tops."

Leona turned to study Tori over the top of her stylish glasses. "Did you have a disagreement?"

She shook her head.

"Did you retire to the bedroom?"

She rolled her eyes and shook her head even harder.

"Perhaps *that* was the problem, dear."

"No. It was the phone call he got after he'd taken no more than three bites."

"Phone call?" Leona echoed.

This time she nodded, her words shoring up the gesture with the kind of answers her head couldn't convey. "From Beth."

"Oh."

For a moment neither said a word, their visual focus distracted by a squirrel scampering across the Green. When she did speak, Leona's words were hushed. "Did he at least keep the conversation short?"

"Relatively, yes."

"Well, I suppose that's a good sign. At least he wrapped up the call to continue your dinner together."

She looked down at her hands as she twisted them inside her lap. "It would have been a good sign, if that's what he'd done."

Leona turned to her once again. "He didn't?"

"No."

"Don't tell me he left."

"He left."

"To be with her?"

Tori switched back to nodding in an effort to keep her voice from breaking.

A gasp of disgust escaped Leona's thinning lips. "Why?"

"She thought someone was after her."

"After her?"

She nodded again.

"How?"

"In a dangerous way. She felt unsafe, prompting Milo to ride to the rescue."

"Who would be after her?" Leona asked. "Other than, perhaps, me?"

Tori's head snapped up and she turned to meet her friend's gaze? "You?"

"You think I like what her presence is doing to you, dear?"

She sucked in her breath as Leona's words took root in her thoughts. "Wait."

"Wait, what?" Leona asked as she looked around at the empty Green. "What's wrong?"

"Please tell me you weren't trying to scare her in the parking lot of the Sweet Briar Inn the other night."

"I wish I'd thought of it." Leona ran her hands down

the pale pink material that draped across her thighs. "Then again, doing that would have backfired as we saw, yes?"

Backfired . . .

"She acted as if he knew what room she was in."

Leona's hands stilled. *"Did* he?"

"He said he didn't." She heard the sadness in her voice but could do nothing to stop it. She'd held it at bay through the circle's entire breakfast meeting and simply couldn't do it any longer.

"Do you believe him?"

"I want to. I really do. It's just that—" She stopped, swallowed, then continued on, her voice adopting a raspy quality. "Well, I wanted to believe Jeff was true, too."

"I know, dear."

She sat up tall on the bench. "Wait. I can't say that. I believe him. I do. Milo is nothing like Jeff."

Leona squeezed her hand. "Let's assume he is telling the truth then, shall we?"

"He is," she insisted.

"Then we have another question to consider."

She looked at her friend. "What's that?"

"Why she'd insinuate otherwise."

Tori's shoulders slumped. "I wondered that all night while I tossed and turned in my bed."

"And?" Leona prompted.

"And I came up with nothing because I just don't get it."

"I do."

"Tell me."

"She's trying to get under your skin."

"She's trying to get under my skin?" she repeated. "But why?"

"To cause trouble."

"For whom?"

"You and Milo."

"For what purpose?" Though the second the question left her lips, she knew the answer as clearly as if she'd dreamed it up all on her own.

"To break you up, dear."

Closing her eyes, she thought back over their meeting at the bakery. She thought about the designs. She thought about the conversation. She thought about the way every male in the room stopped to stare at Milo's former girlfriend.

"He called me when he got home. He apologized for running out."

"As he should."

Her heart twisted under Leona's words. "He did the right thing, Leona. He really did. What would have happened if whoever it was had tried again?"

"She wouldn't be an issue any longer, dear."

Tori couldn't help it, she laughed. But as the sound subsided, she cocked an eyebrow at the deadpan face Leona sported. "You *were* kidding, right?"

"Perhaps. But one thing can't be ignored any longer."

"What's that?"

"You have a problem on your hands. A blonde, blue-eyed problem."

"Maybe it was an isolated thing, Leona."

"Perhaps. Though I suspect your problem just got a lot bigger the moment Milo ran to her aid."

Chapter 14

"So let's take it from the top again, shall we?"

Tori grabbed hold of her left shoulder with her right hand and kneaded the skin beneath her fingers. "Sure, if you want to, but really, nothing is going to change."

They'd been at it for nearly an hour, Police Chief Dallas's chat feeling a lot more like an interrogation minus the swinging overhead light and the two-way mirror with the overeager partner on the other side.

"So you're saying you never actually said you'd strangle Mrs. Lawson, is that right?"

"That's right."

"We have a witness that would say otherwise."

Dropping her hands to the top of her desk, she pulled a pencil from the wooden holder and twirled it between her fingers. "Regina Murphy heard a lot of people saying virtually the same thing. Did she say, specifically, that I threatened to strangle the victim?"

The chief's eyes narrowed on hers. "She said everyone at the party threatened the victim in one way or another—with strangulation being the stated method of choice."

"Well, everyone didn't. All I did was make mention about the rope Milo tied to the tree not being a good idea to have in our sights."

"And you don't see that as a threatening thing to say?"

Her hand stilled around the pen. "No, I see it as a comment that was meant as a joke . . . whether appropriate or not."

"And your friends who actually mentioned the desire to strangle Mrs. Lawson?"

She pushed her chair back from her desk and stood. "You'll have to ask them, Chief Dallas. But, having been there at the party, I'm as certain as certain can be that they, too, were joking."

"Do you find that people often grit their teeth while joking?"

"When they've been pushed to the brink and they're trying to maintain their composure by lightening the atmosphere, yes. And that, Chief Dallas, is what these purported threats you're referring to were all about. Nothing more, nothing less."

He followed on her heels as she crossed her office to the closed door. "Mrs. Lawson is dead, Victoria."

She grabbed hold of the doorknob and turned. "I realize that, Chief, and that is a shame. It truly is. For no matter how offensive and mean-spirited that woman was, no one—no one I know—wished her true harm."

"Someone did."

Yanking the door open she swept her hand into the hall in an indication their meeting was over. "You're right. I'm just not that someone. Neither are any of my friends."

"Time will tell, Victoria, time will tell."

"It always does." She watched as his uniform-clad back disappeared down the hallway and out the back door, his squad car visible in the background. Stepping out into the hall, she turned in the opposite direction, her feet being led forward by the promise of some sanity.

Nina looked up as she entered the main room. "Are you okay, Miss Sinclair?"

She joined her assistant behind the information desk and grabbed hold of a pile of books that were waiting to be sorted. "It's fine. Just a lot going on, you know?"

"Is there anything I can do?"

Slowly she moved the books from the original stacks into smaller ones depending on where they were shelved around the library. "We can talk about something other than Ashley Lawson and Beth Samuelson."

"Beth Samuelson? Who's that?"

"Nobody." She moved the top book onto the history pile, the second onto the mystery pile. "You know what? I want to talk about that donation we got from Curtis in the fall. You know, the two thousand dollars we tucked aside until we got through the holiday season."

Nina's face glowed with excitement. "I've been giving it some thought ever since we got it, tossing around ideas for all sorts of things. I've even kept Duwayne up a night or two bouncing ideas off him."

Tori laughed, the sound and the feeling doing wonders against the tension that had started with memories of Beth Samuelson and re-ignited with Chief Dallas's unexpected second visit. "And?"

"Well, I had some good ones, I really did, but it was Duwayne's idea that I've not been able to forget."

Pushing the various piles to the side, she leaned against the counter. "Tell me."

"Duwayne said that he thinks what you did with the children's room is fantastic. He said it's the kind of thing he would have loved when he was a little boy growin' up in Mississippi. But he also said that it's when you get a little older—like in your teenage years—that books tend to lose their pull."

She nodded. Nina was right. It was a fact of life for the teenage set who were suddenly gaga over anything that didn't include sitting in a room alone. "Go on," she encouraged.

"He started talking 'bout the things teenagers like. Things like getting together with friends, acting more grown-up, feeling as if they've got something to say in life that makes a difference or needs to be heard."

Pulling the computer stool closer, she sat down, her attention riveted on her assistant's words.

"Duwayne thinks that acknowledging those things in the area of books might make them seem less babyish or inconsequential."

"Okay."

"He suggested having a night, maybe once a month, where the library stays open just for teenagers."

"We don't want to be a hangout spot, Nina."

"If it involves books and reading, we do."

She nodded. "Okay, keep going."

"On that night, we host a book club that is just for them. The books they're interested in, the books they want to discuss. We pull up the chairs and sofa, we pop some popcorn or bring in a batch of cookies, and we let them talk about the book they've read. What they liked, what they didn't, what could have been better."

"I like it."

"Book clubs are a grown-up kind of thing. They'll be

drawn to that alone if we can focus it to where they are in life."

Her assistant was right. "And the donation? What's that for?"

Nina's eyes rounded with excitement. "To buy the books they select and, maybe, bring in an occasional guest speaker to increase the excitement."

"Depending on the speaker they can be quite costly," Tori reminded.

"Then we tell the kids that. Let them weigh who's most important. It'll be an unexpected lesson in budgeting."

For a moment she said nothing, her mind rewinding its way through their conversation, stopping to pause on the highlights. And just like that, the answer was clear. "I love it, Nina. I absolutely love it."

"I'd volunteer my time to lead the discussion," Nina offered. "And, believe it or not, so will Duwayne. He thinks a male presence might encourage some of the teen boys to give it a shot."

She nodded, a smile stretching her face wide. "I suspect he's right. Now I love it even more."

Nina's face grew a shade darker as she looked down and toed at the carpet beneath their feet. "I was hoping you would, Miss Sinclair."

"You're going to make a wonderful head librarian one day, Nina." She stepped off the stool and pulled her assistant in for a quick hug. "Your instincts are right on the money."

"Thank you, Miss Sinclair. Though, in this case, it's really more a case of Duwayne's instincts."

"Did you like the idea when you heard it?"

"I loved it."

"Then that's *your* instinct that stepped up to the plate."

She turned back to the piles on the counter, her thoughts already picking through the books in their inventory that might serve as possible kickoff titles for a teen book club. "Shall we put out some feelers?"

"You mean at the high school?" Nina asked in a voice that was suddenly breathless.

She nodded.

"Oh yes! Yes! But"—Nina squared her shoulders with a rare burst of confidence—"can I try my hand at a few posters first? Something that can be hung up around the hallways to drum up the kind of interest an announcement over the P.A. might not accomplish?"

"I think that's a wonderful idea but under one condition."

Nina smiled. "What's that?"

"I get to show it to the board before you hang them up. It's high time you got some recognition by those men."

Chapter 15

Melissa Davis was the epitome of the perfect mom—endlessly patient, always encouraging, and constantly smiling. The fact that she had seven children under the age of thirteen to mother didn't change those qualities one iota.

Being a possible murder suspect, however, scratched two of those certainties off the list.

"Victoria, I was positively awful to Jake Junior this afternoon when the kids got home from school. He set his backpack on the counter to unload his papers and homework then left everything there for just a moment to go help Tommy pump up his bicycle tire." Melissa sunk into the lattice-backed chair across from Tori and slumped her head onto the table. "When I walked back into the kitchen after getting Molly up from her nap, I saw his backpack still sitting there and no Jake Junior anywhere in sight."

"Okay."

Melissa popped her head up. "I called for him to come

back to the kitchen and then told him to get his garbage out of the kitchen. His *garbage*, Victoria."

She reached across the table and patted her friend's hand. "If that's the worst you say over the course of that child's life, he'll be okay. Trust me."

"For some children, maybe. But my kids don't have the manners they have because I bullied them. They have them because Jake and I made the decision long before Jake Junior came along that we were going to raise our children by example."

"You have a lot on your mind."

"That's no excuse."

Tori pushed back her chair and walked over to the cabinet that held various cups and glasses. Reaching past the colorful, plastic, teeth-nibbled offerings, she extracted a tall glass from the very back and filled it with ice water. "Here. Drink this. You don't look very good right now."

"I don't feel very good." Melissa took the glass from Tori's outstretched hand and merely set it on the table, untouched. "As soon as I said what I said, his eyes got all big and his bottom lip quivered and, well, I felt positively awful."

Tori claimed a chair closer to her friend. "Did you tell him that?"

Melissa nodded. "I did. I told him I was sorry. And I think he understood but I just don't know."

"Does he know what's going on?"

"I suspect he does. I think he heard me and his dad talking about it last night after I got the call."

"The call?" Tori leaned forward. "What call?"

"The one from Chief Dallas. Saying he wanted to stop by after the kids left for school."

She felt her stomach lurch. "And did he?"

With a twist of her hands, Melissa removed the ponytail tie from her hair only to gather every last strand together once again and reposition it slightly higher on her head. "He did. He got here around eleven. Said his ten o'clock meeting ran a little later than he had anticipated."

"Meetings are generally scheduled in advance and written on a calendar. His ten o'clock didn't entail either."

Melissa's hand stilled atop her hair. "How do you know?"

"Because I was his ten o'clock and he didn't schedule anything. He simply showed up." She grabbed hold of Melissa's water glass and took a gulp then repositioned it in front of her friend once again. "Unfortunately, my office didn't have the windowless effect of most interrogation rooms."

The woman pulled her hair out of its holder once again, her hands repeating the same pattern—gather hair, wrap with band, gather hair, wrap with band. "You, too, huh?"

"Me, too."

Melissa dropped her hands to the table and slumped against her chair. "Does it make me an awful friend to say I'm a little relieved to know I wasn't the only one being grilled about Ashley Lawson's murder?"

She considered her friend's words. "I'd say it makes you human."

The faintest hint of a smile flitted across Melissa's face only to disappear just as quickly. "Thanks, Victoria."

Nodding, Tori reached for the glass once again, stopping her hand midway. "How about I just get my own?"

Melissa laughed. "You can have mine. I'm not thirsty."

She accepted the glass and held it to her lips once again, the coolness of the liquid helping to dispel the dryness that had started during her own visit from the Sweet Briar police chief. "So what happened?"

"He asked me about the party, again, and I told him,

again." A burst of laughter wafted its way from the back-yard and through the open window. Rising to her feet, Melissa peeked outside, her gaze lingering beyond the con-fines of the cheerfully messy kitchen. "I can't be without these kids, Victoria. I just can't."

"Are you going somewhere?" she asked as she took yet another sip of water.

Without turning, Melissa spoke, her voice dripping with fear. "If Chief Dallas has his way I'll be spending the next kazillion years behind bars."

She choked on her water, the resulting cough pulling Melissa back to the table. "Are you okay, Victoria?"

"I—I'm f-fine. But"—she inhaled sharply—"what's this with the prison stuff? Did he say that?"

Melissa dropped into her chair once again, her shoul-ders rising and falling as she did. "He didn't have to. The questions he was asking said enough."

She thought back over her own encounter with the chief just that morning, the man's pointed questions and skepti-cally raised eyebrows a memory she'd tried to banish as she moved through the rest of her day at work. "Let me guess. He wanted to talk about the things you said regard-ing Ashley Lawson."

"He knew I'd said strangling would probably be my pre-ferred method of killing her. He knew I'd laughed when Caroline Rowen commented on eliminating her for the good of the kindergarten birthday party circuit. And he knew I'd been one of the ones to speculate how best to untie Milo's knot."

Blowing a strand of hair from her cheek, she pushed back her chair and stood. "I got essentially the same thing. Though his statements were tailored to the things *I* said that evening."

For a moment Melissa said nothing as she traced a pattern across the tablecloth with her nail-bitten fingers. When she finally spoke, her voice was strained, her words wooden. "I feel awful that everyone is being harassed because of a party I threw. A party that you and Rose and Dixie and Leona had no reason to be a part of except to lend moral support."

"We were there because we wanted to be there, Melissa." She strode across the room to the window and glanced outside, the sight of her friend's brood bringing a smile to her lips despite the topic at hand. "And I'd be willing to bet Debbie and Beatrice don't regret bringing Jackson and Luke to Sally's party, either."

A snort from Melissa made her turn. "That might be true about Debbie but I'm willing to bet it's not where Beatrice is concerned. That poor girl is terrified."

"Of Chief Dallas?"

Melissa nodded. "Among other things, yes."

"Other things?" she asked as she retraced her steps across the kitchen and leaned against the counter.

"The Johnsons aren't happy about Beatrice's possible involvement in Ashley's murder. They told her they'd give it a little time to see how it plays out but that looking for another source of employment might be a good idea."

She sucked in her breath. "Are you serious? Luke loves Beatrice. And anyone who knows that woman—as his parents should—knows she couldn't hurt a flea."

"You'd think that, wouldn't you?"

"So what's the problem?" She pushed off the counter and rejoined her friend at the table. "Why are they giving her a hard time?"

"Because Regina Murphy belongs to the same golf club

as the Johnsons do and her rage over Ashley's murder is starting to spread around to all the members."

"Ahhh, and now those members are starting to question why the Johnsons are keeping one of the possible culprits in their home, is that it?"

Melissa nodded. "That about sums it up."

"Did Chief Dallas arrange a meeting with her for today as well? Or did he just show up on her doorstep in much the way he did mine?"

"He just showed up. And, if her voice on the phone afterward was any indication, she is absolutely terrified." Melissa pulled her hands into her lap and sighed. "Just like I am—and I imagine everyone else is."

One by one Tori drummed each of the fingers of her right hand on the table only to repeat the process again and again, her mind replaying every question Chief Dallas had asked her that morning while juxtaposing it with those she imagined he asked of everyone else. "Why do I feel like we're part of a witch hunt right now?"

A swell of voices, followed by running footsteps, signaled the rapid approach of six of the seven Davis kids. Lowering her voice to a whisper, Melissa leaned forward. "Because we are."

Tori inhaled Melissa's words just as Jake Junior ran into the kitchen followed by Julia, Tommy, Kate, Lulu, and Sally. "Mom, can we use the sidewalk chalk on the back patio? I want to show them how to play a game we learned in gym class today."

Melissa's face brightened as she drank in each of her children's faces. "Is it a game everyone can play?"

"Yes." Jake Junior smiled broadly as Lulu made a bee-line in Tori's direction.

"Miss Sinclair, Miss Sinclair. I didn't know you were here!"

She motioned the child over to her chair and pulled her in for a hug, the aroma of play dough, shampoo, and cookies that seemed to cling to the little girl's hair providing a much needed boost after a day that had been entirely too long. "I came by to visit with your mom for a little while."

The little girl beamed from ear to ear. "I'm glad."

Jake Junior nodded. "I am, too. Lookin' after the lot of us has to get a mom tired sometimes."

Melissa's mouth quivered. "There's nothing in the world I'd rather do than look after the six of you."

A babble emerged from the handheld baby monitor on the kitchen counter. "That's Molly reminding you to say *seven*, Mommy," Sally said.

"I stand corrected. There's nothing in the world I'd rather do than look after the seven of you."

A second babble brought a chorus of laughter to the room. "And that's Molly saying she's happy you said seven, Mom." Jake Junior planted a kiss on his mom's cheek. "So can we? I promise to pick up every last piece of chalk and put them all back in the bucket when we're done."

Melissa glanced at the wall clock over the sink. "Okay, but only for about thirty minutes. Then it's time to come inside and get washed up. We're having pizza tonight when your dad gets home."

"Pizza?" shouted Kate.

"With just cheese?" Julia inquired.

"And lots and lots of yummy crust?" Sally piped in.

Tori laughed. "Well, Mom?"

Melissa nodded, her trademark happy smile returning to light her hazel eyes. "Yup, just cheese and lots and lots of yummy crust."

Two little arms shot into the air. "Yes!"

And with that they were gone, six sets of sneakers smacking against the floor followed by the sound of the door banging shut in their wake. Tori looked back at Melissa, noted the way her friend's smile was slipping from her face once again. "It'll be okay, Melissa."

Their gazes locked. "But what happens if it's not?"

"Did you kill her, Melissa?"

Her friend's eyes widened. "Of course not!"

"Then it has to be okay."

"Does it?"

She contemplated Melissa's words, let them conjure up memories of her own time as a murder suspect and the stress it had caused in her life. The last thing she wanted was to do it again. Or to watch her friends go through it, either.

Squaring her shoulders, she pushed back in her chair. "It does because we're going to make it so."

"We are? How?"

She stood and wandered back over to the window. Glancing down, she watched Jake Junior draw a large square with four sections onto the patio. Then, with painstaking patience, he explained the longstanding game to his siblings. "We're going to do what Jake Junior is doing."

Melissa, too, stood and joined Tori at the window. "Draw a square?"

"No. Work together." She met her friend's questioning brow with a determined inhale. "To figure out who *did* kill Ashley Lawson."

Chapter 16

Tori flopped onto her back and stared at the ceiling, her own words looping their way through her mind.

We need to work together. We need to figure out who killed Ashley Lawson.

"Since when did you become Nancy Drew?" she mumbled beneath her breath.

Since you left Chicago and moved to Sweet Briar.

Turning her head to the left, she took in the time on the digital clock beside her bed.

10:00 p.m.

Was it too late to call? To give Leona a little comeuppance?

Feeling the first real semblance of a smile since the Davis kids breezed into Melissa's kitchen, Tori reached for her cell phone and dialed the familiar number.

One ring morphed to two and then three before Leona's voice filled her ear.

"Yes?"

"Leona, it's Tori."

"Good heavens, dear, do you have any idea what time it is?"

She pushed away the momentary bout of guilt to lay out the facts as she knew them. "I do. But I also know that your favorite TV show just ended so you haven't gone to bed yet."

"Did you see it? Did you see how completely and utterly fantastic Ray Morgan looked when he took off his shirt and ran into the water to save that poor pathetic wretch of a woman who was drowning?"

She laughed. "No, I didn't."

"It almost made me wish I could be that pathetic if only for a few moments." Leona sighed into the phone. "Then again, if I was, I would make sure I was wearing my most attractive bathing suit and that my nails were at least manicured. I mean, *really*, who would summon a lifeguard like Ray Morgan with the kind of nails that woman had? What was she thinking?"

"It's a TV show, Leona. The woman was a hired actress."

"A hired actress with hideous nails."

Touché.

"Oh, Leona, you have no idea how badly I needed this kind of banter tonight." She scooted her head up to the pillow and pulled her afghan with her.

"Bad day, dear?"

"I've had better."

"What time did he stop in and see you?"

She gripped the phone tighter. "He? You mean Chief Dallas?"

"Who else, dear?"

"Around ten-ish, I suppose. He saw Melissa at eleven and Beatrice sometime after that."

"Beatrice was at noon, then. He got to the antique shop around one thirty and he mentioned having stopped for lunch after visiting with her."

"Visiting? Is that what he called it?" she asked.

"When you offer someone chocolates and wine—as a good hostess should—it's a visit, dear."

"Chocolates and wine? *I* didn't offer him anything."

An exasperated sigh echoed from the phone. "Why ever not?"

"Let me count thy ways," she mumbled.

"Victoria, was that a mumble I just heard?"

She gulped.

"Victoria?"

She swallowed harder. "Um, kind of? I'm sorry, Leona, I just find it hypocritical of Chief Dallas to show up at my workplace completely unannounced, badger me with questions for nearly an hour, and then run off on his merry way, leaving me stressed ever since."

"He is conducting a murder investigation, dear."

A murder investigation.

Determined to wipe away the stress before bed, she allowed herself to focus on the aspect that had perpetuated the late night call to her friend. "Hmmm. Seems to me there's been a lot of that going around Sweet Briar this past year or so."

"I know, can you *imagine* such a thing?"

She felt the grin as it stretched across her face. "You'd think I could after living a few years in Chicago, wouldn't you? But, well, I can't. Sweet Briar is unique in that way."

The silence in her ear made her smile even bigger. "Leona? Are you still there?"

"Did you call simply to gloat, dear? Because if you did, it's most unbecoming."

She laughed out loud. "I wish I could say I didn't but, well, I did."

Leona's voice dropped an octave as she addressed someone Tori couldn't see. "Victoria interrupted your sleep to try and make a point but it's fallen on deaf ears."

She looked at the clock again as a feeling of remorse swept in. "Oh, Leona, I'm sorry. I didn't know you had company."

"Would my baby like a carrot to make up for Victoria's insensitivity?"

Rolling her eyes skyward, she felt the smile return to her face. "Please, pass my sincerest apologies along to Paris."

"Paris, darling? Did you hear that? Victoria is very sorry for her boorish behavior. She realizes the error of her ways."

Boorish? Error of my ways?

"I wouldn't go that far, Leona."

"Shhh. You don't want to upset Paris further, do you?" Leona hissed in her ear.

She stifled back the laugh that threatened to result in her friend hanging up. "Um, Leona? Paris is a bunny. I think he's probably fine with what I just said."

"Well, I'm not."

"Then I'm sorry."

"No, you're not."

"You're right." She let the laugh win, the sound bringing an audible smile to her ear.

"I thought about you this evening when I was taking Paris for a walk."

She closed her eyes around the image of Leona strolling along the town square with a garden-variety bunny wrapped in Egyptian cotton and nestled in her arms. "And?"

"I'd rather hoped the phone call Milo got was from you."

"You saw Milo?"

"I did. We were just getting ready to pass each other on the sidewalk when that silly song he has on his cell phone made Paris's ears bolt upright." Leona's voice grew louder as she returned her full attention to their conversation. "And within no more than thirty seconds he was shoving it back in his pocket and taking off in a sprint in the other direction."

She sat upright on the bed. "Did he look upset?"

"I couldn't tell if he was upset or eager. But, either way, he didn't even acknowledge my presence."

She worked to soothe Leona's rumpled feathers all the while her mind was picking through reasons Milo might have reacted in the way he had. Had his mother fallen ill? Had something happened at work? She gripped the phone still tighter as she swung her gaze toward the clock one last time. "I better go, Leona. I want to make sure Milo is okay."

"You haven't heard from him yet this evening?"

"No."

"You really must train that young man better, dear."

For a moment she considered correcting Leona, but opted instead to let it go. Making sure Milo was okay was higher on her list of priorities than trying to correct Leona's outlandish ways of dealing with the opposite sex. "I'll work on it, Leona. Have a good night and give Paris a kiss for me, will you?"

She flipped her phone shut then opened it once again, her fingers finding Milo's position on her speed dial in short order.

One ring morphed to two and then three.

A woman's sleepy voice answered. "Hello?"

Pulling the phone from her ear, she checked the screen

to confirm whose number she had, in fact, dialed. Sure enough, Milo's name was scrawled across the top.

"Um, hi." She felt her stomach churn and tried her best to ignore it. "Um, is Milo Wentworth there?"

A giggle tickled her ear. "Oh, silly me. I must have picked his phone up off the nightstand instead of my own."

Her mouth gaped open as the woman's voice filtered through her ears and conjured up a face to match.

Beth Samuelson.

"His nightstand?" she echoed.

"Which is beside his bed . . ." The woman's voice dropped to a whisper as she continued. "He's sleeping right now. He's totally spent after . . . well, you know."

She blinked against the burning in her eyes, willed her mind to focus on the realities she knew to be true.

Milo was a good man.

Milo was not Jeff.

Milo wouldn't hurt her this way.

Gripping the phone still tighter she considered her various options. She could demand that Beth wake him and put him on the phone. She could get in her car and drive over to his house and see whatever was going on with her own two eyes. Or she could wait until morning when she could ask him face to face. Sans Beth.

"Tell him Tori called, would you? And that I'll talk to him in the morning."

"Tori? Oh, I didn't know that was you. I could roll over and give him a little poke if you'd like."

She closed her eyes against the image of them lying side by side in his bed. Swallowing against the bile that rose in her throat, she forced her voice to remain even. The last thing she wanted was to give the woman on the other end of the line reason to gloat. She was stronger than that. "No, that's fine. I'll speak with him in the morning."

"I'll let him know when he wakes up. Unless . . ." Beth's voice trailed off only to return in the wake of one of her infuriating giggles. "Well, unless we get sidetracked."

With a heavy heart she flipped the phone shut, her mind at war with her emotions. While there was a part of her that wanted to cut Milo off right then and there, there was another part that wanted to believe she hadn't been wrong about another man. Especially a man who had taken the time to get to know her—her thoughts, her dreams, her likes, her dislikes.

Men like that were rare.

And men like that didn't change their feelings for a person with the flip of a switch or upon the arrival of a woman who had walked out on them well over a decade earlier.

Or did they?

She refused to speculate. For as painful as Jeff's indiscretion had been, it had left no room for misunderstanding or second-guessing. She'd known, by the time she'd left the engagement party, that they were over. And if things were to go the same way with Milo, she needed to know the how and the why. Even if the answers to those questions shattered her heart once again.

Chapter 17

Uncertainty and fear drove her from bed long before dawn, her stomach a nauseous mess. Try as she might, she simply couldn't get the image of Milo and Beth lying side by side from her brain. And even when she tried to come up with some perfectly innocent explanation to make it all easier, reality came knocking.

There was no reason under the sun the two should have been in the same house overnight, let alone the same bed. Which meant the explanation she wanted desperately to hear from the horse's mouth was not likely to happen.

Padding softly across the hardwood floor that led from her bedroom to the kitchen, she willed herself to find the happy place that had been hers since moving to Sweet Briar. The place that had her living her dream job, surrounding herself with the kind of friends people searched for their whole lives, and finding the perfect companion.

"Milo." She waited for the sound of his name on her lips to make her smile, yet it didn't. A sure sign she'd shrouded her heart for the inevitable hurt daylight was sure to bring.

As she rounded the corner into the kitchen, her gaze fell on the open notepad she'd tossed onto the table when she returned from Melissa's, the various scenarios they'd concocted covering every square inch of the top page.

- Perhaps Ashley's death was a magic trick gone wrong (in her quest to save one of Paris's kinfolk, Leona swapped a magician's bunny for Ashley Lawson)

- Perhaps her husband had hit his limit (not hard to imagine)

- Perhaps she'd strangled herself (after her darling Penelope tried on the wrong color)

She managed a laugh in spite of everything, the ludicrous parentheticals they'd insisted on including relieving some of the tension she felt in every fiber of her being.

It'll be okay. It really will. I don't need Milo.

Determined to convince herself of those thoughts, she uttered them aloud. "It'll be okay. I don't need Milo."

"Hmmm . . . that's not exactly the kind of thing you want to hear when you show up at your girlfriend's house bearing a surprise breakfast."

She whirled around to see Milo standing in the doorway between the living room and the kitchen, his left hand clutching a bag from Debbie's Bakery. "What are you doing here?"

His smile failed to reach his eyes. "I wanted to surprise you but, well, I think I'm the one who just got surprised."

Resisting the urge to hug him like she normally would, she dropped into one of the kitchen chairs and shoved the notebook to the side. "I'm betting what you just overheard isn't even close to the surprise I got when I called your phone last night."

"You called?" His face brightened. "I didn't hear it ring."

She inhaled slowly in an attempt to keep too much emotion from her voice. The last thing she wanted was for him to see just how much he'd hurt her. He didn't deserve to know he'd meant so much.

"I suspect you didn't hear it ring because you were sleeping."

With furrowed brows he pulled his cell phone from his pocket with his free hand and stared at the screen. "There's no sign of a missed call."

"That's because it wasn't missed."

He met her eyes. "Then I don't understand."

"It wasn't missed because it was answered. By Beth."

All sign of color drained from his face as his phone-holding hand dropped to his side. "Tori, I can explain. It's not what you think."

"It's not? You mean sleeping side by side in your bed with your old college sweetheart is perfectly normal?"

"Sleeping side by side? What are you talking about? We didn't sleep side by side in my bed. She slept in my bed. I slept on the couch."

She steeled herself against the relief that flooded her being. "That's not what Beth said."

"Beth told you we were sleeping in the same bed?" A flash of pain flickered across his eyes. "C'mon, Tori, isn't that going a little overboard? Beth knows darn well what our sleeping arrangements were."

"I must have picked his phone up off the nightstand instead of my own . . ."

"Which is beside his bed . . ."

"He's sleeping right now."

She swallowed as she focused on the woman's exact words rather than their implication. Everything Beth had said could fit with what Milo was describing, but still . . .

"Okay. Then can I ask why she was sleeping in your house at all?"

He dropped the bag and cell phone onto the table beside her notebook and walked around to her side. Squatting down beside her, he took her hands in his and held them tight. "I got a call from Beth last evening as I was out walking. She was in a panic, convinced someone was out to get her. So I went to check on her, to make sure she was okay."

"And?" She knew her voice sounded curt, maybe even a little harsh, but she couldn't help it.

"When I got there, I saw the soaped threat on her windshield. It was just one word but it was unmistakable."

"What was it?"

"Die."

She stared at Milo. "Are you serious? What did the police say?"

He pulled his left hand from hers and held it to the side of her face. "Beth wouldn't let me call them. She said she doesn't want anything taking away from the announcement about her company."

Tori rolled her eyes. "Her company is more important than her safety?"

"Apparently. I tried to argue, to insist she call, but she was hysterical. And that's not all."

"Tell me."

"The owner of the inn told me someone had called repeatedly that day trying to find out what room Beth was staying in. When he and his employees refused to give that information, they were met with angry hang-ups."

"Was it a man or a woman who was calling?"

"They said it was hard to tell, that the voice was garbled and unnatural." He let his hand drop back down to join hers. "So I did what I felt I had to do to ensure her safety. I brought her home with me."

"You couldn't have sent her to another—" She stopped mid-sentence as the reality that was Sweet Briar dawned. "Okay, I get it. She was scared, there was nowhere else for her to go, and you wanted to make sure she was safe. Is that right?"

He nodded. "I guess I should have called and warned you. I'm sorry."

She said nothing for a moment, her mind trying desperately to accept everything Milo had said against the memories that belonged to Jeff's betrayal.

"I'm sorry if I caused you any hurt, Tori. I really am." He stood, tugging her off her chair and into his arms. "Please tell me you understand."

Did she? Did she really understand why he'd bring Beth to his home?

She did. Because he was Milo Wentworth, a rare breath of fresh air as far as chivalry and compassion went. He'd displayed it to her again and again since they'd met, supporting her through Tiffany Ann Gilbert's murder investigation, her need to stick her nose into the disappearance of Colby Calhoun, and the unfair murder charges against Rose Winter's mentally challenged former student.

Finally she was able to say the words he sought, her voice raspy from the reality she not only wanted but needed as well. "I understand."

The second the words left her lips, his shoulders slumped in relief. "Talk about scaring a person half to death."

"I'm sorry but you have to understand what I heard."

"I do, and I'm sorry. I should have called you and told you. I realize that now. But after I got her situated in my room, I went out to the couch and absolutely crashed."

"At least one of us slept," she teased.

"What? You didn't sleep?" He released her from his arms to study her closely. "Why?"

"Because I thought I'd lost you, for starters."

"You didn't."

"I'm glad." She pointed toward the notebook on the table. "And secondly, I guess the weight of being considered in yet another murder investigation is taking its toll more than I realized."

"Chief Dallas is still sniffing around?"

She sat back down in her chair and motioned toward the one across from hers. "He showed up at the library yesterday for a chat."

"A chat?"

"That's what he called it when he suggested we retire to my office. However, after an hour of this so-called chat, I have to say it leaned much closer to an interrogation."

"I'm sorry."

She tugged the notebook in front of her then spun it around to face him. "I am, too. And for Melissa, and Beatrice, and Leona,"

"How so?" he asked as he leaned forward to examine the notes she and Melissa had made.

"They experienced a chat with the chief yesterday as well. I imagine Margaret Louise, Debbie, Rose, Dixie, and those two other mothers did as well, but I haven't heard confirmation of that just yet."

Milo shook his head as his eyes skimmed the various possibilities and asides they'd drafted out of frustration. "You think the husband could have done it?"

Tori shrugged. "I don't know. I don't know anything about him. Neither does Melissa. But shouldn't he be considered? Isn't the spouse or the parent always a suspect?"

"I imagine. It's certainly more likely than a failed magic trick or suicide by strangulation."

She felt her face warm. "You must think we're awful writing that stuff."

"We?"

"Me and Melissa."

He reached across the table to cover her hand with his. "Awful? Never. I think the two of you just needed a way to relieve some unnecessary tension. Who wouldn't in your shoes?"

She met his gaze before looking back down at the notebook. "We did take a few minutes to jot down some possible suspects."

"Possible suspects?"

"People to investigate."

A smile crept across his face, carving knee-weakening dimples in his cheeks. "People for *who* to investigate?"

"Chief Dallas?" she asked, tilting her head ever so slightly.

He cocked his eyebrow. "Is that the correct answer?"

"No. But it's the answer you want, isn't it?" She flipped over the top page of the notebook to reveal a second page of notes—observations and questions she and Melissa had drafted after they'd had their moment of fun.

"Not really. I want the answer that goes with you. And after what happened with you and the Tiffany Ann Gilbert case, and Colby's disappearance last year, and then Kenny

Murdock a few months ago, I know better than to think you'll leave the investigation to the police."

She turned her palms upward and swept them above the notebook. "How can I when my friends are involved?"

"I get it, Tori. I really do." He pointed to the notebook. "So show me what you've got so far. Maybe I can add or discount something you and Melissa might not know."

Nodding, she began pointing out each name on the list. "First there's me."

Milo scrunched up his eyebrows and leaned close. "Did you kill Ashley?"

She nibbled back the grin that threatened to derail their conversation. "Although the notion was tempting from a frustrated kind of way, no. And I was actually the only person at that party who didn't say I wanted to kill her."

"Okay."

Her finger slid to the next name. "There's Melissa. She was fed up with Ashley but not in an angry way. She was more harried from trying to jump through hoops she felt were necessary in order to ensure Sally's party would pass muster with Penelope and her mom."

"And Melissa doesn't really seem to know how to be angry." He raked his hand through his hair then reached for the bakery bag he'd set on the table. "In all the years I've known her and Jake, I've never seen her get angry with any of those kids. And she's got *seven*."

"Agreed. So the notion that she could wrap a rope around another human being's neck and pull it until the person stops breathing is ludicrous." She pointed to the next name. "And then there's Beatrice."

"I think she's even less likely. She's about as meek as they come."

She considered Milo's words. "I agree. Especially after seeing her at the party. Ashley ordered Beatrice around as if she worked for Ashley rather than one of Ashley's friends. And Beatrice did it, like she was *supposed* to." A memory filtered through her thoughts, making her pose another possibility aloud. "Then again, she *was* upset when Ashley questioned the manner in which she'd dressed Luke for the party."

"Angry upset or sad upset?"

It was a good question—one that made her stop and think.

"I'd say more toward the sad. Beatrice takes great pride in the way she cares for that little boy. I think having Ashley question that made her second-guess herself more than it made her angry."

"So you're fairly confident she's a no, too?" Milo asked.

She nodded. "The same goes for Debbie. I mean, she was furious when Ashley refused to have Penelope seated next to Jackson at the birthday table but—"

"Jackson? Are you kidding me? You'd be hard-pressed to find a nicer kid than Jackson Calhoun." Milo rolled his eyes skyward. "I just don't get adults sometimes."

"I know. But Jackson basically paid homage to Sally and her party, which didn't sit well with Ashley."

Milo held the bakery bag in the air and cocked his head toward the logo. "A woman who makes muffins like Debbie does isn't capable of murder. Not unless her family was threatened."

She cocked an eyebrow at him.

"Threatened with *physical* harm," he rushed to amend.

"I agree." Her gaze strayed down to the next name. "Okay, next we have Margaret Louise."

Milo's hand paused on the open bag. "You don't sound as confident about her."

"Oh, I am, from the standpoint I believe she didn't do it but . . ." Her words trailed off as he pulled a blueberry muffin from the bag and set it on a napkin in front of her spot. "That looks good."

"I'm glad." He reached into the bag again and extracted a large to-go cup. "And your hot chocolate."

"Thank you." Looking down at the cup, she willed her thoughts back to the subject at hand, the guilt she felt over doubting Milo making it difficult to think. "But she was the most vocal about wishing she could strangle Ashley. She said it before the party to Melissa, she said it at the sewing circle meeting prior to the party, and she said it under her breath more than a few times at the actual party itself. Though it was always on the heels of something truly nasty Ashley said or did."

"Yet you don't think she's a viable suspect?"

She stared at Milo as he pulled his own muffin from the bag. "And you could think otherwise? C'mon, Milo, you know Margaret Louise. She may grumble when her family comes under fire and she may be overly protective of her grandkids, but she's also one of the most genuine people on the face of the earth. She wouldn't take someone's life."

"I know. I just felt I should ask."

"Well, she's innocent. But my worry is about the stress Chief Dallas will heap on her thanks to the conversations Regina Murphy no doubt shared." She lifted the muffin to her mouth and took a small bite. "Which moves us still further down the list to"—she looked at the page for confirmation—"Leona."

"Leona," Milo echoed. "Tell me again why she was even

at Sally's party? She's not exactly what could be called a fan of little kids."

Tori shrugged. "But she's Sally's great aunt and Melissa's aunt-in-law and, well, she's nosy. I suspect she wanted to see the woman she'd been hearing about at our sewing circle."

"Ashley?"

"Ashley," she confirmed. "The stuff Margaret Louise shared about her was the reason the next two showed up as well."

She followed Milo's gaze back to the notebook. "Rose and Dixie?"

"Rose was disgusted by Ashley's behavior, there's no doubt about that. But she can also barely open her sewing box by herself let alone hold a rope around the neck of a woman half her age."

"And Dixie?"

"Dixie is Dixie. She doesn't act like she likes anyone."

"Throw in the fact she had an ax to grind with the victim and, well, that ups her dislike factor immensely."

She stared at Milo. "What are you talking about?"

"Nothing major, but certainly a reason Dixie knew and disliked Ashley Lawson." Milo plucked a small cup of coffee from the bag and lifted it to his lips, his eyes closing momentarily as he took a long gulp.

"I'm not following."

He shrugged. "A month or so after she retired from the library, Dixie showed up at a school board meeting asking if she could come in as a reader. She felt her experience as a librarian over the past four decades made her a natural with kids."

"Go on," she prompted, her curiosity aroused.

"At first the board members seemed to like the idea. They even tossed around the idea of maybe paying her a little money to come in a few times a week. Just to assist with the kids in some of the younger grades—kids who might really have benefited from a little extra reading assistance."

"Okay."

"Then they changed their mind."

Tori leaned forward. "Why? It seems like it could have been a win-win for Dixie and the teachers."

"It was. Only the teachers weren't asked for input. The board made the final decision. And according to a few of my sources, there was one member who felt Dixie was too old and too negative to work with the children."

She felt her mouth gape open. "She may be negative with adults but have you seen her with kids? She's amazing."

Milo nodded then followed the gesture up with a theatric shrug. "This particular board member based her decision on Dixie's appearance and demeanor in the room at the time of the request."

"And this board member was . . ." she prompted with the help of her rolling finger.

"Ashley Lawson."

Her hand stilled. "Are you serious?"

He nodded again, this time minus the shrug.

She took a moment to process this latest piece of information—information that had the potential to change things a little. Especially in light of the fact they explained a minor detail she'd overlooked until that moment—Dixie had been less than enthusiastic to see Ashley at Sally's party.

At the time, she hadn't thought much about it, the distraction that was Ashley Lawson making all else pale. But now, in a moment of silence, it all came rushing back. Dixie had reacted with anger when the woman had arrived at the party. An anger she should have recognized as over the top.

Still, it was Dixie Dunn. Seventy-something Dixie Dunn. Formidable as she was, she didn't have the physical strength needed to strangle someone half her age any more than Rose did.

"I still don't buy that she'd kill someone," Tori finally said, the momentary possibility chased away by reality. "I mean, she may be ornery at times but—"

"At times?" Milo echoed. "At times?"

She couldn't help but laugh. "Okay, she may be ornery virtually all the time but she's not a killer. I just can't believe that. I won't."

"Which still leaves you with two names."

"Caroline Rowen and Samantha Smith—neither of whom I know very well." She leaned back in her chair, her fingers tracing the logo on the side of her to-go cup. "What I do know is that Ashley said some not so very nice things about Caroline's little girl on the way into the party. Something about her wretched red hair if I remember Beatrice's words correctly."

"Wretched?" Milo's mouth hung open. "Are you serious?"

She nodded. "This woman was awful, Milo. Absolutely, positively awful."

"And Samantha Smith?"

"I don't know. All I know is that her daughter routinely came home crying from kindergarten because Penelope teased her about everything from the clothes she wore to the games she played. At least that's what Melissa told me, anyway."

"Wait." Milo reached into his pocket and pulled out his phone. With the touch of a few buttons, he held it out for her to see. "I remember that name now. Her little girl's name is Kayla and the parents have been to the school a number of times complaining about Penelope Lawson. Only nothing seems to happen according to them."

"Why do you have her name on your phone?"

"I wanted to remember it. I heard the afternoon kindergarten teacher talking about the situation in the lunchroom a while back and it broke my heart. I decided I'd figure out who this little girl is and make a point of saying nice things to her if I see her in the hallway or out on the playground."

For a long moment Tori simply studied him—the smile lines beside his amber-flecked brown eyes, the faintest hint of her beloved dimples nestled in his cheeks, and the unruly crop of burnished brown hair that begged for a good finger grooming. Milo Wentworth truly was one of a kind. How many men would overhear a little gossip and go out of their way to try and make a situation better?

His cheeks grew pink when she said as much to him. "I hate to see any child ridiculed or ostracized. It's not right."

"Neither is this business about Ashley's murder. I don't believe anyone on this list is guilty."

"You that sure about Caroline and Samantha?"

She tried his question on for size, her answer forming faster than she would have expected. "I guess not. I don't know them."

"Then maybe that's where you should start." His hands closed over hers and tugged them to the middle of the table. "Find a way to get to know them."

"But how? I don't think either of them frequent the library very often."

"Find another way." Slowly, he lifted one of her hands

to his lips and whispered a kiss across them. "Melissa is helping you with this, right?"

"Yes."

"Then get her to have a playdate. The kind where the mom comes, too."

A playdate.

She slipped her hand from his and nudged his chin in her direction, her lips stopping just shy of his. "Has anyone ever told you you're brilliant?"

Chapter 18

Tori was halfway to work when she saw her, the leather portfolio in her hand as much a giveaway to her identity as the cascading golden blonde hair and perfectly chiseled body that could make a runway model feel frumpy. For the briefest of moments she felt her stomach tighten only to be shamed away by the reality her mind and heart knew to be true.

Milo loved *her*. Not Beth Samuelson.

She lifted her hand and waved as the gap between them closed. "Hi, Beth. Beautiful morning, isn't it?"

"Oh. Tori. Yes, hi." The woman stopped beside the white picket fence that encased Sweet Briar's town square and flashed her infamous megawatt smile. "The birds sound so pretty this morning, don't you think?"

"I do."

"I heard them when I rolled over in Milo's bed this—" Beth stopped, pursed her lips together and looked at the sidewalk, the gesture striking Tori as more than a little theatrical. "I'm sorry, I probably shouldn't have said that. I imagine it would be hard to hear."

"Why? He was being a gentleman and looking out for your safety. It's what Milo does and it's one of the many reasons I love him." She gazed down at the tulip in her hand, felt the smile as it spread across her face. "Isn't this beautiful? He knows I love tulips and so he planted some bulbs in his yard last year just for me."

She knew she was babbling but she couldn't help it. She was happy. And after the near sleepless night she'd had worrying about a phantom problem, it felt good to let it out. "He even knows I like the yellow ones best."

Beth tightened her grip on her portfolio. "He knows my favorite flower, too."

Cocking her head a hairbreadth to the side, she studied the woman closely. When they'd first met, she'd truly believed the woman's slightly inappropriate comments reflected nothing more than ignorance. But now, after last night's phone call and the innuendos that had been purred into the phone, she had to wonder how much was ignorance and how much was intent.

"I'm sure he does," she finally said. "He's thoughtful that way."

"Thoughtful," Beth repeated. "I suppose that's a description that works, but if I could only use one word to describe Milo it would be . . ." The woman's words trailed off in favor of a combination giggle and hair toss. "On second thought, perhaps that's a description best kept to myself."

She felt her mouth go dry.

Stop it, Tori. She's just trying to get you unsettled.

Shaking her head free of the images that threatened to drag all her insecurities to the surface, she met Beth's smile with one of her own—the same one that Milo loved. "Perhaps it is. Besides, people change over the years. And it has, after all, been fourteen years since you broke up."

"It's funny how fourteen years can sometimes feel more like fourteen *hours*, don't you think?" Beth flicked her hair over her shoulder and stood even taller, her stiletto heels making her seem more than 70 percent legs. "Oh, I suppose I should be a good hostess and invite you to dinner at the house soon. Are you free this evening by any chance?"

She felt the lump forming in her throat, heard the way it left her words more than a little raspy. "The house?"

"Yes. I love to entertain and Milo has a very nice dining room though"—Beth dropped her voice to a near whisper— "between you and me, it needs a womanly touch, don't you think?"

Before Tori could utter a word, Beth waved her long fingernails in the air. "Though I should probably give Milo a ring and make sure it's okay with him. He might have other plans for us this evening."

"Other plans?" She knew she sounded like an idiotic parrot but it was all she could think to say in the wake of Beth's unsettling comments.

Beth reached out and patted Tori on the shoulder. "But I'll know more in a few hours when we meet for lunch. I'm thinking a picnic might be nice on such a beautiful day, what do you think?"

A picnic?

She swallowed over the lump that threatened to render her completely speechless. "I—I think I better get going, the library opens in thirty minutes and there are things I—I need to do."

The megawatt smile returned to full strength. "I think it's so . . . *sweet* that you work in a library." Beth bobbed her head to the left and then the right, her gaze firmly fixed on Tori's face. "Though I'm not sure how you'd look with your hair in a bun. Your face isn't necessarily the best shape for that kind of look."

Don't give her what she wants, dear.

And just like that, she felt her shoulders relax, Leona's voice in her head spouting exactly the sentiment she needed to hear. If she had had any lingering doubt as to Beth's motives where Milo was concerned, they were officially gone.

Beth Samuelson was out to get Milo. Of that she was certain. What was a little less certain, however, was whether she'd be content to stop at simple innuendos obviously designed and orchestrated to shake Tori's confidence.

Nina met her at the back door to the library with a near face-splitting smile and a long poster tube. "I was hoping you'd get here early."

Tori nodded as she reached past her assistant with the key and inserted it into the lock. "You could have went inside you know."

"I know. But when I was walkin' toward the steps just now I saw you walkin' across the street. Figured it would be just as easy to wait."

"Sometimes it pays to keep walking," she mumbled before pushing the door open and stepping to the side to afford Nina passage.

Nina took two steps inside and then slowly turned, her large dark eyes trained on Tori's. "Is everything okay?"

She lifted the tulip to her nose and inhaled slowly. "It was. And it will be now that I'm here but—you know what? Never mind. My day is only affected if I let it be affected, right?"

"Sounds like somethin' my Duwayne would say."

Squeezing Nina's arm gently, she strode past the woman and into their shared office. "Your Duwayne is a very smart man."

Nina followed, her smile of earlier returning in spades. "I know. In fact"—she pulled three posters from the tube and unrolled them for Tori to see—"he helped me with these all night. He was insistent that the placement of the words and pictures be just so in order to catch the kids' attention at the high school."

"The kids . . ." Her words disappeared as she leaned forward, her attention riveted on the homemade poster Nina had created for the walls of the high school. Bold lettering announcing the book club's creation wound around pictures of some of the most popular teen titles. Scattered around the edges were clip-art pictures of teen-friendly foods like popcorn, ice cream, and soda. "Oh, Nina, I love it. It's perfect."

Nina's face brightened even more. "You really think so?"

She looked again, her gaze sucked in by the visual appeal the poster offered. "Actually, I *know* it's perfect."

"Duwayne is goin' to be tickled when I tell him."

"I'm glad." And she was. Pride was something everyone needed. It gave a person wings to accomplish even greater things.

"Your flower is beautiful." Nina pointed to Tori's hand. "It's even your favorite color."

"You're right, it is." She brought the flower to her nose once again and inhaled, the delicate aroma doing wonders against any lingering tension caused by her encounter with Beth Samuelson. "Milo picked it for me."

"I'm not surprised." Nina placed the posters on her desk. "Where's he been hidin' himself? I haven't seen him here in a few days."

"He—he's busy." She felt Nina's eyes on her and met them with what she hoped was a normal smile. "But everything is fine. He brought me breakfast this morning."

A dreamy look passed across Nina's face. "Most men would sleep until noon on their day off. But yours? He gets up early to bring you breakfast. He's mighty special, that man."

She couldn't agree more. To Nina, though, she simply said, "Sounds like we both hit the jackpot, didn't we?"

"We sure did."

Rummaging in her tote bag for a list of items she needed to attend to out on the floor, her gaze stopped on the notebook. She pulled it out and set it on her desk. "Nina? Can I ask you something?"

"Of course, Miss Sinclair."

She cringed at the use of her surname but knew it was futile to correct her assistant. From day one it had been the way Nina addressed her—on the floor, in their office, and at social events. No amount of reminding, asking, or telling changed that.

"Do you know either Caroline Rowen or Samantha Smith?"

Nina repeated the names slowly. "I'm not sure. *Should* I?"

"I guess not. I just figured that most moms with little kids find their way into libraries from time to time. And other than Sally's birthday party the other day, I've not really seen either of them before except in passing at Leeson's Market or in line at Debbie's."

"Wait." Nina's eyes widened. "Caroline Rowen has that little redhead doesn't she?"

Tori nodded. "Zoe."

"Yes, yes, that's right. Nice little girl. Her mother is always very sweet."

"And Samantha Smith?" She fingered the design on the

cover of the notebook, her thoughts swirling with more questions. "You still can't remember her?"

"What does she look like?"

Thinking back to Sally's party, Tori did her best to describe the woman who'd spent much of the evening hovering around her daughter—behavior that made sense now in light of the information Milo had shared. "She's about my height, short brown hair, big brown eyes, kind of quiet."

Nina stopped mid–head shake. "Does she have a little girl, too?"

"I believe Milo said her name is Kayla."

"Kayla, hmmm." Nina tapped her finger to her lips. "No, I—wait, yes, I do. The little girl is painfully shy. But as hard as her shyness seems to be on her, it seems even harder on her mom."

Tori cocked her head to the side and studied her assistant closely. "What do you mean?"

Walking over to the windows, Nina opened the one in the center. "Well, if this Samantha Smith person is the one I think she is, she was in here about a week before Sally's party. She spent a good ten minutes trying to coax Kayla into the children's room to play with the costume trunk and stage. The little girl kept shaking her head and biting her lip as if she was afraid to go without her mom. It caught my attention because at first I couldn't figure out why the mom wouldn't just go *with* the little girl." Nina leaned closer to the screen and sniffed in the spring air. "But as I watched, I realized this little girl was painfully shy and that the mom was just trying to help her take some baby steps in a safe environment."

"And?"

"She finally convinced Kayla to give it a try but not more

than five minutes later the little girl was back at her mom's side."

Tori leaned against her desk and folded her arms across her chest, Nina's words winding their way through her thoughts. "Do you have any idea what happened? Or do you think she'd just had enough time without mom?"

Nina's lips curved downward. "I didn't hear everything that happened but I know Kayla was upset. And when her mom asked what was wrong, the little girl insisted on whispering the answer. Whatever she said, it prompted her mom to give her a big hug and lead her out of the library empty-handed despite the stack of books she'd set on the information desk just moments earlier."

"Do you think something happened?"

"Possibly. It was that day you met with the board members over lunch."

She thought back to the day in question. "We brought in Dixie as backup, right?"

Nina nodded. "Perhaps she'd be the better person to ask."

"You might be right." Pushing off the desk, Tori gestured toward the hands of the clock that signaled the start of another day at Sweet Briar Public Library. "I'll give her a call later on, see if she remembers anything that might be helpful."

Chapter 19

She followed her lunch as it made its way down the checkout belt, its proximity to the various over-the-counter medications separated by the plastic orange divider Regina Murphy had slammed down as Tori approached the line. The action, in and of itself, wouldn't have caught her by surprise all on its own. After all, the notion of paying for items you didn't want wasn't appealing to her, either.

But when it was accompanied by a raised eyebrow, clenched fists, and a cluck of disgust that echoed throughout Leeson's Market it had a way of making a person feel rather pariah-ish.

The key was how to handle it. Did she keep her mouth shut and let the woman purchase her items and leave? Or did she reach out and try to make polite conversation?

She knew what Leona would say. She suspected Margaret Louise and Debbie and the rest of her friends would concur. But try as she might to keep quiet, she simply couldn't.

"How are you, Regina?"

The woman pivoted on her three-inch heels. "How do you think I am?"

The fists were your clue.

Inhaling every ounce of courage she could muster, Tori pressed on. "I imagine you're hurting. You lost a friend and a business partner."

"Lost is a rather sugar-coated way of saying she was murdered, don't you think?" Regina hissed through clenched teeth.

Tori swallowed back the lump that threatened to leave her speechless. "You're right, it is . . . and I'm sorry." She reached out, rested her hand atop the woman's forearm. "I can only imagine how hard this is for you right now."

"You have no idea." Regina hoisted her purse higher on her arm. "One minute you're moving through life under one assumption and the next . . . Well, you realize you were wrong. About everything and everyone."

"Regina, I know you're upset. I know that what happened to Ashley is horrific and that justice needs to be served but I can assure you that no one at Sally's party had anything to do—"

"People you thought were your friends—or at the very least had your back—can turn on you in an instant." The woman's eyes glazed over as she fixed on a spot somewhere over Tori's head. "I mean, you see someone at church or across the table during lunch or while pursuing a common goal, and you just don't imagine they can hurt you in that way."

"I'm sorry, Regina, I really am." She knew the words were lame when spoken against the kind of hurt that played across every facet of the woman's face, but she couldn't think of anything else to say. Regina wasn't ready to hear the truth. Not yet, anyway. "Have they released her body so her family can plan the funeral?"

Pulling her focus back to Tori, Regina stared at her. "Why? Would that make you and your friends feel better?"

She stepped back, the woman's anger akin to a slap across the face. "Of course not! I just wondered—"

"Well, don't." Regina pulled her purse from her arm and thumped it on the counter. "None of this is your business."

"But I—"

Regina's hand stopped just shy of Tori's mouth. "You belong in jail."

Tori's mouth grew dry as heads in the neighboring check-out lane turned in their direction. Not wanting to cause Ashley's friend any more hurt, she searched for just the right words—words that would take the sting out of a truth that wasn't ready to be accepted. "I'm sorry you feel that way, Regina, I truly am. Like you, I hope that justice is served sooner rather than later. But I also know that pun-ishing the wrong people isn't the justice Ashley or the Law-son family needs at this time. Two wrongs don't make a right. They never have and they never will."

She was halfway through her sandwich when she spotted them on the other side of the Green—Beth in a pair of white skintight jeans with a flowery blouse and Milo in darker denim with a navy and white rugby shirt. They were stretched across the red and white checked picnic blanket Tori had given Milo a few months earlier as a hint of things to come when spring finally revealed itself again.

Only she'd intended it for a picnic of their own.

"Nice lookin' couple, wouldn't you say?"

Tori peeked around the other side of the tree. "Oh, hi, Mr. Downing. I didn't see you there."

"Been sittin' here 'bout ten minutes or so. Thought 'bout sayin' something sooner but you seemed lost in thought with your eyes closed and your head 'gainst that there tree." The man bobbed his head to the side. "Seemed silly to interrupt your quiet time on account of chitchat."

She shrugged. "I always like to chat with you." And she did. The elderly man was one of her most loyal patrons at the library, his twice weekly visits something she not only looking forward to, but treasured as well. "I guess you're right. I was just lost in thought is all."

Mr. Downing chuckled. "Least you were 'til that bee buzzed you out of your respite."

The bee.

"Then you got sidetracked by that young couple over there same as I did." He gestured her attention back to the sight she'd rather forget. "Reminds me of you and your young man."

That's because it is.

Shaking her head free from a path she didn't want to explore, she forced a laugh into her voice. "I guess I just hadn't noticed them before now."

"I confess I didn't either until I followed the path of that bee. Seems he was attracted by their relationship as well."

Their relationship. Milo's and Beth's.

She swung her focus back toward the picnic blanket as the man continued on, his words bringing a catch to her throat. "That's the way me and my Evelyn were nearly every day we had together. We laughed. We joked. We talked. We planned. We simply enjoyed each other's company no matter where we were and no matter what we did. Was that way from the moment we met in school."

He leaned back on his park bench, a wistful smile lifting the corners of his mouth. "Only I got foolish and decided to see if the grass was greener somewhere else. Didn't take me long to realize the mistake I made. Guess you could say I was the luckiest man in the world when she agreed to give me a second chance."

A second chance . . .

"I only hope they have more time together than my Evelyn and I did." He released a sigh from somewhere deep in his soul. "Sure makes me wish I could redo those foolish moments."

His words played in her head, tugged at her heart. "Did she take you back right away?"

"She played hard to get for a few days but I won her heart back in the end."

"How?" she asked as she looked, again, at Milo and Beth.

"By callin' on all the things we enjoyed together—bike rides, long walks, holdin' hands, picnics on the Green . . ."

Picnics on the Green.

She swallowed. Was that what was happening with Milo and Beth? Was she winning him back?

"Thinkin' 'bout your own young man?"

Mr. Downing's words broke through her woolgathering. "I'm sorry?"

He lifted his left knee and crossed it atop his right. "I asked if watchin' that young couple is makin' you think of your Milo."

For a moment she considered the notion of using Mr. Downing's less than stellar eyesight to her advantage, but she couldn't. Instead, she divulged the facts as they were and braced herself for the inevitable.

"If it was any other couple, I'd say yes, Mr. Downing.

But since one half of that twosome *is* Milo, I'd have to say no." There. It was out.

She watched as the man dipped his head forward and adjusted his glasses. "Why, Victoria, it looks as if you're right." Slowly, he pulled his attention from the blanket and fixed it squarely on her face. "It's a foolish period is all. You mark my words."

"Problem is, the foolish period was *hers*, when she broke up with him in college."

He waited as she continued, her words clarifying things as much for herself as for him. "He was crazy about her in school. They were joined at the hip for nearly a year until she broke it off, crushing his heart in the process. Then, about a year later, he met Celia. Two years after that, he and Celia got married, only to have her taken by cancer six months later. Ten years went by—ten years with no real relationship of any kind until I moved to Sweet Briar." She inhaled the courage she needed to reach the point in the story that was now. "Slowly we've built something special, something lasting. The kind of relationship I truly believed was confined to the fairy tale section in the children's room."

"And that's changed?"

Tori shrugged. "I don't know. I certainly hope not. But Beth—the girl he was crazy about in college? She showed up in Sweet Briar a few days ago and seems determined—like you were with Evelyn—to fix a mistake *she* made fourteen years ago." She raised her index finger into the air and pointed toward the laughing woman with hair the color of golden silk. "Alas, operation picnic is in full swing."

He looked toward the blanket once again, his narrowed eyes beckoning hers to follow. "Seems to me he's not bitin'."

"What do you mean?"

Lifting his own finger into the air, he, too, pointed. "I s'pose I was just taken in by the laughin' and the squealin'. But now that I'm noticin', really noticin', it's fairly obvious she's the only one makin' any noise."

Determined to see the situation for what it was rather than what she feared, she forced herself to see the facts—

Beth on one side of the blanket, Milo on the other.

Beth laughing and gesturing and squealing, Milo simply nodding.

Beth using her hands and her body to emphasize whatever she was saying, Milo checking his watch.

"You know something?" she whispered. "I think you're right."

"Fourteen years, you say?"

She nodded. "Fourteen years."

"That ain't foolish, Victoria. That's a sign of something that wasn't right the first time."

She inhaled Mr. Downing's words into her heart, savoring them for what they were. The truth was right there in front of her face, in the one-sided interactions between Beth and Milo. And it was right there in the—

Reaching into her purse, she extracted the vibrating phone and glanced at the caller ID screen, the name stretching her mouth into a wide smile as she looked at the pair on the blanket once again.

"Hi, Milo."

"Hey, beautiful. Any chance you have a few minutes for lunch?"

She winked at Mr. Downing. "Actually, I'm finishing up my lunch right now."

Disappointment filled her ear. "Oh. I was hoping that maybe I could see you."

Turning her focus back toward the blanket, she noted

the way his shoulders slumped as he held his cell phone to his ear. "You can."

His shoulders pulled upward. "When?"

"How does right this very second sound?"

"Right this very second?" he echoed as Beth's shoulders took over the task of slumping.

"That's what I said." She knew she was teasing, being deliberately evasive, but talking to Mr. Downing had boosted her spirits.

"Where are you?"

"Watching you."

"Watching—" He stopped then looked left and right until he finally spied her sitting on the bench at the base of the tree. "There you are."

"Here I am." She heard Mr. Downing chuckle as Milo flipped his phone shut, thrust it into his pocket, and then jumped to his feet, his long legs making short distance of the gap between them.

When Milo reached the tree, he spread his arms wide. "I had no idea you were here."

She closed her eyes as he held her tight, reveling in the feel of his nearness. "I stopped by Leeson's and picked up a sandwich, figuring I'd take it back to the library to eat. But when I walked past the Green, I couldn't resist a little time in the sun."

Slowly he released her, stepping back in the process. "Why didn't you tell me you were there?"

"I'd just noticed you when Mr. Downing"—she swept her hand in the direction of the elderly man on the bench beside the pathway—"started talking to me."

She felt Milo studying her, knew he saw right through her words. "Is that the only reason?" he asked.

"I think so," she said honestly. "I hope so, anyway."

"Milo! Come quick!"

They both turned to see Beth cowering on the picnic blanket, her hand pressed to her mouth. In a flash, Milo retraced his steps, Tori on his heels. "Beth? Are you okay? What's wrong?"

With one hand still covering her mouth, Beth raised her other hand and pointed toward the cropping of trees that lined the northern border of the Green. "Someone—someone was *watching* me."

Milo whirled around. "Tori, you stay with Beth and make sure she's okay." And then he was gone, his feet pounding against the asphalt pathway that wound its way toward the trees.

As he disappeared from sight, Beth slowly lowered her hand to her lap to reveal the megawatt smile that was as much a part of her exterior as the hair that cascaded down her back. "The prince always comes to his princess's rescue, doesn't he?"

Chapter 20

The worry in Nina's eyes said virtually everything Tori needed to know. Dixie's drumming fingers simply filled in the gaps like the thump of a sledgehammer.

"Are you okay, Miss Sinclair?" Nina asked as she walked through the door. "I was getting worried."

"You *do* realize your lunch is only supposed to be forty-five minutes, don't you?" Dixie crossed her arms in front of her chest. "As head librarian you really should know better."

"I'm okay . . . now. And yes, Dixie, I'm aware of how long my lunch break is supposed to be." Tori crumbled her plastic grocery bag inside her hand then tossed it into the trashcan behind the information desk. "Things just . . . Well, let's just say that something came up that was out of my control."

Nina exhaled a rush of air. "I'm just glad you're okay. I was worried, especially when I heard the police siren."

A police siren in response to a false claim.

She shook her head, the action as much to placate Nina

as it was to free her own head of the realization that had come the moment Milo ran toward the woods.

Beth Samuelson was a liar, of that she had no doubt. And the motive for those lies was clearer than ever. Beth wanted Milo and she'd stop at nothing to get him back. Even if that meant lying to the police.

For a few moments Tori had actually considered calling the woman on her trumped-up claim, but in the end, she'd let it go, opting, instead, to sit back and watch the whole thing play out. Even when it resulted in Beth nearly jumping into Milo's arms the moment he returned to the blanket with the police in tow.

When the time was right, she'd tell Milo the truth about his college flame. In front of the police wasn't that time.

"So where were you?" Dixie demanded.

"I—"

"Ms. Dunn stopped by to talk to you about her schedule for story time," Nina stammered by way of explanation. "It wasn't on the calendar."

"Patrons don't follow a calendar. They're to be assisted at any time during business hours and last time I checked"— Dixie turned her wristwatch for Tori to see—"now is definitely in that time frame."

"And that's why Nina is here." Stepping behind the counter, Tori made short work of a stack of returns, her hands expertly sorting them into the correct piles. "But, since you seem to need to talk to me, let's talk. I'm here now."

"Shouldn't we go to your office?"

She shook her head. "As you so nicely pointed out, we *are* in the middle of business hours."

Dixie made a face. "But I—"

"So you'd like to talk about your schedule?" Pulling her

stool over to the computer, Tori clicked a few icons until the branch calendar appeared on the screen. "Right now I have you down for each Thursday morning over the next three weeks. Would you like to take some of those off?"

"No, I—"

"Nina? Could you take next Thursday morning?"

"Of course, Miss Sinclair."

She looked at the screen. "I could take the one after that, no problem."

Dixie stamped her foot. "I'm not saying I don't want to work them. I just wanted to talk about them."

"What about them?" She forced herself to focus on Dixie rather than the smile Nina was attempting to hide.

"I was hoping I could do a story time on bullying."

"Bullying?" she echoed.

"Based on what I saw recently, it's sorely needed. Even if the biggest culprit of all is no longer under the influence of her adult counterpart."

Her fingers left the keyboard. "What are you talking about?"

"Bullying needs to stop. It hurts a child's confidence in so many ways."

She held up her hands. "Dixie, I agree one hundred percent. But what was that about the biggest culprit and her adult counterpart? You lost me."

"I had a little girl wander into the children's room during story time a week or so ago. And while I was reading, I watched this little girl be ridiculed by the nastiest child I've ever laid eyes on. Before I could put a stop to it, the little girl ran from the room in tears."

She heard the gasp as it escaped her mouth. "Wait. Where was I?"

"You were meeting the board for lunch."

Nina pointed at Dixie. "See? I told you Ms. Dunn would be the perfect person to ask."

Ignoring her assistant, Tori focused instead on the elderly woman who stood just inside the circular counter-top that denoted the information desk.

"The perfect person to ask about what?" Dixie groused.

Tori glanced around the room, her gaze skimming across the handful of patrons either perusing books at a table or wandering down the aisles in search of a particular title. "Nina? Can you handle things for just a few more minutes? I'd like to talk to Dixie in my office after all. It won't be long."

"Go ahead, Miss Sinclair. I'm fine up here." Nina stepped around the counter and headed toward the bank of comput-ers near the side wall.

Dixie led the way down the hallway, her penny loafers shuffling along the carpet. "I don't want you to think I was negligent in not stepping in to stop the nastiness that day but, by the time I realized what was happening, the little girl had run off."

Closing the door behind them, Tori motioned toward the two wicker chairs by the window. "It never dawned on me to think you'd been negligent, Dixie. I see how you are with the children every week. You're wonderful."

The elderly woman beamed at the praise. "Why thank you, Victoria. It's nice to know my efforts are noticed."

"It would be hard not to notice. Especially when the children in your story time sections always look so happy." When Dixie was settled into the chair with the lavender cushion, Tori followed suit, claiming the yellow-cushioned chair as her own. "But I would like to know what happened that day. Just so I can have a better understanding."

Without so much as a moment's hesitation, Dixie

launched into the story. "I had a slightly larger than normal group that day on account of a playdate one of the children was having. That child's mother asked if it would be okay if her daughter brought three friends to story time. Of course I agreed. The more children I can reach, the better."

Tori nodded. "I agree."

"Two of the little friends were fine. Polite, respectful, curious about the various books I was reading. But the one was rather standoffish, almost as if she was above the notion of sitting on a carpet listening to stories." Dixie held her hand out and made a little face. "Can you imagine a kindergartener being too good for books?"

"No. Not really. Unless it's something she's been trained to think."

"Then this one was trained very, very well." Lifting her hand to her glasses, Dixie adjusted them to sit more firmly across the bridge of her nose. "I—like the rest of the children—was enthralled in the story I was reading when the little brunette walked in. So it was a full page or two later that I finally realized she was standing there on the edge of the circle listening to the story. Then, before I knew what was happening, the nasty little one had stood up and was standing in front of this new little girl telling her she wasn't allowed to be there, that only certain people could attend story time and she wasn't one of them."

She sucked in a whoosh of air, to which Dixie nodded in commiseration. "I know. Isn't that awful? Before I could say or do anything, the little girl had run off, tears streaming down her face." Dixie swiveled her stout body to the right and leaned toward Tori. "I got up, took hold of that nasty little one's arm, and gave her a talkin' to she won't soon forget. Though I suspect she has other things to worry about these days."

"I'm not following."

"Chances are she's trying to figure out who is going to pamper her now that her mother is gone."

"Gone—wait!" Reality hit like a one-two punch. "Penelope Lawson was the little girl?"

A cloud of anger pushed its way across Dixie's wrinkled face. "I should have realized she was tied to that awful woman. Why, her reactions to books and to *me* were much the same as her mother's."

Recalling Milo's words, she nodded. "I'm sorry Ashley kept you from being a reader at the school. She couldn't have been more wrong and, in doing so, the children of Sweet Briar Elementary certainly lost out."

Ever so slowly, Dixie lifted her head to meet Tori's gaze, a hint of moisture evident behind her glasses. "Thank you, Victoria."

"It's the truth, Dixie."

A moment of awkward silence filled the room only to be chased away by more details of the day in question. "I considered getting Penelope's phone number from the mom who'd brought her to story time but decided against it when I realized the other mom was gunning for Ashley."

"*Other* mom?"

"Yes. The mom who was at Sally's party—Stephanie Smith, I believe."

"Stephanie? Steph—wait, you mean *Samantha*?"

Dixie mumbled the name beneath her breath, trying each version on for size. "Actually, I think you're right, I think it *is* Samantha Smith. I didn't get her daughter's name."

"Kayla," Tori supplied as her mind worked to inventory the various bits of information she'd gleaned from Dixie over the past several moments. "So Samantha came back?"

"I was walking home from story time, contemplating

whether I should ask for Penelope's number, when I bumped into Samantha and Kayla near the park. I recognized the little girl right away—the pageboy-style haircut, the sad eyes, and the same heartbreaking little frown I'd seen as she ran out of the children's room. So I stopped and went over to her and her mother so I could apologize for that little Penelope's behavior and for the fact I didn't realize what was happening until it was too late."

"And?"

"The mother sent Kayla off to play so we could talk. Though most of what she said was hard to understand on account of the crying."

"Kayla got hurt on the playground?"

Dixie shook her head. "Samantha was crying. About the way Penelope has been bullying Kayla for months—at school, at the playground, in the library . . ."

She considered the woman's words, realized they meshed perfectly with everything Milo had told her. "I heard that was happening. It's such a shame, isn't it?"

"You're darn tootin' it's a shame. A cryin' shame if you ask me. *Kindergarteners* bullying one another? Can you imagine?"

"No." It was a simple answer but it was the truth.

"I told her I had half a mind to call Penelope's mother and she told me not to bother. Said it wouldn't do any good. And, had I put two and two together and figured out who Penelope belonged to, I would have understood her concerns a bit more quickly."

"So you didn't call?"

"Samantha said it was a losing battle. When I tried to disagree, she simply spouted that thing about going around and coming around that your generation seems to love to say."

"What goes around, comes around," she whispered.

"That's it. That's what she said. Only she didn't say it quite the way you did just now."

Tori looked a question at the woman. "I don't understand."

"She said it more like this." Gritting her teeth, Dixie repeated the saying, the venom in her voice hard to miss. "'What goes around, comes around. And trust me, Ms. Dunn, Penelope Lawson and her precious mommy dearest will get theirs. Soon.'"

Her mouth gaped open. "She said all of that? Even the part about Penelope and her mom getting theirs?"

"I said she did, didn't I?" Dixie snapped. "In fact, my memory is quite clear on the subject."

"Did you tell Chief Dallas that?"

"Why on earth would I do . . ." Dixie's words trailed off as understanding dawned in her large puppy dog eyes. "You think *she's* the one who strangled that hateful woman?"

Reaching out, she patted Dixie's arm, the gesture as much to calm her own nerves as Dixie's. "I don't know. But it certainly bears a closer look, don't you think?"

"I reckon. Though, if you're right, it bears more than that."

"What are you talking about?" she asked.

Dixie pushed off the chair and shuffled over to the door, her leathery hand grasping the doorknob before Tori had even stood. "If Samantha did it, and I mean *really* did it, there's a whole slew of Sweet Briar women who'll think she deserves a round of applause."

Chapter 21

She'd just put the finishing touches on the dessert table when the first knock sounded signaling the start of the Sweet Briar Ladies Society Sewing Circle. With a quick swipe of her hand across the top of the white linen tablecloth, Tori turned and headed toward the door.

Peeking through the screen door she couldn't help but smile at the sight of the plump woman on the other side juggling three foil-covered plates along with the prerequisite sewing gear. "Margaret Louise, let me help you with that." She pushed the door open and reached for two of the plates. "You're only supposed to bring one thing."

"I know, I know. This one is mine and those"—Margaret Louise pointed at the plates in Tori's hand—"are from Beatrice and Melissa."

She glanced down at the plates. "Beatrice and Melissa? Why? Where are they?"

Margaret Louise stepped inside, her sneakers making a soft thud against the hardwood floor. "They're not coming."

"They're not?"

"No. They're both too upset. Seems Chief Dallas was fishin' in the clouds again today."

"Fishing in the—" She stopped, the meaning of Margaret Louise's words hitting their target without interpretation. "Are they okay?"

"They'll feel better when it quits hurtin'. Just wish I knew when that might be." Margaret Louise dropped her sewing gear onto the floor then took the plates from Tori once again. "And short of that, I'd like to come up with an idea that's horse high, bull strong, pig tight, and goose proof. Anything to put that smile back on Melissa's face again. Not used to seeing that child so down in the mouth."

"I know. I saw it the other day when I stopped by to visit. Sad just doesn't seem to go with her, does it?" A swell of voices on the other side of the screen pulled Tori's focus back to the door. "Sounds like Rose and Dixie are here now, too."

"I'll put these on the table."

"Is there any chocolate?" she asked.

Margaret Louise let out a chuckle from somewhere deep inside her soul. "Do you think I'd show my face in this house if there wasn't?"

It was Tori's turn to laugh as she met the next group of sewing sisters at the door. "Good evening, Rose. Good evening, Dixie. I'm glad you could make it."

"We've got work to do." Rose pushed her way through the door, her trademark cotton sweater pulled tightly around her shoulders. "I found some felt that will work perfect for a chip bag and a strawberry."

"I found some for the lettuce and the cheese." Dixie followed her friend down the hallway only to stop midway and turn. "I want to thank you, Victoria, for the kind things you said yesterday. They meant a lot."

She couldn't help but stare as the woman resumed her path toward the dessert table. Little by little the wall was crumbling around Dixie's tough-as-nails façade, their common love of children and books forging a bond between them she hadn't thought possible. Yet there it was. And she was glad.

"Must I really open the door myself, dear?"

Whirling around, she felt the smile before it even completed its trip across her mouth. "Leona, hi!"

"The door?"

She closed the gap between them with two quick strides. "Oh, sorry. I got sidetracked by Dixie."

"Dixie?" Leona asked as she, too, stepped inside. "Is she nailing herself to a cross again?"

"No, she's not." She heard the disbelief in her voice, felt the contentment that chased it away. "It's getting better. It really is."

"I told you it would, didn't I?"

She looked a question at her friend.

"Don't furrow your brow at me like that, dear. It'll encourage wrinkles."

"Wrinkles? Who's got wrinkles?" Georgina's voice bellowed through the screen just before she yanked open the door and stepped inside. "Are you badgerin' Victoria again, Leona?"

"Badgering?"

She rushed to head off a tiff before everyone could be present for the show. "I set up the dessert table just inside the kitchen door. Feel free to set your dishes down and find a seat for the evening."

"I'm here, I'm here." Debbie peered through the screen, her hair pulled into a high ponytail that only accentuated her already high cheekbones. "Jackson had a lot to say at the dinner table this evening so things ran a little late."

"As good a reason as any, I'd say." She pushed the door open once again, her nose seeking out the woman's covered plate. "Something from the bakery?"

Debbie shook her head. "From my secret stash."

She drew back. "Secret stash?"

"Those are the recipes I try at home. Some make it onto the menu at the bakery, some stay exclusive to the Calhoun household. The kids usually decide which recipes stay exclusive." With a flip of her finger, Debbie lifted a section of the foil and held it up for Tori to see. "Anything chocolate and gooey tends to stay exclusive."

"Chocolate? And gooey?" she echoed.

"That's not what I brought."

She felt her shoulders slump then caught the glint of amusement in Debbie's pale blue eyes. "Hey! That's not nice."

Debbie laughed. "But it was fun. You should have seen your face."

"Ha ha. Besides, Margaret Louise has chocolate."

"She may. But I bet she doesn't have gooey."

"Okay, go. Go put your stuff on the table." She trailed behind her friend, breaking off in the direction of the women already seated in the living room. "So how is everyone this evening?"

"I think the better question is how are *you*, dear?" Leona tilted her head forward and pinned Tori with a stare from atop her glasses.

She swept her gaze across a wide-eyed Georgina, an

abnormally subdued Margaret Louise, a distressed Rose, and a hard-to-read Dixie before focusing on Leona once again. "What? What's going on?"

"You didn't act fast enough, dear."

"Act fast enough? On what? What are you talking about?"

"Milo. And that little hussy he's picnicking with around town."

"Must you always be so insensitive, Leona?" Rose snapped before patting the empty cushion beside her. "Come now, Victoria, come sit by me."

Hussy?

"It sounds to me as if it was a good thing Milo was with that woman this afternoon," Dixie mused. "He may have stopped something horrible from happening."

Debbie stopped midway into the living room, her hands no longer carrying the exclusive treat. "Did something happen at the school?"

"This has nothing to do with the school." Georgina gestured Debbie toward a folding chair to her right and then drew forward in her own seat, prompting the others to do the same. "Now ya'll know I'm not the one to go 'round spreadin' rumors, so you better listen close the first time."

Leona rolled her eyes skyward as Georgina's voice grew hushed. "Seems someone has been lurking around Milo's college sweetheart since she arrived in town. She's been followed in the parking lot of the inn, she's heard the sound of someone trying to pick their way into her room—"

"She did?"

Georgina nodded in her direction. "And she had a threat written across her windshield with soap."

"Good heavens! Why would someone want to do that?"

Why indeed.

"Because she's trying to get her former knight to climb back on his horse and ride to her defense." Leona lifted her chin and grabbed for the stack of magazines Tori had left beside the plaid armchair. "And Victoria here is allowing it to happen."

"I think your shirt is missin' a few buttons there, Twin."

Leona looked down at her silk blouse. "No, it's not."

Margaret Louise snorted. "It's an expression, Twin."

Slowly Leona fixed her gaze on her sister. "Are you trying to say I don't know what I'm talking about?"

"No, I think she's saying you're nuts," Rose interjected. "And I have to agree."

"Oh shut up, Rose," snapped Leona.

Tori held up her hands. "Actually, I have to say Leona is right. Mostly about the first part, and maybe even a little about the second part, too."

Leona twisted her mouth and nodded. "At least you're aware. Though why you're letting it happen is beyond me."

"What am I supposed to do?" She grabbed her sewing box and stack of felt from the alcove off her living room and made her way over to the empty spot beside Rose. "Buy her a one-way ticket out of Sweet Briar?"

"That would be a start."

Rose stamped her foot on the floor. "What are you talking about?"

"Milo's former girlfriend. Though"—Leona stopped flipping pages long enough to meet Tori's gaze—"if Victoria continues to sit back, the former tag may disappear."

Rose gasped.

Dixie clucked.

Debbie looked up from her own pile of multi-colored felt. "That's not a very nice thing to say, Leona."

"The truth hurts. Always has, always will."

"Guess that explains why you wince every time I call you old," Rose mumbled just loud enough for Leona to hear.

Before the fur could start flying, Tori held up her hands. "I believe Leona is right in her belief that Beth Samuelson is trying to get Milo back. I also believe she's right when she says Beth is trying to do it by playing the damsel in distress." She set the wooden sewing box at her feet and the pile of felt in her lap. "Let's be honest: we all know Milo is a gentleman in the truest sense of the word. And no gentleman is ever going to sit back while a woman is in peril. Even if it's a bunch of—of hooey."

Leona's eyebrow rose yet her mouth stay closed.

"Hooey?" Georgina asked. "You really think she's making stuff up?"

"I know she is." She proceeded to fill the circle in on the events of that afternoon, describing in detail the entire picnic scene. When she got to the part about the stranger in the woods and Beth's hidden smile, Leona nodded.

"That stranger never would have been in the woods if you hadn't arrived on the scene, dear."

"I think you're right."

Georgina waved her hands back and forth. "Wait. What kind of person would make up these kinds of claims?"

"A woman who is desperate to correct a gross error in judgment," Leona stated from behind her magazine.

"But what on earth could actually come from makin' that kind of stuff up?" Margaret Louise held up two pieces of felt—one light brown, the other dark brown. "Chocolate chip cookies?"

Heads nodded around the room as Tori entertained the best answer for the first of the two questions. But Leona beat her to the punch. "What can come when a woman makes such claims? Attention? Protective arms? A shoulder to cry on?"

"An opportunity to sleep in their bed?" The second the words left Tori's mouth she realized the error of her ways.

"Did you just say what I think you just said, dear?" Leona finally asked.

"If you think I said she's staying in his bed, you're right."

The woman's perfectly pouty lips dropped open, as did the thinner and less made-up versions sported by the remainder of the group.

"That's it. Milo is off my list of nice people," Margaret Louise sputtered.

"You won't find me offering to read to his class anymore." Dixie shook her head sadly. "And here I thought that man knew the meaning of the word *loyalty*."

"Lousy, good for nothing man." Rose reached for Tori's hand and gave it a gentle pat. "You can do better, Victoria. Just give it time."

"Wait. Stop. Please." She pulled her hand from the felt she was sorting and held it up. "Beth is staying with Milo because of a threat she found on her windshield. And she is staying in his bed. But Milo is sleeping on the couch because he's not interested in turning back the hands of time no matter how badly Beth may want to."

"You believe that?" Leona barked.

"I do. Because I have faith in Milo and the relationship we're building."

"Foolish girl."

"Leona, enough," spat Dixie. "Since when is trust foolish?"

"I would think Victoria of all people could answer that question best."

"It's not foolish, Leona. Not in a relationship with any staying power, anyway. And Milo and me, we have staying power. Which means I have to trust what he says until he shows me differently."

"Having that woman in his home overnight isn't showing you differently?"

"No, Leona. It's showing me what I already know to be true. Milo is a special guy—the kind of man that cares about the people in his inner circle. How can I fault him for exercising the very quality that I love about him?"

"With ease. This is his college sweetheart we're talking about."

"His *former* college sweetheart, Leona. That's the part you're missing."

"Seems to me you're missing the part about his bed, dear."

"So what are you going to do?" Debbie asked, her quiet voice a sudden reminder of the evening's missing members.

"I'm going to bide my time until I feel I should say something to Milo. Doing it any sooner might make me come across as some sort of green-eyed monster. Besides, it's quite likely she'll disappear on her own once she releases those designs of hers into the wild."

"What do you mean?" Dixie asked.

"Her designs are spectacular. And I *do* mean spectacular. In fact, I'd be willing to say they're the kind of thing that will jettison her career to the next level—a level that will take her far away from Sweet Briar, South Carolina."

"Let's hope you're right."

She shrugged in Leona's direction. "And if I'm wrong,

I'll deal with it at that time. In the meantime, I'm going to focus my attention and my efforts on a much more pressing issue."

"What? Was he spotted buying a diamond ring for this woman? Is that what it's going to take to wake you up?" Leona drawled.

"Leona!" Rose stamped her foot again. "Must you be so—so—"

"Rude?" Dixie offered.

"Evil?" Margaret Louise countered.

Rose cleared her throat. "I was thinking more along the lines of awful. Like that woman at Sally's party."

"Ashley Lawson," they all chorused.

"Yes, that one."

Handing a piece of muted pink felt to Rose, Tori nodded her head at the group. "Which brings us to the pressing issue I was talking about. Melissa and Beatrice are not here tonight because they're overwhelmed by the stress of this murder investigation and the fingers being pointed in their direction via Regina Murphy. And after the run-in I had with her at Leeson's this weekend, I can't say that I blame them."

"Run-in?" Georgina echoed.

"She's absolutely convinced one of us killed Ashley."

"You must admit, the timing of her strangulation in respect to Sally's party certainly makes you wonder."

All eyes turned on Debbie.

"Do you think one of us did it?" The surprise in Rose's voice was tough to miss.

Debbie shrugged. "One of us in this room right now? I doubt it."

"What are you saying?" Margaret Louise dropped her

needle into her lap. "You think Melissa or Beatrice is guilty of murder?"

"No. But the members of this circle aren't the only ones who were at that party. Nor are we the only ones to come up against that woman's sharp claws."

Tori thought back over everything Dixie had said in her office the day before, the woman's comments about Samantha Smith stirring up more than a few questions and suspicions. "I have to agree with Debbie."

"You're thinking about that Smith woman, aren't you?" Dixie asked as her hand stilled in the middle of threading her needle.

"I am," she confirmed. "Especially in light of what she said to you after the incident at the library."

"What did she—"

Rose jumped in, cutting Georgina off. "Said to *Dixie*? How about what she said to that blonde thing that showed up halfway through the party?"

"Blonde thing? You mean, Regina?"

Rose nodded. "Right after Regina gave the rest of you a talking to about the things that were being said, that short-haired brunette pulled Regina aside and gave her an earful. I wasn't able to make it all out on account of my hearing disappearing faster than Leona's youth, but I know this much—she despised that Lawson woman even more than the rest of you."

"I didn't despise Ashley," Tori said. "I didn't even really know her."

"Well Margaret Louise certainly despised her, and so did Debbie."

Neither woman bothered to argue.

"And let's be honest, Dixie, you weren't a fan, either."

Dixie nodded. "Agreed."

"And Leona, you weren't wild about her the night of the party—"

"Keep my name out of your mouth, old woman." Leona lowered her magazine to her lap. "Melissa and Beatrice despised her, too."

"They did. But no one more than the brunette."

"You mean Samantha Smith?" Tori sought to confirm.

"If that was the one that went with the mousy little girl, yes."

She considered Rose's words, their missing component a needed piece in the puzzle. "I wish I knew what she said."

"If you really want to know, why don't you just ask?" Leona tossed the magazine onto the coffee table and looked around the room, her gaze narrowing on the various pieces of food taking shape around the room. "I have to say this food project is one of the cuter ones we've ever done."

"We've?" Georgina challenged.

Leona rolled her eyes and grabbed another magazine from the pile. "I am part of this group, aren't I?"

"*How*, we're not quite sure." Rose set her completed piece of ham to the side and reached down to the floor, pulling a piece of dark brown felt from Tori's pile. "The crust on the bread needs to be darker then the actual top and bottom, don't you think?"

"I don't know why I keep coming to these meetings each week only to be insulted for my intelligence."

Rose looked up. "Your intelligence?"

"Ladies." Tori quickly teed her hands together. "What do you say we head into the kitchen and sample everyone's treats before we really get down to business? Abby's and Sophie's birthdays are right around the corner and we've got a lot of food to make between now and then."

One by one each circle member rose from their chair and headed toward the kitchen, the conversation of choice switching from murder theories to pies and cakes. Tori trailed behind the group only to be stopped in her tracks by a waiting Margaret Louise. "Melissa told me about your investigation."

"Margaret Louise, I can't help it. Chief Dallas isn't looking in the right place."

"We're both sittin' in amen corner, Victoria. I just want to help is all."

Help.

"Can you encourage Melissa to invite Zoe Rowen over for a playdate? Perhaps with the right questions, one of you can get a handle on where her mother stood in terms of Ashley Lawson?"

"Okay. And how about Kayla? Do you think we should invite her, too?"

She considered the possibility. "Why don't you wait on that. For just a little while, anyway. Just in case Caroline might be more willing to talk without Samantha being there. And besides, I think your sister is right."

Margaret Louise turned toward the kitchen only to stop mid-step. "Now, Victoria, I realize even a blind squirrel finds an acorn every once in a while, but don't you think you're goin' a bit far?"

Tori laughed. "Be nice."

"Why? Leona was positively awful to you about Milo, tonight."

The smile slipped from her face. "She's just looking out for me in her own way. You know that."

"Maybe. But she still has a stingin' way of doin' it."

She couldn't argue.

"Victoria?"

"Hmm?"

"You mind tellin' me what, exactly, my twin was right about?"

"The stuff about Regina and Samantha."

Margaret Louise scrunched up her brows. "What stuff?"

"That I need to *ask* in order to know."

Chapter 22

"So how was your circle meeting last night?"

Tori leaned to the left and peered around the computer. "I hear you, but I don't see you."

Two large encyclopedias parted in the middle atop a backless shelf to reveal a pair of large, brown eyes. "I'm right here. Someone put M in front of D, and S in front of R."

"You'll have that," she said. "As to your question, it was fine. Operation Play Food is coming along nicely."

"Miss Sinclair, I have to admit, I'm having a hard time imagining play food made from fabric."

Pushing her shoulders back, she took the opportunity to stretch her neck and shoulders, her time spent researching titles for the teen club leaving her more than a little stiff. "I would have said the same thing if I hadn't seen the things Debbie has made for Suzanna and Jackson over the years. She's got bread, ham, peanut butter, lettuce, chips, brownies, pancakes with pats of butter, and that's only the tip of the iceberg."

"Is it hard to make?"

Tori shook her head. "Not really. It's a bit time-consuming since much of it is done by hand, but to be honest, I like that more than the machine most times. It makes me feel like it's really *me* making it."

A large green volume passed in front of Nina's face, blocking her from view momentarily. "Do you think you could teach me how to make things like that?"

"Sure. I don't see why not." She looked back over the list of teen titles one last time before sending it to the printer. As the telltale whir of the machine signaled its completion, she slid off her stool and snatched the still-warm paper from the top tray. "Though, based on the pace everyone was working last night, I suspect these two little girls will have more than enough play food for their birthday."

Nina stepped out from around the shelf and wandered into the biographies, her voice growing more hushed despite the closer proximity. "I was thinking more along the lines of learning to make things like that for my own little girl. Unless of course, it ends up being a boy."

"Okay, sure. I can teach you . . ." Her words trailed from her mouth as the meaning behind her assistant's comment took root in her head. She whirled around to meet the shy smile she'd grown to treasure as much as the Sweet Briar Public Library itself. "Nina? Are you—"

"Pregnant?" Nina whispered. "Yes."

A squeal of excitement burst from Tori's lips as she dropped the printout on the counter and ran into the biography aisle, an unending stream of questions firing their way through her thoughts and out her mouth. "When are you due? How long have you known? Is Duwayne excited? How are you feeling? Do you want to sit down?"

Nina laughed and held up her hand. "Miss Sinclair, Miss Sinclair. One question at a time."

"Oh. Sorry. I'm just—" She stopped, pulled the woman into her arms and held her tight. "Oh, Nina, this is fantastic news! I'm so excited for you."

"I'm glad. I was afraid you'd be worried about your workload increasing around the library. But I promise I won't take too much time off. And maybe I can even bring the baby with me sometimes. They sleep a lot in the beginning, right?"

She stepped back. "My workload? Are you kidding me? Everything will be just fine. And if there are any gaps I need to fill, I'll call on Dixie."

"Ms. Dunn will like that."

"She will." Slowly, her gaze skimmed down her assistant's body, lingering on the tiny little belly mound she hadn't noticed until that moment. "So how far along are you?"

A smile stretched Nina's face wide. "Almost three months."

"And Duwayne?"

"He's beside himself with excitement."

"Is that why you haven't been eating very well?"

Nina shrugged.

"And why you've been feeling a little sluggish lately?"

"I guess."

"You guess?"

"I didn't find out until last night."

"Last night?" Tori echoed.

Nina nodded. "I wasn't really paying attention to the calendar, just figured things got off-kilter a bit when my mamma was so sick last month. But then when I realized I still hadn't started, and put it together with how I've been feeling lately, I started to think *maybe*. Just maybe. So I got a test at Leeson's Market yesterday on the way home from work and took it after dinner. You should have seen Duwayne's face when I walked into the room and set it on his lap."

Tori took hold of Nina's forearm and led her to the information desk. "So, if you're three months along, this baby should be due in late September or early October?"

"That's what Duwayne and I have come up with. I guess the doctor will tell us more."

"Do you have an appointment?" she asked.

"Yes, I have an appointment. I called first thing this morning and set something up for tomorrow afternoon." Nina waved her hands in protest as Tori guided her to the stool. "I don't need to sit down. Really, I'm fine."

She stared in awe at her assistant. "Oh, Nina, I'm just so excited for the two of you. You guys are going to make great parents."

"I hope so. I've certainly learned a lot from watching you this past year or so."

"Me?" She blinked back the confusion her assistant's words created. "You mean Melissa?"

"No. I mean *you*. The way you are with every single child that comes into the library." Nina wandered over to the list and plucked it off the counter. "You're endlessly patient, always creative, constantly cheerful, and exactly the kind of person that's going to be a wonderful mom one day. Just like I want to be."

"You will be, of that I have no doubt." She willed herself to focus on Nina rather than the uncertainty her assistant's words had kicked off. "And I consider myself lucky that I'll have the opportunity to live motherhood vicariously through you."

"Until you and Milo get married and have one of your own."

Milo.

Her shoulders slumped.

"Miss Sinclair? Is everything okay?"

She shrugged. "It'll be fine. Really." Leaning against the stool, she allowed her mind to travel six months into the future. "So? What's your gut? Do you think it's a boy or a girl?"

Nina crossed her arms against her chest. "I think you're being evasive right now."

"Nooo. I'm being a good Auntie Tori."

A smile lit the woman's dark eyes. "I like the sound of that."

She clapped her hands together only to have a few curious heads turn in their direction from the computer bank. Lowering her voice, she closed the gap between them in an effort to keep their conversation as private as possible. "Then it's settled? It's finally settled?"

"What's settled?"

"You're finally going to drop this Miss Sinclair nonsense once and for all?"

A flush rose up in Nina's cheeks. "I—I always called Ms. Dunn *Ms. Dunn*. I guess I just feel more comfortable that way."

"Well, I don't. We're more than just coworkers, Nina. We're friends, too, aren't we?" Without waiting for a reply she touched a gentle hand to the woman's stomach. "And I most certainly don't want to be known as Auntie Miss Sinclair."

"How about Auntie Mrs. Wentworth?"

She drew her hand back. "Let's not jump the gun, okay? Auntie Tori suits me just fine, don't you think?"

Nina grabbed her hand and held it tight. "What's wrong?"

"Nothing. It's all good." She tugged her hand away and wandered back over to the computer. "Really, it's fine."

"Whatever you say, Miss Sinclair."

She whirled around. "Wait. I thought you were going to stop calling me that."

"And I thought you said we were friends." Lifting the printout from the counter once again, Nina skimmed her finger down the list of titles. "You've got some good ones here. Hopefully they'll be enough to entice the high school kids to give this club a chance."

There was no doubt about it, she'd hurt Nina by putting her off and it was easy to see why. While she'd thought nothing of asking the woman details about her pregnancy, Tori, herself, had deliberately tried to hold back details of her own life.

"Look, Nina, I'm sorry. I just don't want to heap my sad story on your shoulders when you have such wonderful news to share."

"And I shared it."

"Okay, I get it. I really do." She looked around the room, noting the activity of each and every patron—the elderly couple on the computers, the forty-something man perusing the newspapers, the college-aged kid hunched over a stack of research manuals at a corner table. "Okay, yes, there's a problem. Only it's not really Milo. Not in the way you must be thinking."

Nina stepped from behind the counter only to return dragging a chair. Positioning it close to Tori's stool, she sat down. "What am I thinking?"

"That we're fighting? Or on the verge of a breakup?"

"You're not?"

"No. I don't think so."

"Then what's the problem?"

She inhaled the answer into her lungs then listened to it

as it poured from her mouth. "He's being maneuvered like a puppet at the moment and doesn't seem to see it."

Nina eyebrows rose. "Maneuvered by who?"

"His college sweetheart. His *drop-dead gorgeous* college sweetheart. She's back in town on business and has her sights set on him. Only he's not responding the way she'd like so she's pulling out all the stops to make sure that he does."

"Pulling out all the stops?"

"That's right." She heard the hint of bitterness in her voice and felt ashamed.

"Like?"

"Like saying she's afraid for her safety every time she knows we're together, landing her overnight accommodations in his home in the process."

Nina gasped.

"Remember how I was late returning from lunch over the weekend?"

"Yes."

"They were having a picnic lunch together."

"A picnic lunch?"

"It was her doing. But halfway through the lunch, he called me and I happened to be on the Green, too. Within three seconds of me being with him, this one starts screeching about someone watching her from the woods."

"So Milo runs off and away from you."

Tori nodded, Nina's recap bringing a burn to her eyes. "And as he's running, she's smiling."

"*Smiling?*" Nina echoed.

"Why not? Her mission was accomplished."

"Tell him, Miss—Tori! Tell him she's pulling his strings. No man wants to be someone else's puppet."

She closed her eye against the memory of their late night phone call the night before, the encouragement of her sewing sisters still fresh in her mind. "I did. Or, at least, I tried to. Last night. After everyone left."

"And?"

"He got quiet. Maybe even a little angry . . . though that's hard to tell for sure with Milo. He's not one to get angry."

Nina's hands rose and fell above her lap. "Did he say *anything*?"

"Just that I was being unfair. That I wasn't the one who saw the soaped threat on her car, that I wasn't the one who saw her shaking in her room at the inn, that I wasn't the one who saw the relief on her face when he invited her to stay at his house."

Nina snorted. "I'll *bet* there was relief."

She waved aside her assistant's implication. "Maybe he's right. Maybe I am over reacting."

"Do you think you are?"

Did she?

Did she really imagine the smile on Beth's face as Milo ran into the woods? Did she jump to conclusions regarding Beth's stay in his house or had there truly been leading innuendos designed to take her in that direction?

The answer was as crystal clear as it was when she had dialed Milo's number before bed.

Beth had an agenda—one with Milo's name dead center.

"No."

"Then what are you going to do?"

She shrugged. "I don't know. Focus on clearing everyone's name in Ashley Lawson's murder; work on this high school book club with you; hold down the fort here; finish up Operation Play Food before Abby's and Sophie's birthdays." She met Nina's eyes before letting her focus drift to the woman's stomach. "And pamper you for the next six months."

Nina nodded, yet said nothing, her eyes wide as she peeked around the library. When her visual inventory came back the same as Tori's, she pushed off her chair and stood. "If Milo loses you over someone this conniving, this calculating, it will be his loss. And he will regret it for the rest of his life."

Chapter 23

It really should have come as no surprise. Pageant Creations, after all, was located out of Sweet Briar, South Carolina, not Manhattan or Chicago, Dallas or Los Angeles. But still, based on what she'd seen of Regina Murphy thus far, Tori imagined a modern office building or even an elaborate storefront of some sort.

Not a converted garage that had seen better days.

Yet there it was, in all its non-glory.

Inhaling every ounce of determination she could muster, Tori stepped out of her car, her eyes drawn to the now empty parking spot in front of the door—a reserved parking spot that no longer had an owner. The sight brought her up short, making her swallow over a lump she wouldn't have expected when she first pulled up.

Somehow, some way, she'd allowed herself to get caught up in all the drama that was Ashley Lawson—the meanness, the pettiness, and the over-the-top one-upmanship. And then, when the woman turned up dead, she'd turned her focus toward finding a way to clear her friends of any suspected wrongdoing.

Yet she'd forgotten something. Something she'd pushed from her thoughts until just that moment, as she stood staring at the pink lettered sign that depicted a side of the victim she'd all but forgotten.

Ashley Lawson had been someone's mother.

And that someone had to be hurting in a way Tori couldn't even begin to imagine. Especially considering the fact that that someone was only five years old.

There was absolutely no doubt in her mind concerning the innocence of her friends in the death of Penelope's mom. Sure they disliked the woman, maybe even hated her. But kill her? No.

Yet someone had.

Someone who strangled the victim inside her own car.

Someone who, as of that moment, had gotten away with murder.

Someone who robbed a little girl of a mother.

And someone who needed to be caught. For the sanity of those who weren't guilty and for a little girl who deserved to know that justice had been served.

She pulled her gaze from the sign and fixed it, instead, on her intended destination. All day she'd deliberated the notion of calling Regina and asking for an appointment, yet, in the end, had opted instead to simply show up, unannounced.

Now, as she turned the knob and stepped inside, she couldn't help but doubt that decision just a little. Especially when she considered the notion that Regina might get upset. Then again, what's the worst she could do? Call Chief Dallas?

"Hello? Is anyone here?" she called as she pulled her hand from the door and let it click behind her. "Regina?"

Her mouth gaped open as she looked around at the lavishly decorated waiting room—the freshly polished wood floor, oriental rug, and leather lounge chairs in stark contrast to the building's exterior. Strewn around the walls were pencil-sketched designs of little girls' pageant dresses and the year they were created, their increasing sophistication evident along with the passage of time.

"Welcome to Pageant Creations, how can I help you?" Regina strode into the room and stopped, her carefully modulated greeting disappearing from her lips as her gaze came to rest on Tori. "What are *you* doing here?"

"I came to talk to you. We got off on the wrong foot with everything going on and I want to apologize. I realize Ashley was your friend and I also realize that it had to hurt to hear some of the things that were being said about her at Sally Davis's birthday party."

Regina's mouth opened only to close just as quickly.

Tori gestured toward the window and the parking lot beyond, her mouth putting words to her epiphany. "I've been so busy trying to figure out how best to convince you and Chief Dallas that my friends are not guilty of her murder that I missed the fact that you lost a friend. For that, I'm truly sorry."

The woman's jaw tightened as a parade of emotions marched across her face. There was anger, surprise, uncertainty, and something else Tori couldn't quite identify. But, in the end, Regina simply gestured toward the hallway from which she'd just come. "I can give you a few minutes, I suppose."

"Thank you." She pointed toward the pictures that encircled the waiting room. "It's amazing to see the way your designs have taken off over the past"—she leaned toward the oldest picture—"five years. It has to be very satisfying."

"It is. Especially now with the likes of Fredrique Mootally noticing Pageant Creations."

"Fredrique Mootally?"

Regina waved her French-manicured hands in the air, beckoning Tori to follow. "Fredrique Mootally is only the most well-known adult pageant designer in the country. He is *the* go-to person for anyone wishing to win Miss America or Miss Universe or Miss Anything for that matter."

Trailing behind the woman, Tori couldn't help but take in the sights along the way—the framed designs found in the waiting room morphing into actual photographs with each passing step. "And now he's noticing your company?"

"He wants to forge a *partnership*. A very lucrative, very prestigious partnership the likes of which will change everything in my life. And I do mean *everything*. Not the least of which is this dump." Regina's pace slowed momentarily as they approached an open door on the left, the narrow gold plaque above the entryway leaving no guesswork as to the room's occupant.

Tori peeked inside, the stack of books and picture frames in the middle of the desk bringing a lump to her throat as Regina's voice continued. "Not that Sweet Briar isn't . . . *lovely* . . . for some people, because I know it is. But I've spent quite enough time here. It's time to move somewhere bigger."

At the end of the hall, Regina turned right, the click of her stiletto heels disappearing as they left the hardwood floor in favor of a plush wall-to-wall carpet. "Somewhere where people know what fashion is . . . and what it isn't."

Tori looked around, her mind absorbing every detail of

the white walls and black lacquered furniture, their overall absence of color offset by the bright red carpet and red-matted artwork. "You don't have to explain. I'm not from Sweet Briar. And while I appreciate many aspects of small-town living, there are quite a few things I miss about Chicago." Leaning forward, she studied the impressionist painting on the wall behind Regina's desk. "Namely the culture—the shows, the galleries, the museums, that sort of thing."

"Then you can appreciate what an association with Fredrique Mootally can bring." Regina dropped into her desk chair. "It's like the difference between cooking hamburgers and dining on filet mignon every night."

Tori nodded, her feet leading her toward the next crop of artwork. "I get that. I really do. And I'm happy for you." She stopped as her gaze fell on a park sign propped against the far wall. "What's that?"

Regina stiffened. "That's something Ashley didn't live to see."

She stepped closer, the red and black signs beckoning to her from across the room. "Penelope's Park? What does that mean?"

"It was the next step in Ashley's ongoing quest to immortalize her daughter's name."

"Next step?"

"You saw the parking spot, didn't you?" Regina flipped her laptop open on her desk and began tapping on the keyboard, her tone rising and falling with each click of the mouse. "Well, the park was the next logical step. She shelled out good money to have Sweet Briar Memorial removed from the sign and replaced with her daughter's name."

"Wow. I had no idea." She soaked up every detail of the sign, imagined it hanging from the metal post she'd driven past countless times over the past year.

"That was the problem. The sign she insisted on erecting in the parking lot kept her happy for all of about two days—until she realized the only people who would see it were people who happened to come to the office." Regina pulled her top desk drawer open and rummaged around inside before finally extracting a brown leather date book. "Then she came up with the park idea. She offered to update all of the equipment on her own dime if the town would rename the park in her daughter's honor."

"Lots of people would see that," she mumbled.

Regina snorted. "You'd think so, wouldn't you? But even before the signs came in, she started talking about how the only people who would see the name were people who came to the park."

She looked from Regina to the sign and back again. "What did she want? To have her daughter's name in lights?"

"Until *that* wasn't far-reaching enough, either, regardless of the mountains she moved, or destroyed, in the process."

Aware of the stress building in Regina, Tori changed topics. "How is Penelope doing? Do you know?"

The tweet of Regina's phone prevented her from answering. "Excuse me. I need to take this." Regina flipped her phone open and held it to her ear. "Pageant Creations, how can I help you? Oh yes, Natalie. I'm fine; how are you?"

Tori continued around the room, her attention vacillating between the artwork in front of her and the conversation taking place behind her, the notion of Ashley's devotion to her daughter more than Tori could comprehend. What happened to hugs and kisses or special trips to the ice cream shop? When did things like that stop being special enough? Did children really care whether their name was on a parking sign?

Regina stood and crossed to the drafting table beneath the window, her hand gliding across an artist's folder. "The first six have been . . . *misplaced*. But I'm sure they'll turn up. Soon. In the meantime, the ones I have are absolute showstoppers."

It was hard not to notice the rise in Regina's pitch. Tori had been there herself, many times. Sure, she hadn't lost a friend in such a brutal way as Regina had lost Ashley, but she knew about trying to shoehorn heartache into a life that insisted on moving along at its usual pace.

"Does it really matter whether there's five or ten, or six or twelve?" Regina argued. "Dynamite is dynamite, isn't it?"

She turned just in time to see the woman's face fall. "That's it? Just like that? No chance to . . . Okay . . . Okay . . . I'll be in touch." For a moment the woman simply sat there, motionless, the tension from earlier replaced by a palpable disappointment evident by one single word. "Damn."

"Are you okay?" It was all she could think to say under the circumstances. "Is there anything I can do?"

Regina lifted the folder from the draft table only to slam it back down once again. "Damn! I wanted this so badly."

"The partnership fell through?"

"You could say that." Regina pushed off her chair and strode across the room toward her desk. "Look, I don't mean to be rude but I've got work to do. If you've got something to say, say it. Otherwise, I'm going to have to ask you to leave. I've got to figure a way to salvage this deal one way or the other."

"I understand." She closed the gap between them, her thoughts jumping to the reason for her visit. "Someone killed your friend and employee. I'm confident my friends are not responsible. But there were other people at that party, people I don't really know. And while I hate to think any of them may be responsible for Ashley's death, it is certainly possible."

"Possible went out the window when I found her in her car with a rope around her neck, don't you think?" Regina dropped into her chair once again.

Realizing the angry Regina was back, Tori cut to the chase. "Can I ask what Samantha Smith said to you the night of the birthday party?"

"Samantha Smith? Who's that?"

She lifted her hands to her head. "About my height, short brown hair, a little spiky at the top. I think she was wearing a denim jacket of some sort?"

"Okay, okay. I remember." Regina propped her elbows on her desk and leaned forward into her hands, her jaw tightening in the process. "She—she told me I had a hateful person working for me, someone who was cruel to children, and that I—along with everyone else at the party—would be better off without her."

"Better off without her?" Tori echoed. "What? Did she expect you to fire Ashley?"

A low, mirthless laugh escaped the woman's lips. "*Fire* Ashley?" Regina dropped her hands to her desk and stood. "Are you kidding me? I was offering her the chance to immortalize her *own* name instead of—oh, forget it, it doesn't matter. That woman was crazy."

"But—"

"It's time for you to go. I am trying to run a company here. A company *without* a head designer I desperately needed."

Chapter 24

Tori felt the smile spread across her face the second she saw the name on her caller ID screen, the momentary respite from her thoughts a welcome relief. Flipping the cell phone open, she held it to her ear. "Hi!"

"I called over to the library and Nina told me you were off today. Where are you?"

"I just left Regina's office and I'm heading home. I'm in dire need of a little chocolate."

"You get anythin' good while you were there?"

"Not really. Except maybe the fact that Samantha Smith may have hinted at the crime that took Ashley's life."

"Then you need to go straight to the chicken pen and start scratchin'."

Her laugh echoed around the car. "Excuse me?"

"Sorry 'bout that, Victoria. I forgot who I was talkin' to for a minute." Margaret Louise's voice bellowed in her ear. "Rather than taking a hint as told to you by someone else, how 'bout you get one straight from the horse's mouth instead?"

"What horse might that be?" She slowed to a stop at the four-way intersection on the eastern edge of the town square.

"Samantha Smith."

She stepped on the gas only to switch to the brake once again. "How?"

"By stoppin' by—hold on a second, will you?"

As she waited, Tori slowly crept across the intersection, her gaze sweeping the grounds of the Green as she headed down one of its bordering roads.

"Victoria? You still there? Sorry about that. Sally had a mini-crisis."

"Is everything okay?"

"Just dandy. Now drive on over here and let's see if we can't get some of those answers we need."

"Samantha is there?"

"Sure as shootin' she is. Seems almost the entire mornin' kindergarten class and their mammas are here."

"And where, exactly, is here? Melissa's?"

"Good heavens, Victoria, of course not. We're at the park—Sweet Briar Memorial Park."

Sweet Briar Memorial Park.

"You mean, *Penelope Park*, don't you?" She turned onto Valley View road and headed east.

"Now don't you get me started on that, Victoria. This is too nice a day to discuss the fact that our city council is three pickles shy of a quart."

"It could be worse. They could be four pickles shy." Tori stifled the urge to laugh as she pulled into a parking spot beside the park. "I'm here now."

"Ooooh, I see you, I see you."

She scanned the crowd of moms and kids to find a waving Margaret Louise on the far side of the monkey bars, her plump form moving alongside Sally as the little girl worked to maneuver each rung. "I see you, too."

"The horse is on the bench when you step inside the gate."

"The horse . . ." Her voice trailed off as she sought out her friend's directions. Sure enough, the short-haired brunette that had been a topic of discussion with Regina Murphy not more than fifteen minutes earlier was sitting on a bench watching her daughter like a hawk. "I see her."

"Why don't you strike up a conversation when you first walk in. And I'll do my best to encourage Sally over in that direction."

"Sounds good. See you soon." She snapped the phone closed in her hand and pulled the key from the ignition. A quick check in the rearview mirror confirmed what she already knew—she needed more sleep and a rapid end to the drama. And while she was at it, perhaps a one-way ticket out of Sweet Briar for Milo's former flame, as well.

Shaking the latter image from her thoughts, Tori stepped from the car and made her way over to the gate, the prospect of talking to Samantha guiding her forward. As luck would have it, Samantha turned in her direction as she approached.

"Hi. Samantha, right?" She extended her hand in the mom's direction. "I'm not sure if you remember me but—"

Samantha stood. "Of course. You're the librarian. The one who helped with Sally Davis's birthday party."

She confirmed the woman's words with a smile and a nod. "That's right. I'm Victoria Sinclair. How are you?"

"I'm good. Thanks." Samantha gestured toward her daughter. "You ever notice how life can turn on a dime?"

She looked from the little girl to Samantha. "Turn on a dime? I'm sorry, I'm not following."

"One minute we were all discussing the merits of disposing of that awful woman on account of her rudeness and her insensitivity, and the next, she's gone." Samantha's hands rose into the air. "Poof! The classroom cattiness and the totally ridiculous birthday party pressure is gone just like that."

"Samantha, that woman is *dead*."

"You're right. And so are my daughter's tears."

Nothing like leading the horse to water.

"Your daughter's tears?" she echoed.

"The tears she cried every single day after school thanks to Penelope's nastiness." Samantha's hands found her hips. "And now that Penelope has been out of school mourning her mother's death, things are so much better."

She knew she was staring, could even feel her left nostril flaring in disgust, but she couldn't help it. It was one thing to be happy your child was fitting in better and quite another thing to gloat about the death that happened in order to make it happen. "Penelope will *eventually* come back."

"But now she'll be on her classmates' turf."

"Her classmates' turf?"

"That's right. And it's going to be one ruled by kindness and acceptance. Not nastiness and selective inclusion."

"Mommy, Mommy, come catch me!"

Samantha held her index finger in Tori's direction, the gesture polite but dismissive. "Well, I better go. It was nice talking to you." And with that, the woman was gone, her feet kicking up pieces of shredded tires as she made her way across the playground and over to the swing set.

"Catch any fish on your line?"

She whirled around to find a grinning Margaret Louise at her elbow. "Excuse me?"

"You get anythin'?"

"You might say that."

Margaret Louise's eyes rounded. "What?"

"Besides the fact she despised Ashley?" she murmured as her gaze sought and found the back of Samantha Smith. "Well, there's also the little matter of her being almost *giddy* about Ashley's murder."

"The playground sure is less splintered."

"Margaret Louise!" She eyed her friend closely. "I realize she wasn't a nice woman, I saw that with my own two eyes. But please tell me you aren't glad she's dead. There *is* a little girl who's been hurt by her murder."

"Ah, don't mind me. Of course I'm not glad she was murdered. But by the same token it's hard not to notice the change in the class dynamic now that she's gone."

She watched as each child headed home, some pulled away by the promise of a cookie, others guided home by the need to start dinner. Yet still she sat, the warmth of the spring sun rooting her to the same picnic bench she'd claimed as Margaret Louise headed home with Sally.

All of the things she'd wanted to do that afternoon—the book she wanted to read, the play food she wanted to make, the flowers she wanted to plant—paled against the desire to simply sit.

And think.

There was no getting around the fact that Samantha Smith didn't miss Ashley Lawson. And no getting around what she'd said to Regina Murphy the night of Sally's party. But was it a hint of things to come? A diabolical plan she intended to execute little more than twelve hours later? Or simply words spoken by a frustrated mom who needed to do nothing more than vent?

"Hey, beautiful. Margaret Louise said I might find you here."

She swung her head to the right as a smile played its way across her face. "Milo, hi! What are you doing here?"

He opened the gate and stepped inside, his hands pulling her to her feet before he even officially stopped at the bench. "I stopped by your house but you weren't there. So I started wandering around, hoping I'd catch a glimpse of your car somewhere." Wrapping his arms around her, he planted a kiss on the top of her head. "When I passed Margaret Louise's place, she called out, said she'd seen you at the park and that you were looking mighty good."

Oh, how she loved that woman.

"And?" she teased, stepping back so she could twirl around.

"You look even better than she said." He caught her hand and pulled her close once again. "I like that skirt on you. It's real pretty."

She glanced down at the tiny sprig of lavender flowers that adorned the A-line skirt, the matching lavender shirt hugging her modest curves. "Thanks."

"No, thank *you*." Lifting her face to his, he kissed her warmly. "Mmmm, I've missed you."

"You've been busy." She sat back down on the bench and patted the open spot to her left. "I figured I'd give you a little breathing room."

"Did I ask for breathing room?"

"No. But you have a lot on your plate right now."

"You mean Beth, don't you?"

She considered denying his claim but, in the end, simply nodded.

He pulled her hand onto his lap and entwined his fingers with hers. "Look, I'm sorry I got a little short with you on the phone the other night but I just don't believe Beth made up that encounter on the Green. Why would she do that? It makes no sense."

Looking down at their linked hands she said nothing. Really, what was there to say? He wasn't ready to hear the truth about someone who had meant so much to him.

"I told her I was heading out to see you and she was fine with it. She understands that you're my girl."

"I never said she didn't understand it. I just said she didn't like it."

"And I think you're wrong."

"Then we'll have to agree to dis—"

The ring of his phone caught her up short. "Hang on a minute. It's Beth."

Of course it is.

"Hey, Beth, what's up?"

She closed her eyes against the words that flowed from the phone, words her mind had predicted the second the phone rang.

"Milo, please, I need you to come home right away. I was sitting on the back deck just now and I heard something."

Feeling his fingers loosen, Tori gently removed her hand from his. "What did you hear?" he asked.

"It sounded like a twig snapping. Like someone was back there . . . watching."

"Where are you now?"

"Inside. With the doors locked. But"—Beth's voice grew weepy despite the smile Tori would bet was stretched across her flawlessly made-up face—"I'm scared. Could you please come home?"

Home.

She swallowed as Milo said the words she knew he'd say. "I'll be right there."

He closed the phone inside his hand and stood, his eyes hooded. "Tori, I'm sorry. I really am. But she needs me right now."

"I know. So go. I'll be fine. I—I've got plans for tonight anyway."

It was a lie and she knew it, especially considering she hadn't actually called Leona or even considered it until just that moment. But it was all she could think to say to keep from crumbling right there on the park bench.

"Oh. Okay. Well, have fun." He took a step toward the gate then stopped. "You have off tomorrow, too, right?"

She forced a smile to her lips. "I do."

"Any chance I can see you after school lets out?"

"Let me see how I'm doing on the circle's project."

For a moment he simply studied her, his eyes depicting a mixture of sadness and disappointment the likes of which nearly broke her heart. When she didn't stand, didn't promise to work as fast as she could, he turned and walked away, his feet leading him toward the damsel who believed distress was a game—a game Milo was too sweet and too blind to realize he was playing.

Chapter 25

She knew she'd get a lecture. It was as much a certainty as the notion that a library had books or a school had students.

And she didn't care. In fact, if Tori was honest with herself, she *welcomed* it. Even *needed* it.

"Leona, can I ask you something?"

Pausing her wine goblet halfway to her mouth, Leona nodded. "Of course. That's why we're having dinner together, isn't it? So you can learn from my expertise in life?"

Her cheeks rose along with her smile. "Actually, we're having dinner because you're my friend and I thought it would be fun to spend a little time together outside our weekly sewing circle meeting."

Leona took a sip of her wine then set the glass back on the linen tablecloth. "Do you think I just fell off one of those turnip trucks Margaret Louise is always glorifying?"

She stared at her friend. "Turnip trucks?"

"You didn't suggest dinner because you wanted to spend

time with me, you suggested it so you wouldn't have to sit home alone—again—worrying about what Milo is doing with that little relationship wrecker he has living under his roof."

All attempts at a half-hearted protest died before they reached her lips. "How did you know?" she finally asked.

"Because I know you, dear."

Blowing a strand of hair from her face, Tori leaned back against her chair, her fingers finding the stem of her own glass and giving it a gentle twirl. "Then what should I do? I tried to make him see what she's doing but he refuses to accept it. He simply doesn't believe that someone he once cared about is a—is a—"

"Conniving little hussy?"

She had to laugh at Leona's description. "Yeah, okay, though I'm not sure I'd have chosen those same words."

"Well, that's the difference between you and me, dear. I call a spade a spade when necessary."

"That doesn't sound like a very belle thing to do."

"When a belle's man is being manipulated, it most certainly does."

"Oh." She pulled the bread bowl closer to her spot and considered its various options. After a quick once-over she selected a pumpernickel roll.

"That, dear, is going straight to your thighs."

Her hand stilled mid-tear. "It's bread, Leona."

"And, eventually, it will end up on your thighs as cellulite. So, too, will that steak you ordered with the cactus butter glaze." Leona sighed dramatically. "And don't get me started about the chocolate concoction we both know you're going to try and order when dinner is over."

She swallowed back the futile attempt at denial. "Come on, Leona, look at me." She pointed at the part of her body visible over the top of the table. "I'm a long way away from being worried about my weight."

Leona nodded, her eyes following Tori's hand as she lifted a piece of bread to her lips. "I remember when my sister used to say that same thing."

Tori dropped the bread onto the plate. "Margaret Louise is beautiful."

"If you can discount all that—extra weight."

"Leona!"

"Don't shoot the messenger, dear."

Tori stared at the piece of bread on her plate, her mind warring with the need to drown her sorrows in yeast and the desire to be proactive with her health. In the end the yeast won out despite the rise in Leona's eyebrow. "I'm sorry, I need it. It's been a long day."

The waitress stopped beside their table and doled out the correct plates—steak for Tori, a grilled chicken salad for Leona. After checking to make sure they had what they needed, she disappeared once again, leaving them to the conversation at hand.

"So what do I do? He isn't ready to listen." She guided her knife through the steak, the sight of the melting cactus butter making her mouth water. "Oh, this looks really, really good, doesn't it?"

Leona rolled her eyes skyward. "I've already voiced my opinion on your order. As for Milo, there's only one thing to do, dear."

She took a bite of steak, savoring the taste as it slid down her throat. "What's that? Scratch Beth's eyes out?"

Leona stopped picking at her salad long enough to level an exasperated look in Tori's direction. "Let's leave the eye scratching to that little hussy, shall we?"

She paused mid-chew. "Then what do you propose?"

"First? That you don't speak with your mouth full."

Tori felt her face warm.

"Second? You don't let her win."

"What am I supposed to do? Lock Milo in a closet every time she calls with another dilemma?"

Leona narrowed her eyes. "That could work . . ."

"Leona! I'm not going to force Milo to do anything."

"You're right. Let's save that for our last resort." Leona grazed the top of her lettuce with the fork as she hunted for yet another piece of chicken among a sea of green. "I was thinking more along the lines of going *with* him when she tries her little games."

"Oh, like she's going to be happy about that."

"Exactly."

She studied her friend closely. "I don't get—wait! I get it now! I accompany him back to the scene of the exaggerated fire, he looks around, sees everything is fine, and then we resume our time together."

"And she's been defeated."

She's been defeated.

Dropping her fork onto her plate, she pushed the half-eaten steak to the side. "You think that'll work?"

Leona's silk-clad shoulders rose and fell. "I don't know. Time will tell. But at least you'll be together which is what you want, isn't it, dear?"

"It is."

"Then we have a plan." Leona made a second pass through her salad only to find a piece of chicken no bigger than her fingernail.

"That wouldn't happen if you'd simply order a chicken entrée, Leona." She laughed at the anticipated eye roll then leaned forward. "He asked if I wanted to come see him tomorrow after school."

"What did you say?"

"My heart was talking at the time and it said I wasn't sure."

Leona pushed her salad bowl to the side in time to pluck a dessert menu from the arms of a passing waiter. Flipping it over, she pushed her glasses higher on her nose and scanned the list of sweets. "Sounds like you almost offered Milo to Beth on a silver platter."

"Almost?"

"Of course. But since you first uttered those foolish words you've had the good fortune of speaking with me. Which means you now realize the error of your ways and you will be waiting on his couch when he arrives home. Preferably in something that will make him forget all about that little hussy." Leona waved their waitress over to the table. Pointing from the menu to Tori, she lowered her voice to a near whisper. "She'll take the Triple Chocolate Overload."

"Leona! I thought you said—"

"Hush, dear. Cellulite worries must, occasionally, take a backseat to jump-starting the libido."

Chapter 26

She was almost done with the tomato when the first reinforcement shuffled up the sidewalk.

"Good morning, Rose."

"It may be morning to you, Victoria, but to an old fart like myself it seems like late afternoon."

Her hand stilled above the red felt. "Why?"

"Because I've been up since the crack of dawn. Been that way since I hit seventy." Rose grabbed hold of the railing and hoisted herself up the three stairs to Tori's front porch. "Just goes to show you how delusional I was in my youth when I used to dream of retirement."

"I don't get it." She pulled the felt to her chest and stood. "Here, why don't you take the rocking chair and I'll move over to the swing."

"Thank you, Victoria." Rose patted her hand then lowered herself to the slatted wooden rocker. "That last year before I quit teaching? I used to imagine being able to wake to the sound of birds instead of an alarm clock buzzing in my ear."

"That's one of my favorite parts of having a day off." Tori sat down on the porch swing and repositioned her latest sewing project in her lap, her hand resuming its blanket stitch without so much as a passing thought. "It's almost magical."

"Enjoy it now while you can. Because in about forty years you'll be woken up by something much more persistent than a chirping bird."

She pulled the strand of red thread through the underside of the tomato then looped it around the outside once again. "And what's that?"

"Your bladder."

"Ahhh." She looked up from the nearly complete condiment. "I'll keep that in mind."

Rose tugged her tote bag onto her lap and reached inside, her pale white hand returning with a piece of purple. Holding it up, she cocked her head toward the nondescript rectangle. "I figured a peanut butter sandwich should have an option of jelly, don't you think?"

She smiled. "Absolutely."

"And I brought a pale yellow color to make a few pats of butter for Dixie's pancakes." Rose reached into her bag once again, this time pulling out a bundle of deep purple embroidery floss. "Now, Victoria, the bladder isn't the only thing you need to look out for when you get old."

"Oh no?

"There's the forgetfulness, the aches and pains in your joints, and the desire to talk about food all the time."

She dropped the tomato onto the table beside the swing and began working on the slice of cheese that was next on her list. "I remember that about my great-grandmother. Whenever she and my great-grandfather used to go somewhere, the food was always the part she talked about. Not the people they saw, not the things they did. Just vivid details about every single food item they saw—whether they actually ate it or not."

"I know. And I swore I wouldn't do it, but I do. It's part of the reason our sewing circle has so much food. Gives Dixie and me something to talk about for the next week."

Tori guided the scissors through the fabric then looked up. "I notice you didn't include Leona in that statement."

Rose waved her hands above the jelly taking shape on her lap. "Leona's not old yet. She's still got a good ten years to go before she's trembling and coughing and shuffling around like me. But don't you tell her I said that, you hear? Half the fun of sewing circle is watching little Miss Perfectly Poised get a little red in the face."

"Little Miss Perfectly Poised?"

"That's one of my nicer names for Leona." Rose set her jelly off to the side before reaching inside her bag for the piece of pale yellow felt and its coordinating embroidery floss. With deft fingers she separated the floss into three strands. "Good heavens, I couldn't believe the way she went at you about Milo and that woman during the last meeting. It's like she can't even fathom the notion of a woman being secure without a man."

"I don't think it's that so much as it is the simple fact she knows he means a lot to me."

"We *all* know that, Victoria." Rose pushed her toes against the ground as her chair began to slow, her normally trembling hands surprisingly accomplished with a needle and thread. "We also all know you're a genuine treasure. If Milo Wentworth allows himself to get sidetracked from that fact, then good riddance."

"Good riddance to whom?"

Tori and Rose turned toward the sidewalk to find

Margaret Louise and Dixie approaching. "Has anyone ever told you you've got elephant ears, Margaret Louise?"

"All the time." Clasping Dixie's upper arm with a pudgy hand, Margaret Louise propelled the retired librarian up the stairs and over to the second rocker. "It's what keeps me in the know on all things Sweet Briar."

"And then she tells me, and I tell you, and you tell Victoria." Dixie nodded toward Rose's butter pats. "Those will go nicely on my pancakes."

"Did you finish them?"

"I did." Dixie reached into her cavernous purse and fished out two small tan-colored circles. "I even made a bagel." After the prerequisite round of oohs and ahhs, Dixie continued. "Georgina brought over her contributions this morning—a bag of chips, a waffle, and a hamburger equipped with all the trimmings."

Tori glanced down at her cheese and smiled. "I think this was such a neat idea. Those little girls are going to have a blast with all of this food."

Margaret Louise dropped onto the swing beside Tori, the motion whipping them both backward. "So what did I miss? Who's leavin'?"

"No one. Why?"

Rose clucked. "She's talking about our conversation regarding Milo, Victoria. The part where I said good riddance."

Margaret Louise stiffened. "Did you two break it off?"

Tori shook her head. "No. Not at all. It's just—" She shrugged her shoulders. "Everything will be fine. I'm going to see him this afternoon. At his house. That way he won't have to travel so far when Beth comes up with her latest diversion."

"Hi, everyone!" Debbie trotted onto the porch with a

large gift bag in her hand. "Is Operation Play Food ready to become Operation Birthday Present?"

"I think so." Tori lifted her cheese into the air then brought it down to rest on top of the pile she'd assembled over the past week. "Beatrice left her food in my mailbox yesterday and Dixie has Georgina's. And Margaret Louise and Rose are virtually done, right, ladies?"

Rose paused her rocker for a moment and held up her offerings. "One last pat of butter to go."

"Thank you so much, everyone. Those two little girls are going to love this food."

"Any word on a job for Colton?" Dixie asked.

"As a matter of fact I saw Eloise just the other day and she said there was a glimmer of hope, though it might mean they have to move out of Sweet Briar." Debbie walked from person to person, quietly gushing over each piece of food she saw. When she finally reached the lone remaining chair, she dropped onto it. "Seems the ones we want to stay, leave, and the ones we want to go, stay."

"Who are you wantin' to go?"

A flash of crimson rose in Debbie's cheeks. "I probably shouldn't say. It wouldn't be terribly kind of me."

"Aw, c'mon, Debbie, every dog ought to have a few fleas," Margaret Louise chided. "It's what binds us together."

Rose pointed toward Tori. "And see? I always found cheese to be very binding."

A chorus of laughter rang up around the porch. "Okay, okay," Debbie finally said. "Well, after everything I've been hearing, I'd like to see that Beth Samuelson leave town."

"It ain't gonna happen." Margaret Louise shifted in her seat, the wooden structure creaking beneath her weight. "That little thing has her sights set on Milo. Saw it just myself at the bakery this mornin'."

"This morning?" Tori echoed.

Debbie confirmed the woman's words. "I saw them, too. And Margaret Louise is right. You can see it in every bat of her eyelashes when she looks up at Milo."

"And what does Milo do in return?" Rose snapped.

"He really doesn't respond. He just acts like his normal self." Debbie pulled a package of tissue paper from the gift bag and held it up for everyone to see. "I figured I'd wrap each food grouping in tissue paper before placing it in the bag. That way, when Abby and Sophie open the package, they'll see the complete pancake set, the complete BLT, the"—she glanced over at Rose's lap—"complete peanut butter and jelly sandwich set, et cetera."

She knew Debbie's description of Milo shouldn't matter. She knew the kind of man Milo was all on her own. But still, it helped to hear that others saw the same thing in his actions.

Without missing a beat, Debbie flitted back to the subject of Beth and Milo. "The first time I saw her, I thought she seemed nice. But I suppose I should have known better when I saw them together. Anyone who can be all syrupy to someone like *that* should be suspect."

"Saw who?" Rose asked, the question a near perfect match to the one brewing inside Tori.

"Beth and Ashley."

"Beth and Ashley? When?"

Debbie stopped sorting food sets and looked up, her shoulders rising and falling in rapid succession. "I don't know. The morning of Sally's party, why?"

Leaning back in the swing, Tori raked her hair into a high ponytail only to let it fall back to her shoulders. "I didn't realize they knew each other beyond a vague professional thing."

"I don't think they did. In fact, I'm sure they didn't because that's how I knew Beth's name when I saw her the next morning while talking to you. I heard her introduce herself to Ashley when they met."

"Did they strike up a conversation in line while they were waiting for breakfast or something?"

Debbie shook her head. "No. It seemed more like they had a meeting. Ashley had a leather case with her and Beth was dressed all professional in a tailored suit and heels. She was friendly with Ashley yet very businesslike. Though . . ." Debbie's voice trailed off as she fixed on some distant place far beyond Tori's front porch. After a moment, she swung her focus back to the group. "By the end of the meeting it changed. Suddenly the businesslike formality was gone and they were acting like the best of friends. Which, at the time, I thought was neat . . . except for the fact it was *Ashley* she had befriended."

"Did you hear what they were talking about?" Dixie asked as Margaret Louise leaned closer.

"No. Sunday morning is one of my busiest days of the week so eavesdropping wasn't really an option. Besides, I didn't know about Beth's connection to Milo at that time so I just figured it was a business meeting. Especially since that leather case Ashley had with her was open on the table for most of the meeting."

Feeling her mood begin to slip, Tori stood and gestured toward the house. "Would anyone like something to eat? Or drink?"

"No. We're fine, aren't we, ladies?" Rose completed her last blanket stitch on her final pat of butter and tossed it across the porch to Debbie. "So where are things with the murder investigation? Does anyone know? Chief Dallas seems to have eliminated me."

"He must think I'm stronger because he's still sniffing around my place." Dixie sat up tall, puffing her ample chest outward in the process. "I suppose the party guests are still his hottest suspects, though he probably should be sniffin' around one in particular, isn't that right, Victoria?"

"What are you talking about?" Rose countered.

Tori returned to her spot on the swing, the change in topic a welcome reprieve. "We're talking about Samantha Smith. She was one of the other moms at the party."

Rose secured her bundle of pale yellow floss with a sticker then returned it to her bag along with the purple bundle. "Now which one was she again? I know I should remember this but I don't."

Dixie jumped in to the conversation. "She's about Victoria's height, short brown hair, large doe eyes, followed her little girl around almost nonstop . . ."

"Ah, yes, I remember her." Setting her bag on the ground, Rose turned her attention to the scraps of colored felt on her lap. "You think she might be behind the murder?"

Tori shrugged. "I don't know. But she's certainly not shy about the positives that have come from the woman's death. Seems they'd had more than a few run-ins regarding Penelope's propensity toward bullying, all of which— including the bullying—have now stopped."

"And it has," Debbie confirmed. "Even Jackson says it's a nicer class now."

Dixie laid each pancake across her lap for a final inspection. "That's all it usually takes, isn't it, Rose?"

"Too bad Samantha couldn't have made the noose just a wee bit bigger and gotten rid of both of them at the same time."

A collective gasp rose up around the porch.

"Good heavens, Debbie, you can't mean that," Margaret Louise protested. "Penelope might be difficult but she's only five."

Debbie's face paled. "I-I wasn't talking about *Penelope*. I was talking about Beth."

"Ain't that the truth. Too bad Samantha didn't know." Dixie stacked Rose's butter atop her pancakes and handed the set to Debbie. "Perhaps she'd have considered doubling up."

"Two hogs for the price of one."

Tori made a face at Margaret Louise, the visual inspired by the woman's comments making her laugh out loud. "I feel like I should be disagreeing at this moment, like I'm being an awful person for not coming to Beth's defense."

"You're human," Rose reminded.

"Besides, I don't think Samantha was even aware of Beth's presence that morning." Debbie wrapped the breakfast food items in the colored tissue paper then placed it in the large gift bag.

Tori sat up tall. "That morning? You mean Samantha was in the bakery the morning of the party, too?"

"She was. But, looking back, I doubt she even noticed Beth. In fact, if I recall correctly, she only had eyes for Ashley."

"Eyes?"

Debbie shrugged off Dixie's curiosity. "*Daggered* eyes. Is that better?"

Chapter 27

While Leona's suggestion was tempting, Tori opted to wait for Milo on his front steps. It was safer that way. Besides, the less face-to-face time she had with his houseguest the better. For all parties involved.

It wasn't that she had a propensity toward confrontation, because she didn't. What she did have, however, was a need to make things right. And Beth's constant manipulating wasn't right.

Milo deserved better.

Unfortunately, in this case, he needed to discover that on his own. She just hoped it was sooner rather than later. For both their sakes.

"Hey, beautiful!" Milo's long legs closed the gap between them in mere seconds, the smile on his face erasing any and all self-doubt that had left her questioning her decision to take up camp on his front step. "What a nice surprise."

She stood and stepped into his arms. "It was your idea, silly."

"One that you seemed to be less than enthusiastic about if you'll recall."

"I'm sorry. I really am. It's . . . Actually, you know what? Let's just forget it. Let's try to enjoy us today."

His arms tightened around her as his lips brushed across her forehead. "Sounds perfect to me. Where's Beth?"

"I don't know. I never—"

"Milo? Is that you?" They both turned to see Beth standing in the doorway, her voluptuous curves showcased by the off-white minidress she wore. "Oh, Tori, I didn't know you were out here."

She waved. "I was waiting for Milo."

"Oh." A cloud passed over Beth's china doll features only to disappear as quickly as it came, replaced, instead, by the runway smile that turned male heads far and wide. "Won't you come in? We love having guests, don't we, Milo?"

Guests?

"Tori isn't a guest, she's my girlfriend," Milo said not unkindly as he held his hand out to Tori. "She even has a key, don't you?"

She nibbled back the smile that threatened to make her look too eager. "So how are you today, Beth?"

"Wonderful. I've been busy cooking Milo's favorite dinner—beef stew and homemade biscuits."

Tori's eyebrow rose as she met Milo's eyes. "Beef stew is your favorite?"

Swooping in, Beth extricated Milo's hand from Tori's and led him toward the kitchen. "Of course it is. Why, I figured that out on our very first date, didn't I, Pooky?"

"Pooky?" she echoed.

"That's been my little pet name for Milo since that very first night, too, hasn't it?" Without waiting for his response,

Beth lifted the lid on her stew pot and beckoned Milo over. "It's just like it was the first time I cooked for you."

"Smells great, Beth, thanks." He leaned over the pot. "And there's enough so Tori can stay for supper, too. Perfect."

Beth's smile faltered a smidge. "I'm sure she has other plans, isn't that right, Tori?"

Tori shook her head. "No, actually, I don't. And I'd love to stay."

"Of course you would," Beth mumbled beneath her breath.

"I'm sorry, can you repeat that? I missed what you said."

Beth's smile returned as she scooted up close to Milo. "I said, I'm so glad."

She resisted the urge to laugh out loud. Perhaps Leona was right. Given enough time, Beth Samuelson would surely hang herself.

Milo reached for Tori once again then lifted her hand to his lips. "Beth, if you don't mind, Tori and I are going to spend a little time together out on the deck."

"Oh." Beth opened the utensil drawer closest to the Crock-Pot and began shifting slotted spoons and spatulas around. "Um, okay, that's a—a good idea. Between dinner and"—she swept her hand toward the scraps of paper that littered the kitchen table—"work, it's best if I stay inside anyway."

It was impossible not to sense the woman's disappointment. And, for a moment, she couldn't help but feel bad for Beth even though she knew Leona would have a fit.

But how could she not feel bad? Milo Wentworth was one in a million. She knew that and so did Beth. Experience had taught them that at very different times in their lives. Tori had come upon Milo after running up against a man who was the complete opposite in terms of honor. Beth, on the other hand, had essentially started with honor and tossed it aside out of youthful ignorance.

Determined to find a way to make things right, Tori wandered over to the table in search of a true conversational topic—something that didn't necessitate Beth's need to prance and twirl in front of Milo. Slowly, she scanned the various sticky notes scattered around, the woman's stick figure fashion show bringing a smile to her lips. "I bet you're beyond excited to get your designs on a runway."

Beth shoved the drawer closed and turned around. "It's almost all I think about."

"It's going to be wonderful, I'm sure."

"Hey, let's talk more about this over dinner." Milo captured Tori's hand in his and tugged her toward the back door. "C'mon, I'm dying to have a little time alone with you."

Halfway to the door, she stopped. "I need to give Nina a quick call first. To check on what time we're meeting tonight."

"You have a board meeting?"

"No. We're just meeting at the bakery to discuss the teen group we're getting ready to start. There's a few details we need to iron out and we thought it might be more fun to do it over dessert rather than huddled around the information desk."

"Okay. I'll meet you outside."

She turned in the opposite direction as he disappeared out the back door, her feet guiding her toward the front room and its noticeably better cell coverage.

"Tori?"

"Yes?"

Beth's heels clicked across the floor, stopping just inside

the hallway. "I'm not sure what you're trying to prove by showing up here like this."

"Trying to prove?"

"Haven't you heard of a little thing called a *phone*?"

"Milo asked me to come over after work."

"Because he's being polite." Beth tucked her hands against her hips. "That's what guys like Milo do when they're trying to let girls like you down easily."

She blinked against the ridiculousness that was Beth Samuelson. "Girls like me?"

Beth nodded, her gaze skimming its way down Tori's stonewashed jeans and simple pink T-shirt. "Simple girls. Prudish girls. Bo-ring girls."

"I don't have time for this." Pulling her phone from her purse, she flipped it open, her thoughts swirling between the desire to remain a lady and the urge to scratch the woman's eyes out. "I'd be careful if I were you, Beth. We don't want Milo seeing your true colors."

A low, mirthless laugh escaped Beth's lips. "Milo sees what I want him to see. Which is rather eye-catching, wouldn't you say?" Beth rose up on tiptoes and spun around in a little circle. "And fortunately for me, I'm in need of a white knight as of late—a role Milo falls for every single time."

"Falls for?" she echoed against a throat that was suddenly tight with frustration. "Are you saying you've been lying about being in danger this whole time?"

"Lying might be a bit strong. After all, I really was worried in the beginning. But, the more he ran to my side, the more I came to realize Milo still cares for me. In fact, all I have to do is cry wolf and he comes running. Which really must beg the question as to when he'll finally give up the charade and drop you once and for all."

"Actually, the only question it begs is how I could be so blind."

Tori looked up as Beth whirled around and grabbed for Milo's hand. "Milo! I don't know what you heard but—"

"I heard more than enough, Beth. Now get your stuff and get out. *Now!*"

Chapter 28

Try as she might she couldn't make herself focus on the list of ideas Nina had put together for their meeting—not the food donations she'd managed to line up from both Leeson's Market and the bakery, not the authors she'd contacted regarding appearances, and not the emails she'd wrangled from the board in support of the program.

It wasn't that she'd lost interest in the notion of a teen book club, because she hadn't. And it certainly wasn't a lack of contagious enthusiasm on the part of her assistant.

No, it was simply the fact that her mind and her heart were somewhere else.

"Miss Sincl—I mean, Tori? Are you okay?"

Nina's voice broke through her woolgathering, forcing her attention from the wounded blonde seated at the corner table in Debbie's Bakery. "I'm sorry, Nina. I was really looking forward to meeting you tonight. We never get to hang out beyond the library's walls and getting a chance to do that sounded like fun. And it is."

"It is?

Tori felt her face warm. "It would be, if I wasn't worried about Milo."

Dropping her clipboard onto the table, Nina leaned forward until she was in Tori's distracted line of sight. "Is he sick?"

"No. Nothing like that. It's just . . ." Her words trailed off as she tried to put words to a reaction she had yet to figure out—a reaction that had him virtually throwing Beth out the door and then asking for some time to himself.

It had worked out in a way, since she and Nina were scheduled to meet, anyway. But still, it was more than a little out of character for Milo. Especially considering none of what transpired had been her fault. She'd tried to warn him.

"So tell me, did she lose her favorite can of hairspray or is she just that unhappy about that bizarre shade of pink nail polish she's wearing?"

Tori looked over her shoulder. "Oh, hi, Debbie. I didn't realize you were here. I thought it was just Emma working."

"No. Tonight's my evening with the books." Raking her dirty blonde hair into a high ponytail, Debbie jerked her head toward the lone figure hunched over a sea of papers in the far corner of the bakery. "So what happened? Why does she look like she just lost her best friend?"

"Because she did." Tori wrapped her hands around her mug and pulled it closer to her body. "Milo kicked her out."

"What?!" Debbie grabbed a chair from the next table over and pulled it up alongside Nina. "Sorry, Nina, but I've got to hear this."

Tori glanced, once again, at the woman who'd put the kibosh on what should have been a nice evening with Milo. "The jig is up."

"What jig?" Nina asked.

Debbie brought her hand to her mouth only to let it drop back to the table just as quickly. "Wait. You mean he figured out she was crying wolf just to get his attention?"

She nodded.

"How?"

"He overheard her saying it. To me."

Debbie clapped her hands in the air. "That's fantastic!"

She cast a sidelong glance in Beth's direction. "Milo is upset. In fact, I've never seen him so angry."

"My Duwayne would have reacted the same way." Nina reached for her glass of milk and took a small sip. "I reckon it has to do with their egos or something."

Debbie agreed. "Colby doesn't like to be wrong, either."

"Wrong," she repeated under her breath. "But I didn't say he was wrong. I just—"

And then she knew. Nina and Debbie were right. She had tried to tell him what Beth was up to days ago. Yet when she had, Milo had brushed the accusations off as being unfounded.

Only they weren't.

"I figured something was up when I passed by her table and she didn't even bother to smile," Debbie mumbled.

Pushing her uneaten cookie in front of Nina, Tori lowered her voice to a near whisper. "Have this. It's calories. And it makes it easier to drink the milk."

Debbie's eyes widened as she sized up Tori's assistant. "You're drinking milk? Why? You hate milk."

"But it's good for the baby."

"Baby? What baby?" Reality dawned in Debbie's eyes as she looked from Nina to Tori and back again, a smile spreading across her face like wildfire. "Oh, Nina, how wonderful!"

Nina beamed.

Debbie pointed at Tori. "How long have you known?"

"A few days."

"And you didn't say anything?"

She shrugged. "It's not my news to share."

"It will be one day."

"Nina, *please*."

"No, Nina's right, you know. One of these days Milo will pop the question and you'll say yes." Debbie scooted forward in her seat. "Then you'll get married and enjoy a little time by yourselves before you're sitting at this same table drinking milk instead of hot chocolate."

"Instead of hot chocolate? Never!"

Debbie and Nina exchanged amused glances. "At least you didn't protest the notion of marrying Milo."

Milo.

She took another peek at Beth. "I feel sorry for her. I really do."

"Why?" Debbie asked. "She's been a thorn in your side since she blew into town."

"Because she truly cares about Milo."

Nina took a larger gulp of milk, her face contorting with distaste as she did. "Lying isn't caring, Miss Sinc—I mean, Tori. If she truly cared about Milo she shouldn't have tried to deceive him."

"I guess. I just think she was desperate."

"But why?" Debbie glanced over her shoulder in Beth's direction. "She's beautiful, she owns her own company, she's got talent from what you've said, and there's not a man she passes who doesn't look twice in her direction."

"Except Milo," she mumbled. "And that's the only man she cares about."

"News flash. He's taken."

Tori and Debbie stared at Nina only to have the woman bury her head in her hands. "I'm sorry, I shouldn't have said that."

"Why? It's true." Debbie reached over and patted Nina on the head. "It's okay to speak your mind once in a while. Really. We don't bite. Though, if she"—she gestured toward Beth's paper-strewn table once again—"doesn't start picking up her mess I might have to resort to biting."

"As if that would ever happen." Tori inhaled the first true sense of peace she'd felt all evening. "You and Nina are two of the kindest people I've ever known."

Pushing back her chair, Debbie stood. "Well, I better get back to my office. Jackson is probably wondering where I am."

Tori scanned the bakery. "Jackson is here?"

"In the office. Colby took Suzanna to see a girly movie."

A wistful expression passed across Nina's face. "It's funny but I find myself thinking more about those kinds of things rather than pink or blue booties and changing tables. I guess I'm just hoping Duwayne and I make good parents."

"You will." Tori reached across the table and patted Nina's hand. "The best."

"I agree." Debbie took two steps backward then spun around, her white sneakers squeaking on the linoleum floor. "If you're still here when I finish with the books we'll come out and sit for a while."

As Debbie disappeared behind the counter, Tori swung her attention back to Nina.

"It's nice to see a smile on her face."

"Who?"

Nina pointed out the window. "Her."

Samantha Smith.

She watched as the woman turned and entered the bakery, the door-mounted bell jingling with her arrival.

"Hi, Victoria! How are you?" Samantha stopped beside their table, her large brown eyes twinkling. "It's a gorgeous night, isn't it?"

"It is." She gestured toward Nina. "You must know my assistant, Nina Morgan?"

Samantha met Nina's hand across the table and shook it firmly. "Yes. Of course. Nina is always very helpful to both Kayla and me."

Nina blushed.

"That's nice to hear." She winked at Nina then motioned to the empty chair vacated by Debbie. "Would you like to sit?"

"For just a moment. I'm just picking up a special treat for Kayla."

As they talked, Tori tried to imagine the woman with a rope in her hands, snuffing the life out of another human being. Was it possible? *Really* possible?

"She doesn't know it, but whoever killed Ashley Lawson did that one a huge favor."

"That one?" Tori echoed as her gaze followed Samantha's to the very woman who had cut her night unexpectedly short.

"Uh-huh."

Tori watched as Beth gathered her things then made a beeline toward the three of them. "Do you think Milo will ever forgive me?"

"I don't know, I guess you'll have to ask Milo that question."

"I didn't make everything up. I really didn't. Someone *did* follow me in the parking lot and someone *did* call the inn asking what room I was in. That was all real. It really was. I guess I just liked having Milo coming to my rescue.

It made me realize, even more, how foolish I was to let him go in the first place." Blinking against the tears she was doing a lousy job of hiding, Beth tightened her left hand around her leather portfolio and shifted from foot to foot. "I know, after what I've done, he'll never look at me *that* way again, but I don't want him to hate me. I really don't."

"Give him time, Beth." She knew it was a lame suggestion, but it was all she could think to say. Especially in light of the fact she couldn't answer for Milo. Any permanent damage Beth had done was between them and them alone.

"Give him time," Beth repeated in a whisper as she reached for her rolling suitcase. "I guess I owe him that."

The bell over the door jingled once again, its quick melodic burst signaling the arrival of yet another familiar face.

Regina Murphy.

She raised her hand in a greeting only to pull it back down to the table as Regina headed straight for the counter, the woman's hurried pace preventing her from noticing anyone, including Tori.

"Well, I better get going. It's been a long day."

Tori stepped off her stool and held her hand in Beth's direction. "I wish you luck with your company, I really do."

A hint of crimson spread its way across Beth's cheeks. "I can see why Milo likes you. You're always so nice."

"I try."

Beth lowered her voice to a near whisper as their hands met. "Please tell Milo I'm sorry. And if he wants to tell me off, I'll be at the inn again tonight before heading back home in the morning."

"I'll let him know."

And with that, Beth was gone, her suitcase bumping

along behind her as she left the bakery and headed down the sidewalk.

"Well, I better get going, too. Kayla is waiting anxiously for her treat." Samantha slid down off her stool and headed over to the counter to stand in line behind Regina. For a moment, Tori simply watched them, her mind wrestling with the irony. Both women had been connected to the victim—one as a mortal enemy, the other as a friend. Or, at the very least, a boss.

A flash of movement jarred her focus to the left, tugging her lips upward in the process. There, sitting underneath one of the tables, was Jackson Calhoun, his dark brown hair groomed neatly to the side save for the little ducktail that stood up in the back no matter what his mother did.

"Jackson? What are you doing?"

The little boy pushed off the ground and ran over. "Hi there, Miss Sinclair! Hi, Mrs. Morgan! Mommy didn't tell me you were here!"

"Well, we're here, aren't we, Nina?" She winked a smile at her assistant. "Only we decided to sit at the table instead of on the floor."

"I like that better, too. The floor can be kind of yucky." Jackson scrunched up his face in disgust. "People drop all sorts of things on the floor. Even pictures." His hand shot upward to reveal a crumbled piece of pink paper.

Pushing his tongue forward in concentration, Jackson unfolded the paper and set it on the table. "Mrs. Abbott wouldn't like this picture very much."

"Mrs. Abbott? That's the art teacher at your school, right?" She leaned forward for a closer look. "Why wouldn't she like your drawing?"

"It's not my drawing. I just found it is all." Jackson

scrunched one eye closed and aimed his finger in the direction of Beth's old table. "Right there, under that table."

"Then make sure you wash your hands after you throw it away. Especially if you picked it up off the ground."

"I will. I promise." He raked his hand over the picture, crumbling it into a ball in the process. "Mrs. Abbott taught me how to draw better people anyway. She said stick people are for mommies and daddies who don't know how to draw."

Chapter 29

There were times when giving a person space was advisable. And perhaps now was one of those times. But that would mean listening to her head instead of her heart and her heart was talking far louder at that particular moment.

Which is why Tori was sitting in her car outside Milo's house instead of heading home as she'd told Nina.

It wasn't that she'd lied, because she hadn't. She'd truly intended to go home after they left the bakery. She'd even steered her car in that direction. But when she was just two driveways from home, she'd turned around, her destination suddenly clear.

Milo was upset, of that she was certain. But he hadn't done anything wrong. In fact, he'd done everything right. He'd given an old friend the benefit of the doubt because experience had given him reason to do just that.

It was easy for Tori and Debbie and everyone else to see Beth's ulterior motives because there was no history to counteract the truth—a fact that had put them at an advantage and Milo at a distinct disadvantage.

She looked up at his house, her eyes drawn to the room on the far left-hand side. It wasn't hard to imagine what he was doing—his long, lean body stretched across his bed while he stared at the ceiling in thought. She'd seen it many times—in the park, on her couch, outside the library . . .

It was his favorite position for contemplating life.

Pulling back on the recessed handle, she pushed the driver's side door open and stepped onto the road, the butterflies in her stomach beginning to flap their wings. For over a year now, she'd felt that flutter every time she saw Milo.

And she knew why.

She squared her shoulders and marched up to his front door, her desire to see him all but squashing the nerves that had threatened to make her heed the notion of space. When she reached the top step, she lifted her fist to the door and knocked.

Then she knocked a little louder.

A light went on in the hallway followed by a flash of Milo's form as he rounded the corner and peeked outside.

"I had to come back."

His eyes fixed on hers through the screen door as a slow, albeit shy smile pulled his mouth upward. "I'm glad you did."

She forced herself to remain rooted to the porch, the voices that had preached space growing louder in her head.

Give it time.

Don't crowd him.

His ego is a little battered right now.

"I'm sorry about what happened earlier. I really am. If I'd known any of that was going to happen the way it did, I would have waited to call Nina."

He pushed the door open and reached for her, wrapping his hand around her forearm and gently tugging her inside. "Why? So I could have continued being a blind idiot even longer?"

She stepped aside as he closed the door then trailed him into the living room and over to their favorite couch, the slight slump of his shoulders reminding her heart why she was there. "Giving an old friend the benefit of the doubt doesn't make you an idiot. It makes you special. Rare, even. And I suspect it's one of the many reasons a woman would track you down after fourteen years in the hopes of rekindling something long gone."

"I wish she hadn't."

Bending her leg at the knee, she dropped onto the couch beside him. "You shouldn't. You had fun catching up with her, didn't you?"

He shrugged. "It was okay, I guess."

"You laughed together, right?"

A secondary shrug segued into a nod. "Some, yeah. But you make me laugh all the time."

She leaned into the back of the couch, her gaze locked on his. "True. And you make me laugh, too. But sometimes it's nice to revisit a point in history that had its share of memories, too. And you guys had memories together."

"Memories I'm starting to question."

"Why?"

"Because no one changes that much and that drastically. That manipulative side had to have been there somewhere even back then, right?"

His words looped their way through her thoughts as she considered their merits. "Maybe. But maybe stuff has happened in her life over the past decade that's made her desperate. Less secure. And by reaching out to you she was trying to reach for something about her that was long gone as well."

"By lying?"

It was her turn to shrug. "That, I can't explain. All I know is what I've lived. And two years ago I thought I'd found someone who could make me happy. I gave him love and trust and loyalty only to have him toss it back in my face with a big old side order of humiliation to boot."

She braced herself against his chest as he tried to pull her close. "Wait. I need to say this. So when I moved here, my eyes were jaded. The last thing I wanted was to find someone who could, potentially, break my heart all over again."

"I would never do that to you."

"I know. And that's because I've found a man with honor and integrity—rare things in today's world. Which is something, I suspect, Beth discovered in the time that's passed since college."

He cocked his head to the left and studied her closely. "Go on."

"See, she had the rare thing from the start and opted to let it go because she naively assumed it was an easy thing to find. Life showed her otherwise."

"And that made her lie to get it back?"

"No. The *desperation* made her lie."

Silence blanketed the room as he propped his feet on the coffee table and drew his hands up to cradle his head. She considered the notion of saying more, of highlighting some of the things Beth had done to back up what she was saying, but she opted, instead, to let the words she'd already said be enough.

Milo was a smart man.

When he finally spoke, his voice was its normal reflective self. "Do you think I was too hard on her?"

"I can't answer that. I wasn't in your shoes. I was only in mine. And mine have been a little uncertain as of late."

He pulled his left arm down and wrapped it around her shoulders, pulling her close. "I hope you know that despite my desire to revisit some fond memories and to spend a little time catching up with Beth, I never had any desire to rekindle our past relationship. I'd be a fool—an even bigger one than I've been these last few days—to ever let you go."

She nestled into the crook of his arm as he continued, his chin bobbing up and down on the top of her head as he spoke. "I, too, have seen what's out there. I've dated women like Beth. I married Celia only to stumble around aimlessly after her death. And after all those experiences, I can truly say I found the proverbial diamond in the rough."

Blinking against the tears his words created, she snuggled still closer, the warmth of his nearness giving her the courage to speak. "Then I guess we're meant to be because I, too, found a diamond."

His face paled. "You did?"

Shifting back, she smiled up at him. "Of course I did. I found you, didn't I?"

"I guess you did."

She lifted her lips to meet his, the feel of his skin against hers giving her the courage to say what still needed to be said. "Milo?"

"Mmmm?"

"Beth asked me to tell you that she's back at the inn for the night. In case you—in case you'd like to talk to her."

He pushed off the couch then reached for her hand, tugging her upward and toward the kitchen. "That's great, but no. I've seen and heard enough of Beth Samuelson for a lifetime. It's best if she gets back to focusing completely on her career."

Her career.

She followed him down the hallway and into the kitchen, her feet guided forward by the lingering smell of a beef stew that had gone uneaten. "Any chance I could get a bowl?"

"Of stew?"

"Sure. Seems a shame to let it go to waste seeing as how it's your favorite and all."

Grabbing two bowls from the pantry, he made his way over to the Crock-Pot. "Can I let you in on a little secret?"

"Of course." She watched as he lifted the lid from the Crock-Pot and spooned its contents into each of the ceramic bowls he'd set on the counter.

"Beef stew isn't my favorite. Never was."

She took the bowl from his outstretched hand and carried it over to the table with Milo close on her heels. "Then why did she say it was?"

"Because it's the only thing she knew how to make and she never inquired otherwise."

"Oh. I see." They sat across from one another at the Formica table, Beth's sticky notes still scattered here and there. "Well, at least she could draw."

Milo paused his stew-laden spoon just shy of his mouth. "Draw?"

She nodded. "That's a talent few people have."

He popped the stew into his mouth and swallowed. "Including Beth."

"I don't understand."

Setting his spoon beside his bowl he reached for the pink sticky note that had claimed Tori's attention less than three hours earlier, the runway of stick people bringing a familiar smile to her face. "This is about the extent of Beth's drawing ability. And even this is an improvement from what she could do when I knew her."

She stared at Milo. "But those dresses she designed. They're mind-blowing."

He tossed the crude drawing onto the table and reached for his spoon once again. "You mean those six dresses she carried around in that portfolio? She didn't draw them. She got them from someone else."

"Wait. She told me she drew them."

"Okay, well then perhaps I can take a little comfort in knowing it wasn't just me, after all. Maybe Beth lies to everyone."

"No. There must be some mistake. She said she drew them."

Milo jerked his head toward the pink sticky note. "*That*, she drew. Those dresses, she didn't. Trust me on this."

Her gaze fell on the six little stick people lined along a makeshift stage, their triangular dresses ill-fitting at best.

Six people.

Six dresses.

She heard the gasp as it left her lips, felt the splatter of stew on her skin as her spoon crash-landed in the middle of her bowl, saw the concern on Milo's face as he reached for her across the table. "Tori? What's wrong? Are you okay?"

"Oh my God! I know who did it. I know who killed Ashley Lawson."

Chapter 30

She ran down the hallway and into Milo's bedroom, the echo of his footsteps close on her heels. "Talk to me, Tori, please. What's going on?"

"Did she leave anything behind? Anything at all?"

"Who? What are you talking about?"

"Beth," she explained over her shoulder as she ran back and forth between the dresser and the nightstand looking for anything that could serve as confirmation of the notion swirling around in her thoughts. "Did she leave anything behind? Anything at all?"

He grabbed hold of her arms and stepped in front of her, blocking her second lap around the room. "What are you doing?"

"Looking for proof."

"Proof? Of what?"

"That she did it. That she killed Ashley Lawson."

His mouth gaped open and he stumbled back a step. "Beth? You think Beth killed Ashley Lawson?"

She wiggled free of his hands and strode over to the closet, yanking it open before her feet even came to a stop. "It makes sense, don't you see? She lied about those designs. She told me she drew them and she didn't."

Milo held up his hands and dropped onto the edge of the bed. "What does that have to do with anything? I thought it was one of the party moms."

"We know it wasn't one of my friends. They don't have it in them to kill anyone. And then I was leaning toward Samantha Smith because, well, she just seemed to be a likely candidate. But now, after what you said about Beth and her inability to draw, it all makes sense now."

"Wait. Please. Come sit. Explain this to me so I can understand."

She ran her hands along Milo's clothes, finding nothing that belonged to Beth whatsoever. Not a shirt, not a pair of pants, not a dropped design . . .

Defeated, she wandered over to the bed and sat down, the flapping of her Milo-induced butterflies rivaled only by the pounding of her heart. "Why would she lie about creating those designs other than to cover up how she got them in the first place?"

"I don't know, maybe out of embarrassment? Or some misguided sense of pride?"

"Maybe, under different circumstances. But if someone in her company had drawn them she'd have simply said that, wouldn't she?"

He shrugged. "I guess."

"But if she got ahold of them illegally, she might be more inclined to lie about the how. To cover her tracks."

"Okay." He rolled his right hand in a gentle motion as he wrapped his left around her shoulders. "Go on."

"We know Ashley was a designer. That's what she did for Regina's company . . ." Her words trailed off as another piece of the puzzle dropped into place.

"The first six have been . . . misplaced. But I'm sure they'll turn up. Soon. In the meantime, the ones I have are showstoppers."

Six designs.

"That's it! Oh my gosh, that's it! The designs she's been saying are hers? They're part of a collection Regina was in the process of using to secure a partnership with Fredrique Mootally."

"Fredrique Mootally? Who's that?"

"According to Regina, he's the top adult pageant designer in the country. Only he won't strike the deal unless she has all twelve designs."

"I'm not following."

"She only has *six*."

"And . . ."

"According to Regina, the other six were"—she shot two fingers from both of her hands into the air and wiggled them up and down—"misplaced."

Reality dawned on Milo's face as he began to see the puzzle the same way Tori did. "You think the six designs Beth showed you are the missing six?"

She stared up at him. "They could be. It certainly makes sense."

"You think she *stole* them?"

For a moment she said nothing, her mind working to piece together the various snippets of facts and suspicions she'd managed to come up with thus far. "I think she killed Ashley to get them."

"Then why wouldn't Regina be screaming foul?"

That's the part she couldn't quite figure out. Unless . . .

"Unless she truly thinks they've been misplaced," she mumbled. Looking around the room, she pushed off the bed and spread her arms wide. "But I need proof. Something we can take to Chief Dallas so he doesn't think I'm a complete nut."

Milo, too, stood. "I'm sorry. I wish there was something that could help but she didn't leave anything behind except . . ." Milo whirled around and headed toward the hallway as he beckoned Tori to follow. "She did use the desk in my office one day after she moved in. She said she was reworking her logo and needed a well-lit area. I don't know if she cleaned everything up that first day—she may have, but I *know* she didn't go in there when I asked her to get her stuff and leave."

"Reworking her logo?" She ran to catch up with Milo as he made a sharp left halfway down the hallway. "Wait. I knew that. She'd considered changing the name of her collection but decided against it."

He nodded as he flung open the door to his spare-bedroom-turned-office. "She said that after monkeying around with a new name, it got her thinking about simply redesigning the current logo to give it more pop."

Stepping into his office she looked around, her gaze skirting the stacks of freshly graded tests and quizzes that covered the first of two desks.

"Here we go. See?" He pointed toward the assortment of computer-generated logos strewn across the top of the second desk, all of them highlighting some variation of a spotlight. Nudging one of the sheets upward with his fingers, he sighed. "Nothing. Nothing that'll tell us anything. Except for the fact she was a bit of a slob when she worked."

Tori looked from page to page, some versions showing a large spotlight to the left of the company's name, some showing it to the right. The best of the group bathed the name in yellow as if the company, itself, was in the spotlight. Pushing the top layer of papers to the side she searched another crop of logos, the stark contrast in both look and feel making her lean closer.

"P. C.?"

Milo shrugged. "You got me."

"Pageant . . . what? Pageant . . ."

"Concoctions? Creations? Children?"

"Maybe. But it couldn't be *creations*. That's what Regina's company is called." She pushed the second layer of papers to the side, her gaze falling on the connecting letters underneath—the P and the C intertwining to create a name that made Tori suck in her breath.

"What?" Milo moved in beside her, his breath warm against her ear. "What is it? Did you find—oh my God!"

She didn't really know how she got home. She remembered telling Milo she'd be fine. She remembered getting in her car and slipping the key in the ignition. She even remembered pulling away from the curb. But the actual drive home?

That, she didn't remember at all.

They'd talked it all through—the things they knew and the things they didn't, agreeing to hash it all out in the morning before work. And it made sense. It really did. They both had jobs to do. But trying to shut her mind down after everything she'd learned that evening was virtually impossible.

Especially when so many of the pieces added up to the answer she'd been seeking since Ashley was murdered and a cloud of suspicion was cast on her friends. The problem, though, was the latest piece. The piece that had Beth contemplating a new name for her company.

Penelope's Closet.

It was hard enough to imagine the desperation that would make one woman kill another over six dress designs. But to steal them and then name the entire company after the dead woman's five-year-old daughter?

That was beyond the scope of comprehension. Far, far beyond.

Feeling the beginnings of a headache taking shape behind her temples, Tori unlocked the front door and stepped inside, her hands instinctively finding the dimmer switch on the living room light. She tossed her keys onto the small table beside the door and headed toward the kitchen, the promise of chocolate and Tylenol guiding her feet.

Why would Beth take that chance? Why would she even consider changing the name of her company to something that might point a finger squarely in her direction? Was she that confident in her flirtatious manipulations? That sure of her knee-weakening smile and giggly voice?

"No. Beth is too smart, too business savvy to make a mistake like that." She stopped in the doorway, her own words bringing her up short. Was that true? Did she really think Beth was too smart for such a gross blunder?

Yes.

"Then why? Why consider the name Penelope's Closet?" She yelled the words into the air, listened to them as they left her lips and traveled around to her ears. "Great. Now I'm talking to myself."

Shaking her head at the ridiculousness that was her, Tori marched over to the cabinet and flung it open, her hands beating her eyes to the stash of chocolate she kept on the second shelf.

She unwrapped the foil-wrapped square and shoved it into her mouth just as the phone began to ring. For a moment she considered letting it go, the need for sleep the reason she'd left Milo's in the first place. But by the third ring she couldn't stand it any longer.

"Hello?"

"The more proper way to answer would be to say, 'Good evening, this is Victoria, how may I help you?'"

"I'm sorry, Leona, I should have known better."

"Yes, you should have. But that's why I'm here. To teach you how to act like a true southern belle."

"You mean like a true southern belle *according to Leona Elkin*, right?"

"Is there any other way?"

She had to laugh in spite of the pounding behind her temples. "No. I guess not."

"Now that that's settled, how did your afternoon with Milo go? Did you take full advantage of your time together?"

"I—uh." Was it really just that afternoon that she sat on his porch waiting for him to come home? It was hard to fathom. So much had happened.

"Don't tell me she wrestled him away again? Good heavens, Victoria, are you remembering to put on your makeup and wear something provocative?"

"Put on my makeup and wear something provocative?" she repeated. "No. I mean, yes. I mean, no."

"You're making my head ache, dear."

"Tell me about it." She inhaled a much-needed sense of calm. "I wore makeup. I dressed in a way that acknowledged the afternoon hour and no, Beth didn't wrestle Milo away from me. Quite the contrary, in fact."

"Ooooh, that sounds promising."

She carried the phone into her bedroom and flopped onto the bed, her body sinking into the fleece bedspread. "He threw her out."

"What?"

She couldn't help but grin at the excitement in Leona's voice. "He walked in on her admitting her lies and he threw her out. Then, as soon as she was gone, he asked if I'd give him a little time to himself, too."

A string of unladylike mumblings filled her ear.

"No, it's okay, Leona. I understood. But I did go back again after a few hours. And things are fine."

"How fine, dear?"

"Good. Wonderful." She rolled onto her side, pulling the phone more tightly to her ear. "Except for one little thing."

She could almost hear Leona's eyes roll over the phone. "It's not anything about us. We're as solid as ever. It's just . . . Well, it's about Beth."

"I thought he tossed that little hussy to the curb."

"He did. Only now I'm thinking we'll need to have her tossed somewhere else."

"She *is* still alive, isn't she?"

"Leona! Stop. Of course she's still alive."

"And she's out of Milo's house, right?"

She reconfirmed that turn of events.

"Then what else needs to happen?"

She debated against sharing what she suspected but, in the end, she relented, the need to talk her suspicions through more than a little overpowering. "I think she needs to be in jail."

"Jail? Why?"

"I think she—"

"On second thought, lying to gain access into a man's home should be some sort of punishable offense, don't you think?" A funny sound in the background was followed by, "Oh, shut up, would you?"

She pulled the phone from her ear. "Excuse me?"

"Not you, dear. My sister, Margaret Louise. She thinks she's funny."

"Margaret Louise is there?" She sat up tall. "What did she say?"

"She said if lying to gain access to a man's home was a punishable offense, I'd be sitting in a cell myself. Many times over. But she neglects to realize that failure to correct another person's mistake is not the same as lying."

"Another person's mistake?" she asked as she nibbled back the urge to laugh out loud. "What kind of mistake might that be?"

"Why, my age, of course. Men think I'm younger all the time. And who am I to ruin their male egos by correcting them about something so insignificant?"

A second noise in the background was followed by a rise in Leona's voice. "Twenty years *is* insignificant."

That did it. She laughed. Hard. "Would you feel that way if they *added* twenty years, Leona?"

Silence greeted her question before Margaret Louise came on the phone. "Um, Victoria? What did you just say? I've never seen Leona so flabbergasted by anythin' in my life."

The laughter died on her lips.

Uh-oh.

"Please tell her it was just a question. You know, a chance to lighten the mood after an evening that was far too long. Okay?" She leaned back against the headboard and closed her eyes, the pain in her head hitting an all-time high.

"What happened?"

"I think I figured out who killed Ashley. Only there's—"

A gasp echoed in her ear. "Who? Who?"

"Beth."

"Beth?" Margaret Louise repeated. "You mean Milo's Beth?"

Milo's Beth.

"Beth Samuelson," she corrected. "Milo's *old* college girlfriend."

"Now, Victoria, I realize you've not been terribly pleased with her arrival in town and I can't say as I blame you but don't you think you might be sniffin' in the wrong hole?"

"I'm pretty sure she stole some of Ashley's designs in order to get some much needed attention for her own company."

A moment of silence was followed by a string of questions, most of which Tori was able to answer. Except one.

"I'm not sure about the motive. Simply stealing the designs with the intent to further her own company doesn't explain why she was contemplating the use of Penelope's name on her logos."

Another gasp filled her ear. "She was goin' to put Penelope's name on designs she stole from her mamma? *After* she murdered her to get them?"

"Now you see my dilemma. It doesn't add up. It'd be like putting a neon sign over your head saying, 'I'm a killer, I'm a killer.' "

"But you said she changed her mind, didn't you?"

"She did. But she *considered* it, Margaret Louise. I saw the logo with my own two eyes."

"Maybe there's a piece we're missin'."

"If there is, I'm not seeing it."

"Hush. Give me a moment."

She kept quiet, a smile playing across her lips as she

imagined Margaret Louise in deep thought while Leona stomped around in the background.

After what seemed like an eternity, she leaned forward and glanced at the clock.

10:30 p.m.

"Margaret Louise, I need to get some sleep. Maybe we could table this until morning? I'm meeting Milo at the bakery at seven and—"

"That's it!"

"What?"

"Remember what Debbie said the other day? When we were finishin' up the last few pieces for Operation Play Food?"

"Um, I'm not sure. What did she say?"

A deep inhale was followed by an even louder exhale. "She said Ashley had a meetin' with Beth the mornin' of the party, remember?"

She sat up straight, Margaret Louise's words ringing a series of bells in her head.

"She said that Beth was dressed all fancy-like and that Ashley had her leather portfolio—"

"Open on the table between them," she finished for her friend. "I remember!"

"And remember, she said they were acting like the best of friends by the time the meeting was over."

She mulled Debbie's words in her head, the accuracy of her memory buoyed by the confirmation Margaret Louise provided. "So maybe Ashley intended to give the designs to Beth and something went wrong."

"Maybe she had second thoughts?"

"Maybe. I just wish Debbie had heard something that could confirm or deny what we're guessing."

"You could ask Samantha. Maybe she overheard somethin'."

"Samantha? As in Samantha Smith? Why would she have overheard . . ." Her words trailed off as she remembered the second part of what Debbie had said. The part about Samantha shooting daggered eyes in Ashley's direction that same morning . . .

Chapter 31

She studied the various morning offerings in the breakfast case—her gaze skirting the bagels and muffins in favor of the cakes and donuts.

It was no use. She was hopeless when it came to food.

"Hey there, Victoria, aren't you up early?"

"Up would imply I slept."

"And you didn't?"

She pondered Debbie's question for all of about ten seconds. "No. Which is why I need that"—she pointed to the caramel-drizzled chocolate-covered donuts on the top shelf—"or, rather, *two* of that, I mean, those."

"Proper grammar is not necessary before seven a.m." Debbie grabbed a doily-draped plate from the counter and carried it over to the case. "Two, you said?"

Tori nodded. "And a large hot chocolate. With lots of whipped cream."

Debbie shook her head. "I don't know where you put this, I really don't."

"Let's hope it stays that way. Though, at the moment, that's the least of my worries."

"What's wrong?"

She glanced over her shoulder at the line, stopping when she reached the count of ten in her head. "I'll catch you up later. When things settle down a little."

"Are you staying?"

"I'm meeting Milo."

"Sounds good. I'll bring your hot chocolate out to you in a minute."

Armed with her plate of donuts, Tori wandered into the dining area, her gaze settling on the table she'd sat at with Nina just the night before. She started toward it only to have her progress thwarted by Milo's arrival.

"Hey there." He gestured toward her plate. "Didn't sleep well, huh?"

"Am I that transparent?"

He grinned. "I just know you."

"You better run."

"Never." Leaning forward, he whispered a kiss across her forehead. "Grab a seat and I'll be right over. I just want to grab a tea."

She had just sat down when Debbie appeared beside her table with her hot chocolate. "I told Milo to sit. I'll bring his tea over so he doesn't have to waste his before-school window standing on line."

"Thanks, Debbie."

"My pleasure." Debbie backed up to allow Milo entry to his seat. "Now you two try and relax a little. You both look as if you didn't sleep terribly well."

She turned to Milo as Debbie disappeared behind the counter, the circles beneath his eyes making her feel more than a little guilty. "You didn't sleep, either?"

He shrugged. "How could I? I've been harboring a fugitive in my home for the past few days. I'm not sure the PTA would approve."

"It's better than a fugitive hanging out on the playground, or showing up for parent night." She tilted her face in the direction of the morning sun streaming through the large plateglass window that faced the center of town.

"Huh?"

"I really thought it was Samantha Smith. She said so many things that made her fit as the perfect suspect right up until the moment I realized Beth lied about those designs. Then, just like that"—she snapped her fingers—"Samantha was off my radar. Though, as Margaret Louise pointed out, she's still tied to the big picture."

He reached across the table and tucked an errant strand of hair behind her ear, the feel of his hand against her face dousing her with a much-needed calm. "What do you mean she's tied to the big picture?"

"According to something Debbie said a few days ago, Ashley and Beth had some sort of meeting here at the bakery the morning of Sally's party. By all accounts it was a business meeting that went very well."

"Did Debbie hear any specifics?"

She shook her head. "No. It was a Sunday morning. She was swamped with pre- and post-churchgoers."

"Ahhh." He smiled as Emma appeared beside the table with his tea. "Thanks, Emma."

When the girl had gone, Tori continued. "Samantha was here that morning. And, apparently, she was very aware of Ashley's presence."

"Okay. Then maybe *she* overheard something."

"May—oh my gosh, that's it!"

Wrapping his hands around his mug, Milo sat up tall, puffing his chest out in the process. "I did good?"

She made a face at him. "You always do good. But what you just said? It's perfect."

"It is *if* she heard something. If she didn't, it's moot." He took a long slow sip of his tea. "So do you think Ashley and Beth had struck some sort of deal?"

It was the same question she'd been asking herself over and over throughout the night. "I suppose . . . Though that doesn't make much sense. If Ashley was happy at the end of the meeting, why would Beth need to kill her?"

"Maybe Ashley changed her mind later on?" Milo posed. "Or maybe she decided to stay on with Regina?"

Stay on with Regina . . .

"Ooooh, you might be right." Slowly, she traced her finger around the floral design of her mug. "In fact, maybe I should talk to Regina first. If she can confirm Ashley changed her mind that might be enough to point Chief Dallas in the right direction once and for all."

"Well, there you go. You've got a plan." He glanced down at his watch and winced. "I better head out. But hey, if I see Samantha when she drops off Kayla, should I ask her to give you a call?"

"Absolutely."

She was just saying good-bye to the last of her story time toddlers when Beth poked her head into the children's room. "Tori? Do you have a minute?"

Rising to her feet, she grabbed the stack of picture books she'd used to captivate that week's participants and headed toward the shelves in the far left corner, the woman's presence making her more than a little wary. "I thought you were leaving town today."

"I am. I just wanted to talk to you first."

She paused in the middle of the aisle then turned around, Beth's tired eyes and disheveled appearance catching her by surprise. "Are you okay?"

"No. Not really. I'm"—the woman shrugged—"disgusted at myself for the way I acted toward you. And I wanted to say I'm sorry."

Of all the things she might have expected the woman to say that was not one of them. "I'm, um, not really sure what to say."

Beth wandered into the room and stopped, her ocean-blue eyes widening as they scanned the various murals that graced the walls. "Wow, Milo wasn't kidding, was he? This room is spectacular."

"Thank you. It's my pride and joy." She deposited the picture books on their appropriate shelves then returned to collect the carpet squares favored by the under-three crowd. "So where do you go once you leave here?"

"Back home so I can focus on getting these new designs into production."

"The designs you drew?"

Beth picked a carpet square off the ground and added it to Tori's growing pile. "About that . . . I didn't really draw those designs."

"Why did you say you did?"

"To make myself out to be better than I am."

Startled by the woman's honesty, Tori gestured her over to the tiny stage that played host to a variety of stories her youngest patrons longed to explore through dress-up and role-play. "Have a seat. It's just about the only spot in the room where you can sit without having your knees pushing against your chin."

"Milo likes substance. He always has. And you"—Beth gestured around—"have substance. If you didn't you wouldn't have been able to dream up a room like this."

She perched on the edge of the stage just inches away from Beth, the woman's prime position on her list of suspects foremost in her mind. "I'm sorry, but I'm not sure what you're getting at."

Beth inhaled slowly. "Milo isn't the kind of guy to be content with just a pretty face. He wants more. I mean, look at you. You're pretty, you're smart, you're well liked, and you have the kind of creativity and passion to make something like this happen." Beth waved one hand toward the stage beneath them and the other toward the classic storybooks showcased on the walls of the room. "What do *I* have?"

"Well, for starters you've got the kind of looks that turn heads for miles."

"Which is all well and good if you want the kind of guy that attracts. Substance attracts substance. I've learned that the hard way."

She considered the woman's words. "But why claim you drew those designs when Milo knew you weren't artistic."

"Because I was trying to earn *your* respect."

"My respect?" she echoed."

Beth nodded. "I wanted you to think I had it on the ball. That I was a . . ." The woman's face turned crimson.

"A what?"

"A threat. Just like you were to me."

"I was a threat? To what?"

Beth nodded again. "To any chance I had of getting Milo back."

Silence fell between them as she worked to process everything she'd heard, the woman's brutal honesty more than a little admirable.

"And so you stole those designs and claimed them as your own just to make me feel threatened?"

Beth's eyes widened in horror. "Stole them? I didn't steal them."

She pushed off the stage and wandered over toward the center of the room. "Look, I know who drew them. And I know you have them. What else am I supposed to think?"

"That they were secured during a legitimate business deal?" Beth, too, stood and began clenching and unclenching her hands by her sides. "Ashley Lawson and I shook on that deal, right there in your friend's bakery. I didn't steal a thing."

"But why would she give them to you? Didn't she owe them to Pageant Creations?"

"Ashley created those particular designs on her own time, something not covered by her current contract with Pageant Creations. So she played it smart. She decided to shop them around. And, well, I figured out pretty fast what would turn the tide in my favor."

"What was that?" she asked.

"The opportunity to name the entire collection after her daughter. The second I made that offer, she practically pushed the designs in my direction."

Penelope's Closet.

It made sense now.

"Most people in Ashley's position would have hinged everything on money. But not Ashley." Beth wandered over to the mural of Cinderella and stopped to study it. "She was far more concerned with finding a way to immortalize her daughter's name. The bigger, the better was her motto."

Shaking off the sense of déjà vu she couldn't quite put her finger on, Tori dove into the one topic they'd managed to skirt thus far.

"So you're saying that her murder less than twenty-four hours later had absolutely nothing to do with how you ended up with those designs? Designs you proceeded to tell me were your own?"

Beth spun around and stared at Tori. "You think *I* killed her?"

The horror in the woman's eyes knocked her off-kilter. "I—I certainly *considered* it. You did, after all, have her designs—the same six Regina needed to secure her deal with Fredrique Mootally."

Beth's face drained of all color. "Fredrique Mootally wants my designs?"

She shrugged. "Near as I can figure, yes. Only the deal is off unless he can have all twelve."

"I was supposed to get the other six. It was part of our deal. Only she didn't have the actual drawings with her when we met, just photocopies. She said she'd get them to me the next day." Beth slouched against the Fairy Godmother. "Wow. I can't believe Fredrique Mootally wants my designs. I had no idea."

She studied Beth closely. "He's really that big?"

Beth snorted. "Big? Big doesn't even do him justice. Try top in the business. And by top I mean T-O-P." Pushing off the wall, Beth headed toward the door. "Maybe I shouldn't have cried wolf so many times after all, huh?"

"What are you talking about?"

"People in my position would *kill* to have that kind of connection."

Chapter 32

She was still sitting in the children's room, staring at the door, when her cell phone rang. With a quick glance at the unfamiliar number, she flipped the phone open and held it to her ear.

"Hello?"

"Victoria? This is Samantha. Samantha Smith. Mr. Wentworth over at the elementary school asked me to give you a call. He said you had a few questions for me?"

She wandered out of the room and into her office, her mind sifting through the mental list of questions she'd crafted when she still considered Beth Samuelson a suspect.

But that was no longer the case. Not anymore, anyway.

"I—I was wanting to check in and make sure that Kayla's experiences at the library have improved."

"Kayla's experiences?"

"Um, yes. Ms. Dunn, one of our volunteers, told me about the—the incident in the children's room a few weeks ago. And I want to assure you that we are taking steps to help minimize such an occurrence again." She knew she sounded lame but it was the least she could do on such short notice. Especially after Milo held up his end of the bargain by asking the woman to call. "In fact, one of our upcoming kindergarten story time sessions is about bullying."

"That's wonderful. Though it's not as needed as it once was. Rumor has it that the little girl who took great pride in being a bully might be moving out of state soon. But even if that doesn't happen, she's no longer being encouraged in the way she once was."

She stood at the window overlooking the library grounds, her mouth traveling down a path completely independent of her conscious thought. "You really believe Ashley Lawson encouraged Penelope to be mean?"

"I do. Though I don't think Ashley believed that's what she was doing. I think she just wanted to elevate that little girl above all the rest. But by doing so, she was teaching the child that she was more important."

It made sense. How many other kids had their name on a parking sign? How many kids had playgrounds renamed in their honor?

"Ashley just didn't know when to stop. No party could ever be big enough, no outfit could ever be fancy enough, no friend could ever be good enough for her precious little Penelope." Although Samantha continued speaking, it was a different voice and a different set of words that began playing in Tori's mind, a similar yet juxtaposed sentiment that had her sharing her days' old question aloud once again.

"What did she want? To have her daughter's name in lights?"

Samantha laughed. "It sure seemed that way, didn't it? First the parking spot where she worked, then the park, then who knows what was next."

"Penelope's Closet, that's what." Realizing her mistake, she started to recall her words only to swallow them again as Samantha's voice filtered through her thoughts.

"It's like I told Regina at Sally's party that night. She's better off without a woman like that working for her. I mean, really, do you think six designs are worth being affiliated with someone who doesn't know the meaning of the word loyalty?"

Six designs.

A chill shot down her spine as the enormity of what she was hearing hit her with a one-two punch. "Regina knew that Ashley was taking her designs elsewhere?"

"Of course she did. I told her myself."

"You—" She slapped a hand over her mouth as the pieces of the puzzle finally began to take shape. Regina knew Ashley had betrayed her. She knew the deal with Fredrique Mootally hinged on having all twelve designs.

But why kill her?

Because she could.

The moms at Sally's party made that easy.

"Oh my God," she whispered as she slammed the phone shut in her hand. It all made perfect sense. Regina had been at the party. She'd heard what Melissa and Beatrice and all the other moms had said, allowing her to point her bloody fingers in their direction.

A direction that kept the focus off her.

Nina's voice emerged from the speaker beside her phone. "Miss Sinc—I mean, Tori? Milo is on line one."

"Uh, okay." She reached across the desk and hit the top button. "Milo?"

"Hey, beautiful. You're never going to believe who just called me."

"I—I have no idea." Dropping into her desk chair, she

raked a hand through her hair. "But Milo I think I figured out who—"

"Beth. She actually called to tell me someone is trying to run her off the road. Can you believe it? Like I'm going to jump in my car and—"

She sucked in her breath as yet another dose of reality rushed in. Regina had killed Ashley because of the last six designs—designs she still needed in order to forge a partnership with Fredrique Mootally.

Only there was one little problem.

Beth had them.

"Do it, Milo!" she screamed. "Find her! Now!"

His laughter echoed around the room. "C'mon, knock it off. A person can only cry wolf so many times before—"

Jumping to her feet, she ran toward her office door, the pounding of her heart drowning out the rest of his words. "Milo, please! This time there really *is* a wolf!"

Chapter 33

They were all there—Leona, Margaret Louise, Rose, Melissa, Debbie, Beatrice, Georgina, and Dixie. All eight of her sewing sisters in the throes of what they did best.

"Can you imagine the gall of that woman?" Margaret Louise grumbled. "Standin' there at my grandbaby's party, givin' us a piece of her mind, only to up and take our idea and try to give us credit for the outcome?"

"We were the perfect alibi."

Melissa pinned Dixie with a disbelieving eye. "*We? We?* You were barely on Chief Dallas's radar for longer than a minute. Beatrice and me? We still feel his breath on our necks, don't we, Beatrice?"

The shy twenty-something nodded from her stool on the other side of the table. "But it's okay now. And that's all that really matters. Well, that and the fact that I get to stay on as Luke's nanny."

Leona pushed her teacup into the center of the table. "The most important thing is that Victoria has a bit more time on her hands. We're going to need that to revisit some of our lessons."

"We do? Why? I thought I was starting to get this southern thing down pretty well."

Leona slowly shook her head. "The southern thing? Perhaps. Though there are times I still see a bit too much of your city ways for my taste."

"My city ways?" she echoed.

"What else would you call this innate desire you have to corral criminals?" Leona's chin rose into the air in defiance. "You most certainly didn't learn that here."

She had to laugh. "I didn't? Really? Because the last time I checked all those criminals—as you call them—were corralled *here*, in Sweet Briar."

Leona peered over the top of her glasses. "On the heels of your arrival from Chicago."

Rose rolled her eyes.

Dixie shifted in her seat.

Georgina cracked a grin. "Are you saying that Victoria brought them here with her?"

"These things didn't happen until she showed up, did they?"

"Oh, shut up, Twin." Margaret Louise slid off her stool and came around the table to give Tori a hug. "I, for one, can't imagine Victoria not being here. She's brought a much needed breath of fresh air to both our sewing circle and Sweet Briar."

"I second that," said Rose.

"As do I."

Tori met Beatrice's timid smile with one of her own. "Thank you, ladies. It's nice to know that at least some of you are glad I'm here."

"I'm glad you're here, dear. I never said otherwise. But

I do think we need to go over a few things about Milo. Especially in light of that foolish move you made today."

"Foolish move?" piped in Debbie. "You mean the one where she saved Beth's life?"

"Saved Beth's life by sending Milo to her rescue."

"What did you want her to do, Leona?" Georgina challenged. "Stamp her feet and tell Milo he couldn't go?"

"Milo didn't *want* to go. Victoria *made* him go."

"Because the woman's life was in danger." Dixie forked a piece of cake from her plate and brought it to her mouth. "I think that goes to show just how special Victoria is."

Tori swallowed over the lump that rose in her throat. Somehow, some way, things were starting to thaw between her and Dixie. And it felt good.

Real good.

"Which is something I've known from the very start."

Tori whirled around in her seat to find Milo standing less than two feet away, a strange smile on his lips. "Milo, I didn't know you were there."

"I was counting on that."

"You were?"

He nodded, his feet closing the gap between them as his focus remained trained on her face. "I was also counting on finding you at home . . . alone. Only you weren't there."

"That's because she's here. With us." Margaret Louise tugged her still closer, planting a kiss on the top of her head. "She saved most of our necks by pluggin' away 'til she figured out the truth."

"Lulu calls Victoria the expert finder-outer." Melissa reached across the table and patted Tori's hand. "She says there's nothing in the whole wide world her Miss Sinclair can't find."

Milo cleared his throat to reveal a voice that was unnaturally raspy. "Actually, there's one thing."

She swiveled in her chair to meet his gaze head-on. "There is?"

He nodded. "Though just the other night you claimed you had, only you hadn't. Not the right one, anyway."

One by one she looked from Milo to Margaret Louise to Melissa to Leona to Rose to Debbie to Georgina to Beatrice to Debbie to Dixie and back again, each face sporting the same look of confusion she felt on hers.

Except Milo.

His face was simply unreadable.

"I don't know what you're talking about," she finally said.

Reaching for her hand, he tugged her off her stool and into the center of the room, the bakery virtually empty except for the members of Tori's sewing circle. "Remember what you said about finding me?"

"About finding you?" She felt her brows furrow only to settle back to normal as her memory filled in the missing blanks. "Yes, I remember. I said I'd found the diamond in the rough when I found you."

"And do you know you almost gave me a heart attack at first?"

She stared at him as the confusion returned. "Milo, I'm sorry, I don't know what you're talking about."

Dropping to his knees amid a burst of squeals, Milo glanced over at Margaret Louise and shrugged. "My apologies to Lulu."

"*Lulu?*"

"Hush, Victoria," hissed Leona. "There's a time and a place for all those silly questions of yours. But now is most definitely not that time, dear."

"What is everyone talking—"

The words disappeared from her lips as Milo reached into his back pocket and extracted a red velvet box. With careful fingers he opened it and held it in her direction. "I'd intended to do this in private but, once I got here, I realized I couldn't have picked a better spot if I tried."

She gazed down at him through lashes that were suddenly tear-dappled. "Milo, I—"

"Let me finish." He reached up, pulled her left hand down, and entwined his fingers with hers. "It was here, in this very bakery, where we had our first date. And it was in front of these exact people that I began falling in love with you. So, when you take all of that into account, you'll realize there really isn't a better place on earth for me to ask this question."

"What question?" she whispered as the butterfly brigade took flight in her stomach once again, their constant presence tied to all things Milo.

"I said *hush*, Victoria. He's getting to that."

Margaret Louise clapped a hand over her sister's mouth. "Don't mind her, she won't make another peep."

Shaking his head softly, Milo tightened his grip on Tori's hand and smiled up at her as if they were the only two people in the room. "Tori? Will you do me the great honor and pleasure of becoming my wife?"

Sewing Tips

- Use a pencil sharpener to sharpen a dowel rod, and then soften the tip with sandpaper to create a handy tool to help add stuffing or turn items.

- Felt is a great material for children learning to sew because it is a firm fabric and even large stitches will hold it together.

- Machine stitching on felt can be difficult to remove without damaging the project, so it is wise to use pins to secure the pieces and to double-check measurements and placements before sewing the pieces together.

- The blanket stitch and the whipstitch are nice decorative stitches for hand sewing felt projects. Even stitches provide the most attractive results.

- Use a smaller needle when working with felt. Larger needles create larger holes which don't disappear easily.

- Felt is a nice material for craft sewing projects, but because of the way it is made, it doesn't stretch easily so it may not be the best choice for clothing that needs some ability to stretch.

- When felt is stretched, it will lose its shape and irreparable holes may also be created.

- The edges of felt do not fray when cut and look good straight or pinked in many crafts.

- When sewing by hand, cut your thread in 20-inch lengths to help prevent tangling.

- Place a thimble on the second finger of your sewing hand to assist in pushing the needle through the fabric.

- Aim to keep stitches small as large stitches will tend to create gathers in material when pulled too tight.

Have a sewing tip you'd like to share?
Stop by my website,
www.elizabethlynncasey.com,
and let me know!

Sewing Patterns

Felt Food Patterns

Experience:

Some sewing experience is helpful.

Materials:

   Craft felt in a variety of colors
   Embroidery floss in a variety of colors to match or com-
      plement felt colors
   Thread in colors to match or complement felt colors
   Quilt batting or Poly-Fil
   Cardboard for making templates
   Washable fabric marking pen or chalk
   Sharp scissors
   Straight pins
   Needle for hand sewing

Directions

Use cardboard to create templates.

Trace around the templates onto felt using a washable fabric marking pen or chalk.

Use two strands of embroidery floss when hand sewing.

Bread Slices

Cut two 4-inch squares of ivory-colored felt for each bread slice. Cut a rounded edge on each corner. Cut quilt batting the same size and shape. Cut ½" x 17" strips of tan-colored felt for crust. (If you are using 8 ½" x 11" craft felt, you will need to cut two ½" strips and overlap them as you sew them to the ivory felt.) Use a whipstitch to attach the tan felt strip to the ivory square, overlapping and securing the end. Place quilt batting in the center. You may need to layer more than one piece depending on the thickness of the batting. Add the other ivory piece to the top of your bread slice and whipstitch it in place.

Lunch Meats

Cut two 4" circles of felt in colors for the lunch meat of your choice. Pin circles together and machine stitch near the edge or use a blanket stitch to sew by hand.

Cheese Slices

Cut two 4" squares of orange-colored felt. Pin squares together and machine stitch near the edge or use a blanket stitch to sew by hand.

Peanut Butter or Jelly

Create a blob shape to fit within a 4" square bread slice. Cut two blob shapes in tan or purple felt. Pin shapes together and machine stitch near the edge or use a blanket stitch to sew by hand.

Rippled Potato Chips

Place two pieces of ivory-colored felt on top of each other. Machine stitch lines every ¼" to create the look of rippled chips. Cut 2" x 2 ½" chiplike ovals from the rippled felt. Machine stitch around each chip near the edge.

Chip Bag

Create a bag for chips with two pieces of felt 4 ¾" wide by 5 ½" tall. Use pinking shears along the top edge. To create a logo, sew a strip 4 ¾" wide by 1 ¾" tall across the center of one piece by machine or by hand using a whipstitch. Cut a 2 ¾" circle and place it on top of the strip and sew in place by machine or by hand using a whipstitch. Place front and back sides of bag with right sides together. Pin in place. Sew around the sides and bottom of bag by machine. Clip corners. Turn bag right-side out.

Chocolate Chunk Cookies

Cut two 3" circles of tan felt. Cut scraps of dark brown felt into small rectangles about ¼" x ½" to resemble chocolate chunks. Sew small dark brown rectangles onto one of the tan circles using a whipstitch. Sew tan circles together using a blanket stitch, leaving a space for adding Poly-Fil. Continue sewing closed.

A new Needlecraft Mystery from *USA Today* bestselling author

MONICA FERRIS

Buttons and Bones

❖ ❖ ❖

Owner of the Crewel World needlework shop and part-time sleuth Betsy Devonshire heads with friends for the Minnesota north woods to renovate an old cabin. But beneath the awful linoleum is something even uglier—a human skeleton. Betsy's investigation leads her to the site of a former German POW camp, a mysterious crocheted rug, and an intricately designed pattern of clues to a decades-old crime.

penguin.com

NOW AVAILABLE IN ONE VOLUME

Sew Far, So Good

Three Needlecraft Mysteries
From *USA Today* Bestselling Author

MONICA FERRIS

Crewel World needlework shop owner and part-time sleuth Betsy Devonshire has a knack for stumbling upon dead bodies—and it's entangled her in more than one knotty situation. Here in one volume are three of Betsy's adventures as a not-so-seamless investigator.

Unraveled Sleeve
A Murderous Yarn
Hanging by a Thread

Free needlework patterns included!

M528T0709